--◆{ The Houses of Belgrade }◆--

Jack O'Connell
Seattle
28 July 1994

The Houses of Belgrade

Borislav Pekić

Translated by Bernard Johnson

Northwestern University Press

Evanston, Illinois

Northwestern University Press
Evanston, Illinois 60208-4210

Translated from Hodočašće Arsenija Njegovana. English translation
copyright © 1978 by Harcourt Brace Jovanovich, Inc. Northwestern
University Press edition published by arrangement with Harcourt
Brace Jovanovich, Inc. All rights reserved.

Published 1994

Printed in the United States of America
ISBN 0-8101-1141-1

Library of Congress Cataloging-in-Publication Data

Pekić, Borislav, 1930–
      [Hodočašće Arsenija Njegovana. English]
      The houses of Belgrade / Borislav Pekić ; translated by Bernard
Johnson.
            p.   cm. — (Writings from an unbound europe)
      Originally published: New York : Harcourt Brace Jovanovich,
            c1978.
      ISBN 0-8101-1141-1 (pbk.)
      I. Johnson, Bernard. II. Title. III. Series.
PG1419.26.E5H613   1994
891.8'235—dc20   93-47920
                                                              CIP

The paper used in this publication meets the minimum
requirements of the American National Standard for Information
Sciences—Permanence of Paper for Printed Library Materials,
ANSI Z39.48–1984.

*Make thee an ark of gopher wood; rooms shalt
thou make in the ark, and shalt pitch it within
and without with pitch . . . And, behold, I,
even I, do bring a flood of waters upon the earth. . . .*

—Genesis

The Houses of Belgrade

Since I have now reached those years in which man's allotted span comes to its natural end, and moreover since my health is no longer of the best, I, Arsénie Negovan, son of Cyrill Negovan, *rentier* here residing, have decided, being fully lucid and in possession of all of my mental faculties as prescribed by law, to set down this testament, and in it to state my final, incontestable will regarding my movable and immovable possessions, and whatsoever may concern their preservation as follows . . .

Being of advanced years and in declining health, I, Arsénie Negovan, son of Cyrill Negovan and owner of this property, have come to the decision on this third day of June, 1968, being fully lucid and with all my mental powers unimpaired, to compose my testament on the basis of the right I have by law, and in it to divide up my movable and immovable . . .

Bearing in mind all that I experienced in the course of that evil morning, and being conscious of the serious threat that very soon I shall be in a position where in all probability I shall be unable to express anything at all, most particularly my legal will, I have lost no time nor allowed myself respite . . .

As I take up my pen to explain in more detail this haste to write my will—haste for which my advanced years and my

declining health are only a pretext—it will be best for me
to begin without the hypocrisy of so-called introspective reflection and by admitting that on that morning, which I'm
convinced was decisive for the course of my hitherto unevent-
ful life, I was very upset, filled with anxiety, not to say disturbed. I hadn't been in what for me, a man of substance and
Vice-President of the Chamber of Commerce, was such an ex-
ceedingly unseemly state since 1941, when I formally submitted my decision to retire from my business affairs. For it
was already apparent to even the feeble-minded that those
who were left with the decaying Monarchy around their
necks were rushing headlong to destruction. So I entrusted to
that misalliance of my wife, Katarina, and the family lawyer,
Mr. Golovan (former King's Counsel) while still myself retaining overall control, of course—such matters as the routine
collection of rents and loan interest; all that degrading business connected with the presentation of promissory notes
which had expired as a result of broken leases; and even
that more attractive aspect—the only one among all the
financial advantages which allowed one something unselfish,
passionate, and truly constructive: the maintenance and ex-
pansion of the property owner's capital.

But considering my careful, self-centered mode of life and
advanced years—they total seventy-seven, unfortunately,
and I hadn't crossed my threshold during the last twenty-
seven—everything that I had in mind to undertake immediately upon my wife's departure (for which she had already
largely prepared herself), and that required from me a much
more substantial sacrifice than that which I had made long
ago in resigning my active functions, was without doubt near
to remaining simply a mournful fantasy reserved for some
more courageous year. Indeed, almost the same distress had
seized me in 1919 when I first encountered the Bolsheviks
in the eastern suburbs of Voronezh during a ghostly raid by
Semyon Mikhailovich Budyony's Red Cavalry, with their

pointed green-felt caps, and their leather overcoats strapped tightly round by the many bands of their cartridge belts. With that immediacy peculiar to the Negovans, I had understood that I had no wish ever to encounter them again, even in some benign form, even among the harmless *nonpareilles* announcements from the Soviet Union. That same distress seized me yet again in 1924 (and with this, except for my feelings of shame at the March Putsch, the list of my states of exceptional anxiety is completely exhausted), when I took possession of my first house, the first of those noble, luxurious, excellent model buildings which today, I hope to the satisfaction of all, embellish the capital.

In the feverish anticipation of at last being alone, I had dragged the armchair to the western window earlier than usual. At that observation post (although the term firing position would have better suited that fat, turret-shaped dormer window jutting out over the grimy, worn roofs of Kosančićev Venac, and the aggressive mood in which I took possession of it) I would stay sometimes from noon on, until dusk, spreading its black dust down the river, impeded any further contact with the view and the New Township, whose construction I had continuously followed through binoculars of varied type, size, and range. The day before yesterday I was "on station" early—thus did I designate my favorite armchair when it stood up close to the window; in any other position it lost that honorary appellation and reverted to the anonymous status of furniture—I was, I say, "on station" from dawn on, running the risk that Katarina would notice my agitation, interpret it as an outward symptom of my illness, and put off her departure for the spa.

I even pretended not to notice Mlle. Mélanie Foucault, who was sitting behind me, sterilizing surgical needles in a tin bowl; or rather, seeming totally absorbed with the area I was scanning with a pair of Mayer artillery binoculars, I manifested a complete absence of respect for the presence of my brother's housekeeper. At a favorable moment I would ask for George; yes, that would do, if only to conform to the established rules of that senseless game in which I and his combined companion, nurse, and maidservant indulged ourselves—a game providing still further confirmation of my already ample observations of the general's way of life. But now, I confess, I restrained myself. In the ensuing quarrel which would undoubtedly get out of control, I might have given myself away. On any other occasion, care for my considerably undermined health and my mood—which was as changeable as the sun's movement in the heavens—would have been welcome, even though I usually countered such care with ill-humored refusal; now, however, any excessive interest in my person could easily have turned into a trap which could end my plan before it had even started. For it was necessary, more than necessary, for me to be left without surveillance as soon as possible, and for my solitary morning to be assured of Katarina's absence in order to be spent exactly as I intended.

But I just couldn't restrain myself. When Katarina again came into my room in search of the tortoise-shell combs to put in her hair, I impatiently inquired why, if she were really going on a journey, she hadn't packed the day before.

"Some journey!" she said before going out. "I'm going to Vrnjce and you call that a journey!"

Then Mlle. Foucault said, "Madame Katarina isn't going until tomorrow, Monsieur Negovan. For the moment we're only going shopping."

"For me," I replied, "crossing the threshold is a journey, Mademoiselle Foucault. Outside the house, everything's a journey."

And so, in the irritated anticipation of my wife's going out for a reason which, in these exceptional circumstances, in no way aroused my curiosity (normally I liked to be informed about everything), I went on investigating that part of the plain which, cut in half by the river Sava, stretched off to the west and ended in a yellowish, sulfurlike glow at the edge of the horizon. My view of the plain was set by a dark oak window frame which formed an extended rectangle around an airy canvas—oak that, dried by the June sun and the pearl-colored dusk, looked for all the world like some gilt-encrusted frame. The changing picture in that oblong frame, resembling a coat of arms composed of four identical fields, was shielded by a double barrier of glass whose clarity I cared for meticulously with a chamois cloth. A third glass wall belonged to the complex mechanism of the lens of my most powerful binoculars. Its brass chain clinking, it crawled across the window; whenever it stopped, it bored a large medallion, stamped with a cross with minute divisions on it, out of the magnified landscape.

During the long period of time that I had dedicated my-self to it, the view had changed gradually but continuously before my eyes, making me aware that everything was being transformed with the same insistency—not just that part which was in my vicinity but all the rest too, all that area I couldn't verify with my own eyes because of the limiting frame of the window, the range of my binoculars, and my voluntary immobility. Nevertheless, the changes which grafted themselves naturally on one another—like those of a tree from one year to the next, continuing imperceptibly like sleepers of some unending railway line—were not rude or unrestrained enough to cause me the kind of bewilderment, disbelief, or aversion that you feel when, returning home after a long absence you find your family changed, in-tolerably different from the attractive faces which hastened your return. Although I was present at these changes, even taking part in them from afar, I hadn't lost the inborn Negovan capacity for awaiting and accepting new features only with suspicion until they had been subdued, assimilated, *digested,* as it were—just as hungry amoebae absorb life from around them, making it part of their own composition, and in so doing of course transform it in accordance with their own characteristics, simultaneously separating out the harmful, indigestible portions. On the contrary, my integration with the changes was conditioned by the fact that I had already assimilated the majority of them, especially the appearance of newly built-up areas, and adapted them to myself.

The changes have gone on everywhere, except on the river. Only the age-old water, with its constant color and unhurried, tranquil flow, gives to the view that consistency without which its transformation, however otherwise imposing, would be to the highest degree suspicious, in the light of that inbred wariness of which I just spoke.

The embankment is paved with rough granite slabs and little mounds of flowers which change color every three months, while in the center is a glistening flight of steps which for some reason attracts my attention, even though there is nothing exceptional about them, just a few pale-colored steps with a break halfway down, nothing more. Then comes that clumsy construction of broken lines—like a concrete silo under a triangular glass roof, before which, surprisingly enough, no grain wagons have ever been unloaded; an inexplicable building, quite unsuitable for leasing, which I wouldn't own even if it were given to me, despite its favorable position facing the delta and the War Island. Then the King Alexander Bridge, now completely rebuilt. And high above everything, I see an arrogant palace with its asbestos shine, which is said to belong to the royal government—those monarchists really know how to spread themselves!—and which my binoculars, quite impartial in their magnetically attracted service, hold briefly in their hostile eye, then leave to pass on over the scantily tree-lined avenues and gardens, and alight rapidly on the New Township which, with its useless parks of wasted foundations, is the destination of all my imagined wanderings.

From my somewhat oblique vantage point at a kilometer's distance, the newborn town has the untidy look of an unfinished model. With a certain nostalgia it brings to mind that heap of matchboxes, cubes, cardboard towers, and paper greenery which I used to see in Jacob Negovan's studio whenever I dropped in to ask my enterprising cousin how his plans were coming along. The buildings themselves bear no resemblance to those I built through Jacob's architectural firm or selected for purchase through the legal firm of Golovan & Son. They are somehow sad, poignant, abandoned, as if just barely managing to get along despite the great company of their fellows. They are all identical, empty, hardly giving any sign of life; their flylike eyes, lit by the morning sun, remind me piteously of a dovecote with its little glowing lamps. Most of all—and this is what causes me the greatest difficulty—they are quite impersonal, with nothing noteworthy on their expressionless façades to set them apart physically or spiritually. No individuality. They are not truly ugly in the accepted sense of the word; they are simply without character. Humped together in the plain, they are pitiful to look at, lined up like a despondent column of convicts whose individual identity has disappeared inside their coarse prison clothes.

None of my houses could suffer such a sentence. They were all personal, highly independent, and exceptionally conscious of their own architectural uniqueness—sometimes, I'm not ashamed to say, even of their own arrogance. Those intended for the masses also had a quality which distinguished them from the rest. Squat, close to the ground, built with unbaked clay bricks and roofed with ordinary tiles—they might be said to deprive their tenants of everything except a cavelike shelter—even these possessed, perhaps in their very unseemliness, something peculiarly their own. But those new buildings on the other side of the river in no way counted on the honor of attracting or pleasing the eye. One might have been deceived into thinking that they were too proud for that. I doubt it. They are not indifferent to the unfavorable opinion which their ponderous aspect has aroused, they have just become resigned to it, they have come to terms with their own unsightliness. They exude an air of inhuman fatalism which, ugly as it is, must sadden the heart of any true property owner.

I had studied those houses closely over a long period. I had to admit that from a purely commercial viewpoint they were extremely efficient, more efficient even than my own houses. In my houses too much expensive space was used up for no purpose at all. If the furniture that encumbered them were removed, they would look like the empty caverns of the Pharaohs' tombs. Their ceilings were excessively high, like domes above a church nave (the living area below averaged five hundred cubic meters), and their disposition was irrational, vainly wasting expensive space on entrances, hallways, corridors, verandas, terraces, and balconies, turning the house into an impassable labyrinth dear only to the hearts of children. (I say this despite the fact that I myself spent a childhood among just such mysterious alcoves, transformed by my own imaginings.) These superfluous rooms did nothing to raise the rentable values in proportion, and the excessive size of the stairs simply ate up useful space, not to mention the area wasted on coal elevators—yes, coal elevators! —and on cellars, storage rooms, attics, laundry rooms, and porches. And then, the building materials: the finest stone, the hardest wood, the best plaster, the most durable paint. Marble from Venčac—sometimes even from Carrara! Porcelain, mahogany lamps, plaster rosettes, ceramic floors, wall paper made in Prague! Finally, all those decorative and expensive eaves, loggias, oval niches in which we placed impressive standing figures, and the charming alcoves, chains, balustrades, candelabra, bas-reliefs with mythological scenes, and ornaments—all that stone flora and fauna which at my insistence blossomed from the façades of my houses.

You could have got an extra floor out of each and every one of those houses with no trouble at all, and on each floor you could have squeezed out at least one more apartment. Assuming an average monthly rent of 500 dinars for the four two-story apartment blocks, and reckoning in, of course, that possible third story, one could have collected, after taxes and upkeep, about 4,500 dinars monthly, or 54,000 a year. If this calculation were applied to all my houses, I could have collected more rent in one year than what I've earned until today. But I never allowed myself to sink to the mere taking of profits with the same coldly calculating approach as do the present-day owners.

Indeed, it would have been futile for me to bother with something irrelevant. I was no longer capable of doing anything worthwhile for my "old ladies," as I called them. This was not because any such venture would have demanded a considerable contribution, or because it would have run into administrative barriers (my influence, though long unused, is still considerable), but because any such adaptation, conversion, or extension would have undermined that fatherly relationship which had grown up between myself as the guardian, and each house as my ward. As we grew old together, we also grew to understand each other and began to behave like an old married couple. It was the kind of relationship which I had never managed to preserve with any living being, with the partial exception of Katarina. Such a disloyal act could have seemed like getting rid of a long-time servant at the very moment when, completely exhausted by years of faithful service, he had become undesirable.

But with those imposing buildings in the silent circle of my binoculars I still had nothing in common. I had not ordered or financed their construction. Perhaps, I can't deny it, I had once been of two minds about buying them up. I say "perhaps," for even then I didn't believe that I could make any real contact, not to say alliance, with them, although as an experienced owner and landlord I couldn't entirely exclude the possibility.

Running my inquiring gaze down the curve which like some sleepy many-headed snake was formed by the largest of the buildings, I often asked myself what I really knew about them. I had never been near them, touched or inspected them from any side other than the front which was visible from where I was; I had never sniffed their walls to sense and memorize that special smell which—despite the lime, concrete, plaster, and paint—is the property of every house. Indeed, the only thing I was sure of was the pragmatic concept behind them—a concept which I had never respected or blindly agreed with, but which I am somehow inclined to take into consideration. I was fortunate that, thanks to the position of the window overlooking the river, I was obliged to give them my attention and, restraining my prejudices, to watch the growth of their sinewy family. I thought: I'll always have time to buy them, if it comes to that. First just one, of course. I'd buy that light, chalk-colored one or that pockmarked one on the other side of the railway line. Houses are like people: you can't foresee what they'll offer until you've tried them out, got into their souls and under their skins. If they don't come up to expectations, I said to myself, I'll sell them. If they show up well, I'll keep them. Then I'll buy the others, until the whole new district is mine and I can make them independent and individual so that they're known by a *name* and not just referred to in passing as a general concept: *subdivision, new suburb, quarter, region, blocks,* or *district.* I'd think about that when they were really mine, entered in the land register under the name of Golovan. I must confess, despite all the advantages that it would offer by way of revenue, I've never been able to possess a house which I wouldn't have the courage to show to my friends and clients and, touching its dignified façade, proclaim proudly: "This belongs to me!"

I could foresee that very soon I would no longer be able to contain my impatience at Katarina's continual postponement of her departure: first one of her cotton gloves was missing, then she wanted advice about which brooch to pin on the ribbed pleat of her blouse, then she kept wandering about in search of her baskets, then again she had trouble making up her mind among her various hats, which apart from such rare sorties aren't worth fussing over. Although I was sure that they were all used to my sullenness, I was afraid lest my rudeness toward our guest be interpreted as resulting from my illness, officially diagnosed as heart trouble. And so, with a sigh of resignation, I put the Mayer on the shelf with the other binoculars and asked Mélanie the question which she had evidently been expecting, since she had the answer ready and waiting.

"*Eh bien,* Mademoiselle Foucault, how is my brother George today?"

Mercilessly rolling her *r*'s in her throat and catching them with the tip of her tongue, the spinster answered hesitatingly that, thanks to God's mercy, it could be said that *Général* Negovan was on the whole well, very well in fact, that he hadn't been constipated recently or suffered those many and painful disorders of his digestion about which she normally informed me whenever she visited us.

All this time she was looking somewhere past me, and with an ardor worthy of an angler, fishing the needles out of the bowl and holding them up before that empty gaze. In the gray depths of the room, they glistened like precious stones fashioned in the shape of miniature lances. Then she plunged them back into the boiling water.

Listening to this familiar and monotonous lamentation— which frankly irritated me rather than aroused my sympathy, for I knew how little patience my brother had with it all—

I asked Mélanie why she looked somewhere past the person she was talking to whenever the conversation came around to George, as if the general were spying on her with some internal magic eye which took in everything concerning him and that only she, thanks to some mysterious sense akin to a keyhole, could see and understand. This might explain her wandering gaze, which had to be brought into direct focus with whatever the woebegone George was really feeling at the time. So I added peevishly:

"Well, I suppose it's because he doesn't get about enough, he's holed up between those four walls and doesn't budge."

It was a pitiless game with the old nurse's loyalty, but I had no choice. If I wanted her to go away quickly, I had to put her spaniel-like attachment to my brother—which, I was certain, was mixed in the final analysis with doubtful and almost certainly unrequited tenderness—to the test.

"It really strikes me as quite unhealthy—*absolument malsain*—for him to spend his days in that box. It's particularly unhealthy for a royal general who counts upon going down in history books."

As I had foreseen, Mlle. Foucault became agitated. The syringe shook with the rhythm of the old maid's anger as it was filled with the oily yellow medication.

"And you, why don't you ever go out of this house, Monsieur Negovan?"

"I'm an owner of property, a renter of houses, mademoiselle." Whenever possible, I avoided comparisons with commerce. "*Je ne suis pas un soldat!* My affairs can very well be carried on from here. Indeed, I would say that they can be carried on better from here. The further removed one is from one's place of business, the better. But wars, Mademoiselle Foucault, wars cannot be waged from behind a desk. I'm not saying they can't be planned from behind a desk, but wars are waged on a battlefield. *Au champ de bataille*. And, I imagine, usually waged instead of planned."

Under the stress of her intense feelings, Mlle. Foucault answered in her own language. *"Mais on ne fait pas la guerre, monsieur!* Thank God, we're not at war."

"Really," I said passively, "I don't know anything about that, I don't read the newspapers or listen to the radio. I've no idea what wars are going on at the moment, or whether there are any at all. I don't build up my beautiful houses, Mademoiselle Foucault, so that some blockheads of generals —with due respect to my martial brother—can try their stone-breaking machines out on them, but if there is a war going on somewhere, I'm sure that he's participating in it, moving little celluloid flags over the map and pushing cardboard tanks over plaster molds of the terrain. Now tell me how does the general plan to win further promotion in the service?"

"Monsieur le général cannot be promoted any higher," she said sternly. "He is . . . well, retired."

"Nous y voilà!" I exclaimed, still trying to draw Mélanie's bypassing gaze.

Of course a promotion was impossible. Not because he was retired, but because he was dead. He's been buried these twenty years, for two decades, in the family vault at the New Cemetery (Concession No. 17), where I, who am so different from the other Negovans, will certainly not allow myself to be buried.

Indeed, it was quite incomprehensible to me that they should have surrounded me for the last twenty-seven years and with the best of intentions with a kind of barbed-wire fence. All of them: Katarina; this penniless Auvergnate who is a kind of memorial to Franco-Serbian brotherhood-in-arms, the friends and relations who come to visit me; that harebrained but useful lawyer; even Isidor, Isidor hardly ever comes now—all of them really imagine that, thanks to their naive conspiracy of silence, I know nothing of what's going on outside; that I don't know of my brother's funeral;

that because I don't go out of the house—not so much because of the threat to my health, but more from mistrust of the future—I'm prevented from knowing about anything or anyone of them, from participating, from taking any action, even from living.

In all honesty, I heard about George's demise quite by chance. I could barely make out the words. They were broken, hardly penetrating the bedroom (Katarina's indisputable kingdom), and they were not intended for me even though they concerned me in the highest degree, since they were about my brother's wretched and quite unbefitting end. They further demonstrated the family accord never to tell me anything, an agreement which I had mutely legalized and in fact required of them. From the conversation I concluded that the general had perished as a result of a still unexplained but fateful misunderstanding in connection with his passion (oh, those tormenting Negovan passions!) for General Staff games. Afterward I in no way let on that I knew about the general's inglorious fate, but as a result of that otherwise welcome misunderstanding I sometimes got myself into that situation in which I now found myself: of asking after my dead brother, which I did with the same unswerving sternness and careless sarcasm as when my brother was alive, and on this occasion spurred on by the desire to get rid of Mlle. Foucault as quickly as possible.

In any case I felt no particular commiseration. On the contrary, all I felt was bitterness. When I thought about my brother, no endearing images of childhood sprang before my eyes, and those real ones, the daguerreotypes in the album with its silver, flower-shaped binding, I had thrown out to make space on the shelves for my account books. However much I tried, I couldn't conjure up from memory a single touching moment of brotherly solidarity, yet it would be inadmissible to say that I was indifferent to George's fate. So as usual I said without dissimulation that my brother, who had chosen a career which no one in the family had pushed him into—on the contrary, we had all tried to deter him from it—*ipso facto* had chosen a heroic death as its inseparable, natural, and so to speak crowning act, and that a military career without a warlike death is a good beginning without a fitting end, a meal without spice, a trick, an illusion, *une tromperie, une tricherie.*

"So you tell me he's gone into retirement?"

"You know very well he has!" answered Mlle. Foucault, holding a tuft of cotton in her bony fingers, and pushing it sharply into the neck of the alcohol bottle.

"He isn't dead?"

"*Non, monsieur!*"

"*Vous voyez,* if he *is* retired, then how does my respected brother hope to die a martial death?"

Since Mélanie was at the limits of her patience, I knew that however much she had prepared herself for this visit, my provocation would get through to her sufficiently for her to throw in my face that her untouchable, *son bien-aimé et courageux général,* whatever else I might think about him, had died a warlike death—without a weapon in his hand, it's true, but still laid low like any other soldier by shots from a rifle, at the door of his house, exactly as if on the exposed earthworks of the trenches, and in defense of something the poor wretch considered the hallowed essence of his warrior's profession. Moreover, spurred on by my malice, which such duels only inflamed further, she would tell me all the rest that she kept to herself—all that in theory for my own good had been kept silent—so as to demolish me once and for all. Yet she had promised Katarina to respect "Arsénie's special condition," so now she could only go on torturing herself, or get up and leave. But she seemed to be stuck to the chair. She just went on squeezing the piece of cotton, and the sharp smell of alcohol filled the room. To hide my agitation, I selected a Graetz from the collection of single-barreled binoculars which I used in strong summer sunlight because of its blue-tinted eyepiece, and set about wiping the lens with a chamois cloth.

"You ought to get ready now," she said with the unimpassioned tone of an executioner.

Although she had been giving me injections for a long time—very skillfully, I must admit, and without excessive pain—I still felt humiliated after each session. I was not ashamed to bare myself before a stranger; I was too old to be shy, and anyway I did it cleverly, turning onto my side and using both hands at once so that I exposed only a very limited area of skin, hardly big enough for a thorn. No, it was that intolerable feeling of dependence which sometimes also gave my relationship with Katarina the form of open hostility. And so, taking up the required position with as little movement as possible—with my knees on the seat, my chin on the back of the chair, and my hands behind my back firmly gripping my infinitesimally lowered trousers—I expressed the hope that she would be careful and forget about our passing misunderstanding while giving the injection.

I couldn't hear her. The rubber soles of her old-fashioned lace-up shoes were noiseless. But I sensed her standing behind me.

"At Salonika I used to give injections to Field Marshal Franchet d'Esperey, in his behind, Monsieur Negovan, and he never accused me of clumsiness."

"I'm not complaining either," I said in a conciliatory tone. "I'm no worse than your puffed-up generals!"

Generals who go into retirement, generals who get demobilized, who allow themselves to die, to be buried as civilians, and who never earned a single dinar that was spent on them. But when *they* come, there will be nobody to defend us. I shall have to kneel then, too, and not in a Chippendale armchair, but in the gutter in front of the house—and it won't be Mlle. Foucault standing behind me, but some gangster with an automatic.

A feeling of coolness passed through the skin of my back; I hadn't even felt the needle.

"I saw them in Russia, Mademoiselle Foucault, all those generals, those overpaid Czarist peacocks. I saw the red rabble ruffling their scented feathers, wiping their behinds with their medals, now that we've got down to behinds." The life-giving liquid was coursing through my body. "Or perhaps my brother thinks he can hold them back with cardboard tanks and tin fortifications?"

"For God's sake, Arsénie!" said Katarina, coming in. At last she was dressed to go out. "Just for once, leave Mademoiselle Foucault alone."

"She passed on a greeting from George," I said, counting on this to explain my coarse behavior. The realization that the two women were finally going to leave me alone and that I could put my plan into action—the plan which for the second time in twenty-seven years was to change my life radically, almost turn it upside down—excited me. Hurriedly I pulled up my trousers and reverted to my original position in the armchair.

"He's got those pains in his stomach again," said Mlle. Foucault. "I suggested to him that he get more exercise. There's no likelihood of his getting better if he goes on lolling about within four walls."

Mlle. Foucault got up. She could no longer stand listening to her adored general being spoken of as if he were alive. She angrily bundled the instruments into her tin box.

"I'll wait for you on the porch, Madame Negovan." She went outside without even looking at me.

"You were talking to her about Russia and the Bolsheviks again," said Katarina reproachfully.

She put the little boxes of drops and pills (which I was

to use in her absence if I felt ill) on a one-legged table with a striped top of black and white onyx flecked with streaks of dried coffee. The room, covered with flowered wallpaper with gold stems, was heavy from the smell of medicines, Katarina's oriental tobacco, varnished walnut, and parched paper. The atmosphere was thick, motionless, and gray, lending the triumphant face of Saint George and the scaly dragon a sickly appearance and the color of smoke. She pulled the coffee table up to my armchair, so I could reach it in case of need.

"She has to get used to it."

"We're used to it already. You've talked so much about Russia that I've lived through a whole revolution."

"You haven't lived through anything yet. You should have been in the Ukraine in 1919 to live through something!"

I glanced at the mirror. She was putting on her black hat like a flat English tin helmet. Instead of the scaly shell of enamel on the mirror's smoky back, flaming provinces flashed through it filled with frenzied mobs rushing toward me.

"They'll be here too if things go on like this! They *are* here, everywhere, all around us."

"I know, I know."

"They're only waiting for a secret sign from Moscow to crawl out of their underground lairs. They're ragged, filthy, bearded, and enraged—yes, enraged! In their bloodstained hands they'll be carrying scythes, hammers, red banners, and placards with demands written in red Russian letters to take away everything from us!"

Power, I thought, security, honor, hope, and our houses, my beautiful houses.

"And they'll speak Russian! Katarina, Russian! They'll sing Russian songs and they'll kill in the Russian way with a bullet in the back of the head. And they'll give us affectionate Russian names: you'll be called Katya, Katyusha, and I'll be called heaven knows what."

I felt a slight pressure beneath my rib cage, and put my hand there to find the source of the pain. While I was searching for it, Katarina was already fumbling with the medicines.

"They'll call me Arsen . . . Arseny . . . Arsenyushka . . ."

"Why are you always thinking about *them?* You know it undermines your health!"

Deftly she unwrapped a pill from its cellophane covering. I put it under my tongue and gently pressed it against my palate. My mouth was filled with a bitter taste. I managed to stay motionless. I was covered with sweat and breathing unevenly, but the pain had stopped because I had put the pill under my tongue. With that pill under my tongue I had nothing to fear.

Exhausted by the sudden feeling of helplessness, I eased my back into the padded depths of the armchair and sank into its warm softness, thinking how cruel it would be if something happened now, with such important work awaiting me. I glanced carefully at Katarina, who was bending anxiously over my helpless shoulder. I waited to hear what I had feared all day, something I myself had provoked by my careless behavior.

"Arsénie, shall I put off my trip?"

"I'm all right now."

"Wouldn't it be better if I stayed home? I'll go down and tell Mélanie."

I repeated that I was all right.

"Are you sure?"

"I've never felt better."

"You look tired."

"It's the weather. You just go on out."

"As you say. But I'll stop off at the Mihajlovići downstairs. I'll ask one of them to come up."

I searched hastily for a good reason to prevent that. "No,

please don't! They'll complain again about their rent being too high, and they'll ask for repairs."

"But they've never done that."

"All tenants are the same."

If I had thought sensibly—as I hadn't had time to do—it was an excellent reason for any landlord but me. Having once become involved in property ownership, I understood and exercised it as a branch of the architect's profession. How else would all those wonderful architectural ideas have been realized, if I hadn't financed them? Money in itself never meant anything to me. It was a tangible recognition that a house for which rent was paid was of a corresponding value—though in reality, its value was often greater. But money in my affairs was more a mental than an economic category. Particularly in recent years, which were heavily beset by that crisis of which Katarina and Golovan informed me with unnecessary meticulousness, it was not unusual for me to forgo the rent from impoverished tenants, when I could be sure—again through Katarina and Golovan, acting as my representatives—that the tenants were making faithful efforts toward the upkeep of the leased houses, and had treated them with due respect over a long period. I had not really waived the rent—I was not by any means rich enough for that—but had simply allowed its payment to be postponed.

"What are you going to do this morning?" Katarina asked attentively.

"I don't really know. I'll probably sort out some old leases. Perhaps I'll finally get around to reading that Viollet-le-Duc History of Housing which Isidor gave me."

She bent over and touched my forehead with her lips. My forehead was cold and sweaty, with droplets of amber dew. It was always like that after a heart attack. I well knew the smell of that sweat. It was bitter, salty, and warm. With the years it had become more intense, but it hadn't changed in essence. Nothing had really changed or worsened in me since that day at the cathedral doors when we were introduced to each other. Over Katarina's bent shoulder, the mirror held me in that humbling certainty. The massive Roman nose between its two hollowed cheeks was still hooked. The narrow, pinkish line running across its root came from my pince-nez. Every day Katarina brushed and combed my gray hair and sprinkled it with lavender water; even now it was only thinning in places. The eyebrows were strangely dark, pitch-colored. I had a gray look about me. Mousy. The mustache was the color of wet ash, and drooped from my upper lip like tousled braiding. Yes, gray was my color, silver and gray.

I watched her putting on her coat. She did it quickly, decisively, methodically, unlike anyone else. She would never take it by the collar, put one arm into one sleeve, the other into the other sleeve, and finish the whole operation with an adjusting wriggle which settled the coat comfortably around the body. On the contrary, she began the process where others finished it: she first threw the coat across her back, then pushed both arms into the sleeves simultaneously, and with a supple movement lifted it onto her shoulders with a single jerk. The whole of Katarina's nature was evident in this detail, the manner in which she put on her coat: that commanding Turjaški nature, hers by birth, aggressive in a masculine mold, of that inveterate kind which must do everything at one go, immediately.

Unexpectedly I felt pity—I can't say remorse, but gentle commiseration—for her unenviable position in this house. I was afraid I had made a mistake in allowing Katarina to protect me, actually to believe she was protecting me in a way which is quite irrational for me, even monstrous in its finality and totality, and which has made me withered like this, helpless, dependent. Perhaps I would have acted more correctly if I had told them to let everything follow the course which God intended—as indeed, without my knowing it, her elder brother-in-law, the suffragan Bishop Emilian, had suggested. I knew, and that aroused my pity most of all, that she was torn by fear that some penetrating fact, some careless hint (just like the one that was going to take me out of the house the moment she was gone), some suspicious circumstance or unforeseen event, would break through and split open the protective shield they had forged for me with such great care. She feared that, completely unprepared, I would become a witness of reality, and that this reality, according to their limited reasoning, would bring about my annihilation. I knew also that, caught up in their agonizing game, they had to keep from me the enormity of the economic crisis which was raging outside and which, incidentally, could be deduced from the public works on the other side of the river. So great is their naiveté, they forget that my experienced eye could recognize the recession from minor and extraneous features: for example, the fact that my otherwise fastidious second cousin Maximilian has been going around in one and the same suit for several years; that, theoretically, in accordance with my desire for economy, we long ago dispensed with the aid of a servant; that, because of my condition, we haven't celebrated Saint George's day for quite some time; and most of all, that my tenants, with the inexplicable exception of the Mihajlovići, have been in such difficult circumstances that I have extended to them all that once exceptional principle whereby those who contribute to the upkeep of their apartments temporarily do not pay us rent.

"All right, Arsénie, I'm going now," said Katarina. "I'll see to it that I'm back by three."

"You don't have to hurry on my account."

"The shops are only open until three and I have to pack."

Before she shut the door, I straightened myself up in my

together. Of course I thought about Simonida, for what could arouse me to action more than the misfortune which threatened that noble and gentle being? Of the danger itself I had heard quite by chance, from a conversation in whispers between Golovan and Katarina behind the door of my wife's room. They had forgotten to close it and I heard them mention Simonida with apprehension, foreboding nothing good, and this ominousness was further confirmed by my wife's request: "Don't say a thing to Arsénie about all this." In the hope of learning more details, I had carefully pulled myself toward the door and pressed my ear to the keyhole as if to an earpiece, ready to move hastily and be found once again near the window, armed with my binoculars, should the two of them suddenly come out. Thus I learned with fear, despair, and fury that my Simonida was to be demolished and most probably replaced, and that the decision had already been signed by the responsible authority.

My last-born, the lovely Greek Simonida with her fine, dark countenance, her milky complexion beneath deep blue eyelids, and her full-blooded lips pierced by a bronze chain, African style. Simonida with her old-fashioned perfumes, penetrating, heavy, moist like musk, hung about with the ornaments given her by her spiritual father, the War Ministry engineer and architect Danilo Vladisavljević, and with those whitish streaks across her body characteristic of both convalescents from kidney disease and old houses. In 1925 she was without exaggeration the finest-looking building in the vicinity of Kalemegdan Park, a real family dwelling with large, comfortable, dark, warm, wonderfully unpredictable spaces inside, with secret rooms, and not in the least resembling today's termitelike architecture, those cell-like stone beehives which I could observe from the window. Simonida was especially dear to me, for it was she who had taught me that between possessor and possessed there is possible a deeper and at the same time nobler relationship than the purely financial one. It is to Simonida's credit that I ceased to be a landlord in the accepted and hated sense of the word, and that, instead of a seignorial, enslaving, and gangsterlike attitude, I created toward my houses a mutually possessive relationship, something more akin to polygamy.

It was with Simonida that I began to give the houses names. First just ordinary names, then personal ones. They had to be distinguished, just as living beings are distinguished, by real characteristics, and not by the names of the streets where they were built (even though I picked their company for them), or by the tenants who occupied them (even though I tried just as carefully to give them the inhabitants they merited), or by the level of the rents which were paid for them. But I always chose feminine names. I didn't do this because, in our language, the words *house, block, palace, villa, residence,* even *log cabin, hut, shack,* are all of feminine gender, whereas *building, country-house,* and *flat* are masculine, but rather because I couldn't have entertained toward them any tenderness, not to mention lover's intimacy, if by any chance they had borne coarse masculine names. While still looking at the drawings, I found appropriate names for the constructions I financed, although I often changed them when the buildings were finished.

When I bought houses already built, I would go into a careful analysis of their peculiarities, but in a quite different and much more fertile way than my professional colleagues, which earned me much criticism and mockery. The houses would be christened even before I had paid for them, then registered in the name of Negovan and entered on the property owner's map hanging on my office wall. This meant that I had definitely decided to buy them. I had recognized something personal, individual, exceptional in the houses offered for sale, something without which they would have had no value for me. This way I could look at them, busy myself with them, and communicate with them as if they were alive, which in fact they were. In the course of time they would be transformed by extensions or conversions, their defects would be remedied or their advantages added to, and they would change with aging as I did myself. In a certain way, I think, and I'm not ashamed to admit it, they were a chronicle of my life, my sole authentic history.

And now they wanted to pull one of them down, Simonida, and in her place, at the junction of Paris and Prince Mihajlova Streets, they intended to put up one of their tin garbage cans.

Yes, I thought, they're quite capable of it. It's as if they were Bolsheviks. Perhaps they are secret Bolsheviks waiting for a sign from the Kremlin to rush in and pillage. If I don't do something they'll raise their hands against my Simonida. I haven't the slightest doubt on that score. They tried to pull that sort of trick back in 1931. Lamartine Street at Kotež Neimar had to be straightened. George was living at No. 7a. Several houses which jutted out were threatened, among them the one I had named Katarina. It was named for Katarina because certain features of that thin, narrow house, as well as its simplicity and rationality, coincided with the character of my wife. What I undertook on that occasion I would have done for any house belonging to me. Not just for Katarina. I went to the Town Hall and demanded an annulment of the demolition order. Another street was designated for widening and other houses were pulled down, but my Katarina has remained in its place right down to the present day.

They're clearly assuming that I've lost all interest in my affairs since I ceased to control them personally. But they're mistaken! Arsénie Negovan isn't going to stand by with his arms folded and watch them tear down his beautiful houses. No, sir. I still have some influence. It's true that I seldom use it, but I still have it. In this town they can't treat a Negovan as if he were a nobody, a peasant who's just come down from the hills! Particularly if one takes into account that in my own way I'm one of the builders of Belgrade, one of those people who in civilized countries have streets named after them. No, I thought, they won't be able to harm my Simonida; I'll find a means of curbing them, I'll direct their destructive eye onto some other building which doesn't deserve to live.

First of all I'll go to Paris Street. I'll find out what's happening there. Judging from the conversation between Katarina and Golovan, the demolition hasn't started yet, but it will start soon. Very soon. They'll have to use the dry weather to get the lid on their tin garbage can. I know how these things are done. There isn't a single man in the building business who could put one over on me. Not the insatiable architects, nor the dishonest contractors, not even the slippery construction workers from Trsnotrava, to say nothing of pompous little civil servants. I decided, therefore, to go to the responsible authority once I had made sure that there was no simpler way to save Simonida. From the authorities I expected no problems at all. I knew people at the Town Hall. They would remember me from the times when I used to go to them to get the seal for my contracts. Nor had I anything to fear from higher authorities; there, my name was sufficient. Unfortunately, the difficulties didn't come from that direction. And it was a question not only of Simonida. But so as not to confuse the issue, I'd take things one by one.

I straightened myself up slowly, in stages. The sharp pain beneath my rib cage had long since passed, but it had left a weakness in my muscles which had to be overcome by movement. It was as if I were lifting a heavy sack of sand onto my shoulders. Yet when at last I had stretched myself out, the weight seemed to have disappeared. I felt quite sound, and if it hadn't been for a certain stiffness in the joints caused by my lengthy immobility, I'd even say that I felt a certain exhilaration, a renewed youthful élan. This pleased me, for the adventure—that's the only word for all that I intended to do—required a stronger physical condition than is allotted to a seventy-seven-year-old ravaged by a stormy life.

First I checked if the outer door was properly locked, and as a further precaution I latched the chain. Then I went into the bedroom to choose the suit in which to go out. Opening the creaking doors of the oiled walnut wardrobe, I expected to see before me the dim contours of seventeen once powerful Arsénie Negovans hanging on an iron rod. Their smooth, crumpled shoulders would be drooping down dejectedly so that the hard skeletons of the coat hangers could be made out beneath, glistening with the transparent crystals of naphthalene, soft as hoarfrost. The sharp smell would sting my nostrils; coughing, I would fan the wardrobe doors back and forth several times to disperse the smell, though this would achieve nothing, since the smell certainly penetrated the wood. The ghostly ranks of cloth would tremble with the sharp swinging of the doors, and quite clearly I wouldn't be able to bring myself to touch them since inevitably, if I put one of the suits on, it would look unreal, like a dried human skin from which the flesh had been shaken. It would remind me again of the photograph in George's war album: a single gibbet, erected out of iron tubing in the shape of an enormous Greek letter π, from whose crosspiece the Austro-Hungarian soldiers had hanged Serbian peasants. The hanging bodies were crumpled like the suits on the hangers. I recalled another sight, too, that hadn't particularly moved me at the time: at some abandoned Ukrainian station (was it called Solovkino?), I'd seen a grapelike cluster of five people who, evidently for the sake of economy, had been hanged on one rope with five separate wire nooses around their necks.

Now I'd feel that I had to choose between seventeen dead doubles, each of which was the coffin for one section of my life. For some I could still tell which year of the seventy-seven was buried there; the majority, though, would bring nothing to mind. I couldn't even say where and when I had had them made. Of course the color and the texture of the material would remind me of the season of the year; but whether I was married in those tails darting out of the cavern of the wardrobe like a snake's forked tongue, or in the morning coat with the lizardlike back, I simply couldn't remember. The morning suit I used for official morning visits; it would be too serious for this sort of private stroll. But I didn't want to put on just anything. This was to be my first time out in twenty-seven years. I was going to visit Simonida, I had to take account of my appearance. As far as the weather was concerned, I could dispense with an overcoat and put on the double-breasted blue with the white pin-stripe, although the light brown Ulster would be less conspicuous. I was afraid that the trench coat would hang too low: I had shrunk considerably since my heart trouble.

But in fact I was given no choice: when I unlocked the wardrobe only a single suit was hanging from the rod, wrapped in a cloth cover and sprinkled with naphthalene—the black one which I wore for funerals and, not without superstitious prejudice, avoided for all other ceremonial occasions. I had no time to imagine what Katarina had done with the sixteen others; perhaps she had sent them out to be cleaned. I put on the thin summer trousers, the black vest, and the black jacket with the buttons covered in dark silk. I could, it is true, have worn one of the only two which I used with my house jacket and kept in the wardrobe with the registers, but they were too ordinary for this occasion. And I could hardly hold it against Katarina that she had left me without a suit; she didn't know I was going out, and those two were quite enough to wear in the house. Moreover, she took good care of the older, abandoned ones: in spring and autumn she aired them at the window, brushed them, and sprinkled them with snowy naphthalene powder, then put them back in the wardrobe with a certain veneration, almost as if she were putting them in a tomb. And now she had sent them to the cleaners. My good Katarina! Even though her meticulousness condemned me to go to Simonida in a suit which boded evil, I was thankful to her for that unspoken certitude that one day I would go out of the house again.

From the drawer I took a white poplin shirt with mauve stripes, and a hard shiny rubber collar and cuffs. Then I expertly knotted an ash-gray silk tie and attached it to my shirt with a gold pin, its head dark as night with a precious alexandrite diamond. From Katarina's jewel case I took a pair of hollow gold cuff links like filigree tennis balls. Several more of my valuables were scattered about the box, but there were none of Katarina's jewels. Suddenly I was seized with a terrible premonition. Ignoring it, I hoped that for greater safety she had transferred the jewels to the wall safe under the icon of Saint George. But they were not there either. Nor could I find them in her desk. I had nothing more to hope for; quite clearly Katarina had deposited her jewelry in the bank. Despite my resentment toward banks and their thieving activities—and she must have known of my attitude from my open feuds with all the eminent bankers of the kingdom—she had probably, from an irrational female fear of loss, entrusted her jewels, our jewels, our valuable possessions, the possessions of Arsénie Negovan, to people to whom I wouldn't even have entrusted my excrement! So that's it, I thought angrily: we'll have something to talk about when she comes back from town.

I retained the linen I was wearing, but put on black socks, then my pointed black Bally shoes. In order to hide the seams, which were slightly cracked from standing long unused, I pulled on gray spats with a thin, darker edging. To all this I added two handkerchiefs hemmed with lace, arranging the smaller one in my coat pocket; light-blue gloves flecked with green; a light cane with a handle in the form of a silver greyhound's muzzle; and after short reflection, a Panama hat whose wide Boer brim gave me a bohemian appearance, and which with its air of holiday relaxation compensated for the gloomy significance of my suit.

Bearing in mind an old man's infirmity and my lack of practice in those slow actions which make up the art of dressing—the tie had to be tied in a pleated knot and pinned to the shirt front as a butterfly is pinned to a cardboard base; the buttons had to be pulled through the holes in the cuffs, which were stiffened from lack of use; the laces had to be threaded into the shoes, and the spats tugged on—and bearing in mind also my fear of being discovered, I, in fact, dressed myself quite quickly and neatly. However, I hadn't once turned around to look in the mirror, being quite determined to view myself only when everything was in place. So at last I gathered up gloves, stick, and hat and went up to its crookedly hung, framed surface, marred by smoky streaks, to see how I looked in the suit which I had almost certainly worn last at the funeral of Constantine Negovan.

Of my eight fellow pallbearers, opposite me is Jacob Negovan, son and heir of the deceased. Behind us, barely keeping his dignity under the weight of the hexagonal oak coffin, wriggles Timon, representing the dead man's absent brother Kleont, and the contractor's first-born son, Daniel Negovan. The massive rear of the coffin is being hustled along by two of Constantine's construction foremen with such unstoppable force that the nailed-down coffin sways as we charge down the steps of the chapel, and threatens to run away with the honorary pallbearers and descend like an avalanche on the hired musicians listlessly playing the Funeral March, and on the silent company gathered around the black and silver coach, to which are harnessed four black horses with the feathered mourning plumes fixed to their leather halters.

I can hear Timon, with the sharp-pointed ornament on the coffin lid painfully scraping his chin, telling the over-zealous bricklayers to slow down: "You're not carrying a load of bricks on a building site, damn it!" The pressure from behind slackens off. Once again we're carrying the coffin more slowly, though with every step we still stagger along the black carpet like an eight-masted boat pushed over a black wave by a wind from the stern.

I have no feeling for anything else but the dangerously increasing weight of the coffin; I am conscious of nothing save the orientally ornate chains, glistening in the damp October mist. From the sides of the coffin hang eight bronze handles entwined with thick gilt branches which only make it more difficult to carry the coffin, since my fist is too small to get a firm grip on them. Level with the lid, which is the color of burnt coffee, spread silver roots and palm fronds in riverlike profusion, recalling for Constantine, the architect, our Moskopolje origin; between them, gleaming islands of three-limbed, rhomboid-shaped bronze plaques alternate with silver arabesques, rolls, medallions, and gilt haloes from which the metal faces of angels shine as from a darkened window right up to the clasps, from which clustered silver lace falls motionlessly, caught up in places in loops of bulging yellow grain the size of ripe peas. I cannot see the legs, rolled in the form of scrolls, but one of them, the one beneath my handle, bangs against my bent knee at every step.

We move to one side, turning on the spot like a team of horses stuck in the mud, and place the coffin on the low catafalque, facing the gaping glass innards of the hearse. Then those on the left, headed by Jacob, come around to our side, and we line up along the right edge of the coffin so as to be able to take up the handles again immediately after the funeral oration, and lift the coffin into the coach. With my handkerchief I wipe away the sweat mixed with rain; the rain is no longer falling but is stationary in the murky air, lying on it like a veil of leaden drops. The musicians in their mournful capes press their instruments to their black chests: deadened movements of gold, from which here and there flutter damp, crumpled note sheets hung on wire hooks. In the darkened depths of the chapel somebody's hand—probably Katarina's—adjusts the folded-back draperies which cover the empty bier. The greasy dark yellow, brown, and mud-colored candles, cut by the funeral attendants' scissors, smoke and hiss and choke in their wax.

Out of that murky cavern lit only by the amoebal flames, there moves toward me a wax procession of mauve flowers, oval wreaths with shaking leathery greens around their crowns of blooms, and a huge copper-bound cross on the horizontal member of which is inscribed: *Constantine, son of Simeon Negovan, 1867–1936.*

Up into the movable black pulpit climbs the permanent secretary to the Ministry of Housing, G.K. He places a folded sheaf of paper on the reading stand, discreetly changes his glasses, impatiently tugs at the umbrella held over his head, coughs noisily to clear his throat, and begins the funeral speech. I can hardly hear him. Young Fedor Negovan, that irresponsible offspring of George's, stands behind me whispering: "Make thee an ark of gopher wood; rooms shalt thou make in the ark, and shalt pitch it within and without with pitch." I ask him to stop, but with redoubled sarcasm he goes on declaiming: "And, behold, I, even I, do bring a flood of waters upon the earth, to destroy all flesh, wherein is the breath of life, from under heaven; and every thing that is in the earth shall die." I try to get away from his silky, thick, almost feminine alto, but cannot move because of the group of mourners pressing around the bier. "And the Lord said, I will destroy man whom I have created from the face of the earth; both man, and beast, and every creeping thing, and the fowls of the air . . ." The measured posthumous praises of Mr. G.K. are corrupted at the very moment when they reach my ear by a distorted echo: ". . . for it repenteth me that I have made them." I turn toward the brazen culprit as far as the compressed space allows: "Will you shut up at once!" He looks me up and down like some object he has chanced upon, placidly, knowingly. "I can, Uncle Arsénie, but it won't help. God had the Negovans in mind, too—in fact, I think he had them especially in mind." "I don't care what you think." "I'm sorry about that, Uncle," he answers mockingly, "but at the moment you're not in a position to choose who you talk with." "I'd gladly box your ears!" I'm angry, and this to my discomfort inspires him: "No you wouldn't, and you can't even move your hand. Besides, Uncle, you're not sure how I'd behave: perhaps I'd repay you in kind. Actually, I've always wanted to hit a real, authentic Negovan. You're not the one I had in mind, but you'd do." "Why did you come to his funeral at all?" "For pleasure." "To see how we die?" "Yes," he admits straightforwardly, then coughs: "But even for me, if it makes any difference to you, it's not very pleasant. Don't you think that bureaucratic windbag could get on with his farting? Constantine won't be any better off because we've caught a cold." He is stand-ing on tiptoe to try to stop the wet from seeping through the cracked leather of his shoes. "Where are your galoshes?" I say maliciously. I'm not sorry for him; the voluntary poverty of a Negovan who had, so to speak, totally cut him-self off from the family and become an anchorite to humiliate us publicly only makes me angry. But this is not enough for Fedor. He wants to make me worry as well. "I haven't got them any more. Sophia made them into slippers." I hear him cough again. "For herself, of course," he adds. "That's in keeping with her name." I'm pleased that he's given me the chance to insult him. But quietly and with evident enjoy-ment, he agrees: "Yes, she's a bitch, a born bitch. That's what attracts me. With Sophia you feel as if you're sleeping with a garbage can."

From the front door came the adagio notes of a soft tune, followed by the shrill ringing of the bell, which in no way made me more disposed to welcome visitors. I was of two minds as to whether to respond at all. But I didn't have the nerve not to. Everyone knew that because of my condition there was always someone in the house, and I was afraid that my not answering the door would be inter- preted as if something had happened to me, particularly if it was Mr. Mihajlović, our most kind and attentive neighbor whom Katarina had prevailed upon to drop by in her absence.

It was indeed Mr. Mihajlović standing on the threshold. I peered through the glass peephole as through the eyepiece of one of my binoculars, not daring to let him into the hall lest my clothes puzzle him and start him thinking, but deem- ing it even less advisable to send him away rudely. So I had to find a means of reassuring him, and if possible, of getting rid of him. I thanked him for his attention and told him that I was all right, and that his kind offices weren't needed be- cause I had to lie down for a while. I was fully conscious that the more I talked, the greater the risk that the dark, portly, unkempt man in a worn vest pulled over striped pyjamas would conclude that I was not all right. First, because my voice had begun to tremble and break at just the wrong moment, and because I chose words which were more and more the emaciated synonyms for what had already been said; and also because I had begun to tap my fingers on the wood in apprehension as well as irritation. Finally, I said that I was going to bed at once, that I was undressed, that in fact I had been lying down when he had rung. At last I forced him to apologize fervently for disturbing me, which apologies put a stop to the complicated explanations that I could no longer sustain. When at last he had gone, and I had shut the brass cover of the peephole, I was as exhausted as if I'd been through another heart contraction.

I put in my wallet the documents which would prove my legal ownership to Simonida's tenants, who up to now had dealt only with Katarina and Golovan. Then I clipped my pince-nez to my vest pocket, figuring that after such strict isolation I would certainly be surprised and upset by something or other, perhaps even revolted, and looked for my pocket watch—not the Longines which I used every day, but the gold one engraved with the threefold tower of sapphires which was the property owner's symbol.

All I had to do now was to pick out a pair of binoculars that would slip easily under my coat. The Mayer which I most often used because it was light as a feather—I could not consider because it was too cumbersome. The small Mayer, the 6x30, was too heavy, and the artillery binoculars were clad in an iron suit of armor. The Zeiss prismatic 8x80 was just right in size and weight, but its range finder was damaged. And of course in this instance none of the single-barreled ones would be of any use. It is true that one or two of them would be easy to carry: some were even collapsible —their rings could be pushed into each other like the soft folds of a caterpillar—but unfortunately they would have attracted attention by their artificial appearance, and that would have caused more harm than good. Going over the whole collection, I suddenly remembered that Katarina had just what I needed. The opera glasses which we had bought in Budapest were a beautiful little instrument made out of ivory or some darker imitation, with a chrome rim around the bone body of the eyepiece and the lens and, what was most important, a light-colored handle which, while normally folded like a carpenter's rule, could be mounted on the body between the two barrels, and so make the whole instrument much easier to manipulate.

Of course, these pygmy-size binoculars were not particularly strong; one might even say that they were short-sighted. But since the objects which I wanted to bring nearer would hardly be farther away from me than a theater box from the stage, a longer range would have been of little use; and there was the added advantage that along with the handle it could be stuffed into an ordinary cloth bag. The only difference was that the theater box would be in the street—perhaps some bench in Kalemegdan Park, if it were near enough to Paris Street and if, of course, it were sufficiently solitary for such a tender meeting, since onstage across the street would be playing only one heroine, my Simonida. That was why it was wise to take the binoculars. When I got there I would want to look her over from close up. But my eyes, wearied by those forlorn buildings on the left bank of the Sava, would never allow me to go right up close to her intimately and examine her—not only to look at her but to scrutinize her, just as at the first meeting after a separation one takes one's wife's face between one's palms and examines it at length, comparing it with hesitant, nostalgic memories.

However, what I was really going to find I couldn't possibly foresee. Although I strove sincerely, while making my final preparations to go out, not to think about Simonida, nevertheless from time to time I found myself letting my imagination run on, ordering incomplete and sometimes hardly formulated suppositions, as if cutting from an enchanted picture book damaged photographs which only partially realized all the possibilities passing through my mind. Who knows, perhaps I would find her firm, solid body decrepit, her face wrinkled and lined with creases; perhaps she had lost her freshness and inspiration. Well, all right, everybody gets old, houses too have their life span, and not even the best of care can save them from eventual decay; but Simonida could not possibly be in that condition yet. Simonida wasn't yet fifty; next December she would be only forty-three. That isn't old for a house. It's the prime of life.

Why, then, was she being pulled down?

That was what I had to establish. I'd become accustomed to this problem through my experience with the two-storied Katarina. It was torn down for reasons which had nothing to do with the house itself. For just as people who have done nothing at all wrong are got rid of simply because they stand in the way of something, so houses too are destroyed because they impede somebody's view, stand in the way of some future square, hamper the development of a street, or traffic, or of some new building. Yes, even though they are quite innocent—still in good repair and often, alas, in their prime—houses suffer execution because they hinder some more elegant construction, a building with a stronger spine, a building which lays claim to their place, their site. So Simonida didn't have to be too old or fatally, incurably ill, for the decision to do away with her.

But what if she was? What if she were horribly ill—it couldn't be old age—and it had been hidden from Arsénie Negovan? Arsénie had been told: Simonida is quite all right, you should see how firmly she stands, how superior she holds herself among all those youngsters, all those empty-headed upstarts of concrete, steel, and glass. Modern buildings have outgrown her but they cannot outstrip her. What mixture was she painted with that the color needed renewing so rarely? What was she built with to be so resistant? But now she has been stricken down by some mysterious disease, she's falling apart, her stone is porous and disintegrating, her lintels are cracking, her walls crumbling, her stucco peeling like burnt skin, the wood at her heart splitting; nobody has lived in her for a long time, the occupants had to be evacuated so as not to be buried alive. But Arsénie was told—for he could see that Simonida's rents weren't coming in—that her tenants were in financial difficulties, and that no money should be expected from them for a long time to come; but you don't need money, do you, Arsénie?—you collect houses, not money, you're an owner of property, not a moneylender.

And suddenly everything had become possible. Since Katarina and Golovan—albeit for my own good—had tried to hide from me the fate which now threatened Simonida, why wouldn't they with still greater reason have kept me in the dark for years regarding her true condition? And also of the condition of others about which, in that fateful sense, nothing had been said? Why had the money from the houses dried up all at once? It's because of the crisis, Arsénie, I was told. Crises never affect everyone, Katarina. Outlay for repairs, Arsénie. Repairs are never carried out all at once, Katarina.

Once I had lost confidence in Katarina, I could no longer remain calm regarding other information offered me about my houses, my beloved houses.

I went up anxiously to the property owner's map. This was a blown-up plan of Belgrade, drawn in India ink on a background of snow-white draftsman's paper, on which the names of streets, squares, districts, and suburbs were marked in red, other geographical features in green, and the heading typed and stuck across the upper left-hand corner where the map ended toward Umka. As a basis I had used *An Alphabetical Index, Compiled from Official Data from the Municipal Land Register, T. D. No. 25728/33,* which had been edited and published in 1934 by St. J. Sušić, and *Belgrade Street by Street, A Guide and a Plan,* 1933, by the same compiler. Changes in street names, at the time when I still took an active interest in my affairs, were written in ordinary pencil, but clearly. At each spot where I owned a house there was a tiny cardboard flag, lemon-yellow or sky-blue depending on whether the house was bought or built under my direction. Each little flag had on it information about the name of the house, the district and street where it was situated, its number, the year in which it was built, the names of its designer and builder, the size of the plot of land, the number of stories and the style of the building, its investment value, its living area, the number and category of its apartments, and last but not least its rent.

I hesitated before the pictorial map like a worried general before a plan of his positions under attack, before the map which resembled my brother George's headquarters sections, those useless copies of wars. Only on this map it was not phantom tank columns which were moving forward, nor phantom companies which joined battle, nor phantom bombers which razed towns to the ground. There was no record of ruin and destruction on this map, but only of building and preservation of what was already built. It was a picture of creation and not of destruction, and I stood before this model of my threatened possessions gripped by the fear that I might arrive too late, that during the time I had spent as a hermit, isolated from evil, irremediable misfortune had already befallen Sophia, Eugénie, Christina, Emilia, Serafina, Katarina, Natalia, Agatha, Barbara, Daphne, Anastasia, Juliana, Theodora, Irina, Xenia, Eudoxia, Angelina, and on their whole breed, as had now happened to the most beautiful of them all, my good Simonida.

Here in front of an ordinary drawing, a street plan in a bamboo frame, as if in front of some family altar, I felt remorse that I had abandoned everything I'd lived for to the care of others—even though at that time there had been strong reasons for my decision: the riots which had almost cost me my life. I felt remorse that in a cowardly way I had believed that I could keep myself from danger by cunningly dropping out of sight as if dead, instead of taking the bull by the horns as all true, stubborn Negovans would have done, resisting, fighting, retreating in order to advance again, until victorious or slain in battle.

Fortunately, I now again felt young and determined, just as when I had gone out into the town to contract the work for my first house with the builders. I turned back the page on the church calendar—it was June 1968—and without bestowing a further glance upon the room in which the open shoe boxes lay stranded like stricken ships, I went out.

And once again, by the gong at the front door of the house, I found myself in one of those distressing moments of my past.

Here come the first bombs. They're falling slantwise. They seem to come from nowhere, swarming down magically out of the white honeycomb of the sky. Black holes open in the cloudless air. The aircraft can't be seen. Not even their silver trails, ribbons of silver paper like the tail of a kite floating behind. They must be hidden by the upper arch of the east window, through which I'm leaning. The explosions are soundless. I pay no attention to them. I leave them to George. I'm certain that, shielded by the eaves above the balcony in Lamartine Street as by some stone umbrella, my brother, with the same binoculars—provided, of course, that Mlle. Foucault hasn't yet dragged him away to the shelter—is watching the Allied squadrons and subjecting to withering criticism their frivolous formations, their badly chosen bombing runs, their ineffectiveness.

I myself, on the other hand, am attracted by the bombs. The round, moving, shaking azure veil in the binoculars is crisscrossed with projectiles like flying dots, like the wayward petals of a giant iron flower which has fallen apart high above the roofs, and is now scattering itself over the earth in slow, hesitant fragmentation, casting its seeds over the thick, powder-dry, smoke-filled furrows. Katarina pulls me away from the window—"You must go down into the cellar, Arsénie"—but I won't give in, I cannot leave my houses. I go on trying to guess in what area the bombs will fall, which of my houses is in danger. This is difficult, all the more so because my wife is at me to come away from the window. At first I think that the raid is over the Third and Fourth Wards, above the heads of Agatha, Juliana, and Barbara; then, carried by the wind, it's all falling on Sophia, Chris-

tina, and Simonida; then from the right, from the direction
of the railway station, comes a crash like the tearing of
gigantic dry tree trunks, which I can hardly make out. Now,
with Katarina trying to get me to go down into the cellar,
I'm leaning across the sill of the west window, from which
I can catch a glimpse of the balustrade railings on Angelina's
roof. Luckily, Angelina is unscathed, wreathed in a fiery
mist but apparently undamaged. Unfortunately, from this
distance one can't tell if she's been hit in the back. Behind
her the detonations move on, lightninglike, downriver; it's as
if along the shore, between the blades of the railway line,
some invisible beast whose red paws are raising clouds of
soot-colored dust is moving forward in convulsive bounds.
The giant grows weak before reaching the top of Senjak
hill. Calmer now, I have time to explain to Katarina why I
can't go down into the shelter while my houses are in danger,
why I have to stay where I can give them courage even if I
can no longer save them, but that I have no objection to
her going down, and promise that I'll follow immediately.
In the meantime a second invisible giant with a roar follows
in the smoke-filled track of the first, directly onto Senjak
ridge, where Eugénie stands alone and unprotected. A third
rumbles away to the right, its heavy footsteps stamping
across the river, and buries itself in the Sava embankment.

Beside me stands Major Helgar, Bruno Helgar from the
ground floor. *"Um Gottes Willen, Herr Negovan, das ist ein
Wahnsinn! Hören Sie nicht den Luftalarm? Man muss in den
Keller hinabsteigen!"* "It's very easy to go down into the
cellar, but why don't you stop them?" I shout. "They'll destroy my houses! Haven't you got some way of making them
stop this bloodletting?" "Our antiaircraft defenses are in action, Herr Negovan. We are doing everything we can."

With Katarina's gentle support, Helgar drags me away
from the window. "Don't be foolish, Herr Negovan, you can't
help your houses. You'll only get hurt yourself." "Am I im-

portant?" "And who'll be left to take care of the survivors?" asks Katarina. "Who'll repair those that are damaged?" There's some sense in that, *lato sensu,* and I'm obliged to accept it. I let myself be led down the stairs, which are shaking as if a powerful motor is buried beneath the stone—a furious dynamo which keeps grinding to a halt with a muffled explosion, then continues its pounding with redoubled force—and I am taken into the laundry room, away from the vaulted edge of the concrete trough which is faintly lit by a dimmed oil lamp. Seated on an upturned linen chest, I suddenly feel as if the maddened machine is all around us, around the mildewed walls which are shaking off plaster and cement, and which tremble as if in the grip of a fever. Major Helgar takes a slim metal flask from his pocket. The raid had caught him in the bathroom: his officer's jacket is thrown over his pink torso, overgrown with curly bristle the color of corn, and his cheeks are covered with a white, dried layer of shaving soap, like a clown interrupted while making up. He offers me the brandy, confessing that for such occasions— *für diese besondere Gelegenheiten*—he has prepared a dozen such containers (empties from some army medicine for rheumatism) which are both solid and light.

I decline his offer.

"My husband doesn't drink, Major," explains Katarina. She wraps me in a blanket which she had been carrying when we were still arguing, when she still wasn't certain whether I'd agree to come down, and when I was still certain that I wouldn't move from the observation post until the air raid was over and all my houses safe.

"I won't drink with you, Major."

"Why?"

"You can guess." The motor around us slows down, then starts rumbling again.

"Because I'm a member of the occupying forces, I suppose. *Ein einfacher Eroberer, nicht wahr?*"

"No. It's because you're a soldier. Because of your war and not because of your occupation, Major."

"Well, the war is as much yours as mine, Herr Negovan! We're only two sides of the same bitch of a war."

"You're mistaken," I counter emphatically. "This war is not mine!" I'm shouting above the detonations which now merge into a single incessant rumbling. "A man who builds houses or owns them cannot be party to a war. For him all wars are alien."

My tenant's lips open and shut in short jerks. He is talking, not to me but to Katarina, whom he is urging to get away from the outer wall and take shelter beneath the concrete trough. In that continuous torrent of noise, I'm striving to pick out from the single impervious mass of sound, from the middle of the acoustic cube in which I'm imprisoned, the scream with which my houses collapse—to distinguish the death rattle of Theodora at Dedinje from the agony of Alexandra at Vračar.

I ask Major Helgar—as a soldier, invader, and destroyer he ought to know—if every house dies as it lives, or if, like people, in death they cease to be distinguishable from one another. Instead of answering, without the slightest respect he pushes me rudely under the trough, and then he too squeezes in sideways.

I might easily never have recalled that barrage of noise. In fact the very next day after the Easter raid in 1941, when I was brought an exhaustive account of the damage—which, thank God, was far less than my panic-stricken estimates— I began to exclude that ill-favored raid from my conscious memory; or rather, I compressed it into a relatively ill-defined area of my memory, a cocoon which only under the pressure of extraordinary circumstances could be broken open. Thus of all the raids, there remained only a condensed impression in which an indefinite feeling of horror predominated over the most impressive scenes, and I would never have relived it in such frightening detail had I not again come down the same steps, and had that disintegrating pressure not at last been exerted. This time, of course, I didn't continue down into the cellar but went out into the street, reflecting on the creaking gate which needed oiling.

The ground floor shutters were flung wide open; I had to move off quickly to avoid the kind Mr. Mihajlović, whom I hoped I had left in the certainty that I was resting in bed. I rounded the corner of Srebrnička Street, from where, stealthy but unhindered, I could take a good look at the house in which I lived, and which from the window I could only see at an angle. Near it a gas station had been installed. On both sides of a prefabricated hut, in which all sorts of brightly colored cans with strange labels were displayed, stood four squat blue-and-white gas pumps with thick hoses twined around them.

Even now I probably can't explain why I never felt the need to give 17 Kosančićev Venac a name. Viewed from the street, the house had no special qualities. On a fine-grained brown plane, consisting of three vertical fields above a raised plinth which was pierced by three horizontal cellar windows, rose the ground floor and the second story, separated by two medallions in the shape of stone insignias in relief. On the third level a wooden door bound with forged iron opened onto a semicircular patio, while the whole building was topped by an almost flat roof, bordered by a balustrade with closely set railings in the form of stone skittles. It was natural that my own habitation should not inspire me in the same way as Simonida or the uninhibited, not to say lascivious, Theodora. Nevertheless, despite her lack of visual appeal, she possessed something unique. Since this was not visible from the outside, you had to go around and down onto the embankment, and look at her from the river, to see what it was that set her off: she possessed the finest orientation on the plateau of Kosančićev Venac, and her windows, facing west and overgrown with ivy, offered an unequaled view over the Srem plain.

From the window everything seemed new, *different*. But with the exception of the gas station, nothing on Srebrnička Street had actually changed. Not even the Turkish cobble-stones had been replaced by macadam—something I had tried to get done before the war. Whenever I'd thought about this sortie, I'd always envisaged myself on some unfamiliar corner, groping about helplessly like a blind man who taps the objects around him with his white walking stick, search-ing for traces of the past from which to orient himself. There was, I will admit, something childish in my behavior in those imagined surroundings; a grown man shouldn't have suffered the kind of agony I brought on myself. What's more natural than a town being transformed from year to year, built up and demolished. Had I not myself contributed to its meta-morphosis, had I not myself pulled down single-story cot-tages to build my houses in their place? Still, whenever I had tried to apply this reasoning to my imagined outing, after wandering for some time unimpeded through the transformed but still recognizable streets, I'd always end up at that inevitable and fateful corner (it was built of reddish brick, faced with whitened edges; the angle of the pave-ment at the corner was railed off with an iron chain of heavy, rusty links, whereas on the opposite side, which al-ways remained incomplete for me, there was a square with an elliptical asphalt promenade) —that fateful corner on which everything suddenly became unknown, strange, hostile.

I can't say that the fear of that brutal corner disappeared after I'd taken a few steps, but that fear was put into per-spective. I convinced myself that even if I did stumble upon that corner, the actual experience would be far less shatter-ing than the imagined one. To develop some defense mech-anism, I had to pay special attention to everything that dif-fered in the slightest from the picture of the town I had carried with me when I had irreversibly withdrawn from public life, to everything which during my absence had been built, added to, set up, changed, removed. And of course not only to houses, although they obviously dominated my interest, but to companies, advertisements, traffic signs, kiosks, shops, cars, and perhaps (why not?) even people.

And so, entering Zadarska Street, I stopped to read on the decrepit sloping roof of a battered old house, in crooked, chalked letters: "Reconnaissance Detachment Toza Dragović." I took this simply as a novelty and not, as might have been expected, a reason to feel disturbed, in that so many years after the war this puerile visiting card of some reconnaissance company of the Royal Army had not been erased, but remained to deface the house.

In the triangle between Srebrnička and Zadarska streets there was a bench which had been squeezed between the wall and a gnarled chestnut tree with such force that its slats, studded with large-headed nails, seemed to have grown right into the tree trunk. It looked as if, because it had served as a seat for so long, one end had reverted to its original form; or as if, by some strange quirk of reversed metabolism, the tree had put forth worm-eaten, flattened branches which parodied human handiwork. I was familiar with that deformed bench, too, only previously it had been surrounded by a small garden which now, still defending inch by inch the approach to the house, was being gradually pushed back by the street.

But the house itself held evil memories for me, not in its outward appearance, which was still fairly well preserved and solid, unmarred by any foreboding cracks, but because of a fullness which is characteristic of T.B. victims, people rotting away under a deceptively healthy exterior; it reminded me of the tragedy of Agatha. What had brought a serious crisis upon Agatha were my relations with Major Bruno Helgar, the only German whom, since he lived in the requisitioned flat downstairs, I had been forced to see with any regularity. Given the hostile attitude to the Occupation, my own forebearance couldn't be understood, still less approved of, without the knowledge that the entry of the Germans into Belgrade—in other respects a cause for lamentation—didn't affect me materially. I was sorry, of course, that it had come to this (despite the fact that I had criticized the government for their adverse attitude, and especially because of the provocative street riots which led me so irrevocably to seek a safe asylum in my home), and I of course shared the general unease with which one awaits an administration whose legal mechanism is unknown and whose measures of government cannot be foreseen. But with the exception of the cessation of building activity (I had already on my own largely given up the buying and building of houses), and the requisitioning of accommodations (which also in no way troubled me, for the Germans, in moving out the former inhabitants, took care of my possessions with truly Teutonic scrupulousness; given such an attitude to my houses, the question of financial compensation, although important, was never decisive for me)—with these exceptions, then, the only conflict between us arose as a result of the raid of April 6, 1941, in which the poor, blameless Agatha suffered. The other houses came out of it with minor damage—some were untouched—but Agatha perished, even though her position was not prominent, nor was there any tempting military object nearby.

However, that part of her fate which was the most unusual (when shall I ever stop mourning her?), and which made her a precursor of that solid house on Srebrnička Street, was that the mortal wound she had suffered that April went unnoticed. In the obvious sense of the word, there was no wound; nevertheless, for three full years thereafter, Agatha was in fact dying as she looked the very picture of health. She was expiring silently without any signs of weakness, without a single cry, without that cracking, grinding, and splitting which betray decaying buildings, until at Easter 1944 she gave way and, untouched by any bomb, collapsed of her own accord like a tower of cards. Seven tenants were crushed under her ruins, and the inquiry which was opened on a petition against me by their relatives took as its starting point the ignorant, base, and of course quite erroneous premise that property owners in their pursuit of profit rent houses which are dilapidated and liable to fall down. The inquiry categorically cleared me of that repulsive suspicion. Experts affirmed that Agatha, up to that time a perfectly sound and well-preserved building, had been seriously but unnoticeably damaged internally in the first German bombing—something like a human visceral hemorrhage —so that before she suddenly collapsed she was undermined from inside, decomposed, shattered; they affirmed that the owner had absolutely no way of knowing this and that in that year, 1944, a single distant shock had been sufficient to demolish her. There was no doubt that the house in front of which I was now standing would end up in the same way. And having made this observation, I was ready to proceed along Zadarska Street toward Topličin Venac.

At the line where the cobblestones gave way to a radical band of asphalt and I came out of the shade into the sun, I had the disturbing impression of leaving behind a forsaken region where eternal stillness reigned, broken only rarely by a sound of unknown origin, by some indistinct voice, the dense noise of the wings of a startled bird, the muffled squeak of a gate at the mercy of the wind, or a ship's siren. I had the impression that the area which I had passed through so far was nothing more than an annex, an unusual continuation of my room; that the sidestreet with its close-set walls was only the corridor leading out of my house; and that the sunlit opening at its end, marked by a square metal sign warning me that I was entering the blue parking zone, was the door through which I would leave. It was as if I had still to take the first step toward Simonida.

I immediately told myself that my worry could not have been occasioned by the crowds I had encountered after step-ping out of an empty street. Those people were quietly going about their business; indeed, most of them could have lived in my apartments without my losing self-respect. But I was no longer among them, among my own clientele, for suddenly I found myself in the midst of quite different people: again for the nth time and who knows at what cost, it was March 27, 1941; once again I was hurrying to Stefan's auction and once again I came upon an unruly mob.

People were milling about in all directions, banging into one another, pushing each other aside like badly directed billiard balls. I had to get out of their way for most of them seemed not to heed where they were going, but on bumping into one another changed their course and with the same surefootedness set off in a new direction determined by the chance collision. It was as if they were bumping against muscular rubber mattresses from which they were flung back still more wildly, and then whirled around bemused in an elastic cage composed of invisible springs. But all of them, densely packed and growing denser as more arrived, were moving down toward Brankova Street and the concrete apron in front of the King Alexander Bridge, where a three-deep cordon of police was waiting for them. Not even those rioters whom the volcanic pressure at the center had driven into my street as into an empty sleeve, were by all appear-ances grateful at being squeezed out of this frightful mill whose grinding stones, turned by the mill wheel of hate, crushed, pounded, and ground them. No, with visionary blindness they again hurled themselves into it, pushing into the moving current of flesh as into plastic clay, and again merged with it in a ritual ecstasy which deprived them of control over their limbs. There could be no question of any individuality or reasoned initiative here: thus assimilated, faceless, depersonalized, they rushed on toward the bridge, deprived of any individual movement or personal choice of the direction which the demonstration was taking. It was as if all the separate strength of their previously independent bodies had been gathered together by a single all-absorbing superbody or omnibody which, freed from individual cares and restraints, was smashing and destroying everything in their now unburdened name.

Loyally subordinating themselves to this unifying force, they linked arms in a solid trellis of fists and pushed forward as if boiling over from a white-hot cauldron of discontent and despair. The participants in these demoniacal rounds were constantly replaced by others; sidelong tremors broke apart their single-line chains, tore at their links, replaced them with more resistant, firmer ones. Those who were pushed aside, after having been battered for a time by the oncoming ranks, would grab on to other lines, for which it appeared a lesser strength was sufficient, for they were out of direct range of the constraining blockage, lower down at the approaches to the bridge.

Stretched up over the mob were poles bearing the Yugoslav and Serbian flags. (One of them was red, yes, completely red like newly shed blood.) They were carried between two masts and looked like a bloodied bandage which had just been unwound from a giant's forehead. I felt myself once again in the outskirts of Voronezh, in the midst of an evil mob of rioters, their ranks like rows of coal-black, sodden hovels. It was 1919, the White General Marmontov had already retreated across the Don, and under the protection of the riflemen of Budyony's Sixth Cavalry—who, clustered together into smallish, perhaps even fortuitous groups, looked down from their horses with soldierlike indifference, half-dozing—the mob was dragging frightened, stunned people out of porchways: people in dressing gowns, kaftans, fur coats, cloth cloaks, field overcoats, waterproof capes, and coats with sable collars—from their appearance, respectable middle-class folk and even, I fear, property owners who, as was later explained to me, were counterrevolutionaries, Denikinites, Black Hundreds, and black marketeers. They were beating them with staves and forcing them to crawl in the gutter before their own houses, which they did quite earnestly, even so to speak committedly, while they were battered in the clinging autumn mud with the same staves, pickaxes and hammers. Then the crowd moved toward other houses where the wailing, like that of a forlorn and abandoned dog, awaited them.

Now, today, I beheld placards of brown paper, cardboard, and cloth on which slogans were inscribed in black and red oil:

DOWN WITH THE ANTIPEOPLE PACT!

LONG LIVE THE ARMY!

DOWN WITH THE GOVERNMENT OF TRAITORS!

DOWN WITH FASCISM!

DEATH TO THE GERMAN HIRELINGS!

BETTER THE GRAVE THAN BE A SLAVE!

BETTER WAR THAN THE PACT!

All this I could understand (though not of course approve), since in those conceited sentiments there was much more of a national, Slav, Kosovo, Salonika-front spirit than of revolutionary intent. But among the protests, and especially among the demands, were some which by their radical Bolshevik line took me back to Voronezh and that macabre railway halt of Solovkino. The troublemakers—undoubtedly Moscow stooges—were brandishing placards on which I made out with amazement:

DOWN WITH THE CORRUPT BOURGEOISIE!

WE DEMAND A POPULAR FRONT!

DEMOCRATIC FREEDOM FOR THE MASSES!

LONG LIVE OUR RUSSIAN BRETHREN!

WORKERS, UNITE SOLIDLY IN THE STRUGGLE FOR OUR COMMON CAUSE!

UNION WITH THE USSR!

ALL POWER TO THE PEOPLE!

Which was only a more cunning way of saying: all power to the Soviets, all possessions to the nonworker rabble!

One might think that for my own peace of mind I would have chosen a roundabout route for my visit to Simonida, a detour which would lead me away from that howling procession of hysterical fiends gathered from all sides on the afternoon of March 27, 1941, on Pop-Lukina Street, and still surging down it right up to the present day as if awaiting me, as if again blocking the road in front of me. I had been afraid only of that single corner in my dream, yet here I was now stopped by a familiar stone angle with a passageway, into which I had retreated to avoid being trampled down. Could I have reached Simonida by the more accessible Paris Street? I must say at once that it would have been impossible, just as it had been impossible at that first, real encounter. I had done all I could do to get away from them! I had gone around the corners on the vertical line which joined Kalemegdan Park to Nemanja Prospect. Yet each time I came up against the procession I tried to outflank it, keeping to streets which were parallel. No good! It flowed along densely in an all-blanketing layer which settled upon pavements and houses, just like vacuoles and minute bubbles of protoplasm which feed through their skin, consuming open space. And every minute I was in danger from that jellylike, voracious mass, one of whose extruded sleeves, having penetrated into the sidestreets, might suck me in like a stream of gelatine that in sliding down a glass absorbs sprinkled droplets from all sides.

That, then, was the reason why even now it made no sense to look for another route to Simonida. Between me and my threatened house serried ranks of riffraff, whom nothing could disperse, were still passing; in fact they were there only in my irritating memory, and their phantom procession was no longer under the control of the real laws of pressure and compression, but of some kind of laissez faire, protected by memory, over which only I had a certain influence. Only I, therefore, could eliminate them, although the term "eliminate" could in no way be taken literally, for it was not my aim to erase my events from my memory; I could have done that only by eliminating their living results! Rather I desired to reconstruct them in the transforming light of new consciousness, bearing in mind the forthcoming meeting with Simonida, over whose uncertain position they perhaps had a fateful power—to reconstruct them unhurriedly, objectively, as it were *outside my own self,* and to show myself that my decision to withdraw from society had been at the very least premature, irrational, unfounded, in short mistaken, and that but for that decision I would today have been free of the need to defend my embattled domain.

I believe, however, that it would be useful to look back a little and explain why I hadn't returned home immediately on coming face to face with the demonstration. I can safely assert that among the property owners there was not one (and I knew them all well, and had maintained professional relations with the most eminent of them) for whom the safety of his own skin wouldn't have been more vital than his work—work in that higher sense which doesn't depend on the size of income or the index of growth, but on the character, capacity, and depth of feeling which together are put into it.

Such men increased their possessions either through inertia, to be secure in old age, or simply to strengthen and solidify their personal or social integrity. They didn't do it to augment their property as such, or in any way to become identified with the things which belonged to them, so that they should merge with these objects of commercial control into an indivisible whole, be absorbed into a mutual lymphatic system for the flow and flood of capital, feeling, will, rent, ideas, instinct, profit, hope, beauty, revenue, passion, and the remaining forms of living—a unity of two otherwise opposite beings in which, as in ideal love, it would no longer be possible to distinguish possessor and possessed, owner and owned, and where the very act of possession would be so completely reciprocal that sometime, perhaps in some perfect world, it would become one with the act of self-perception.

It goes without saying that my professional friends were far from the ideal concept of property ownership. The exception, although in a completely different sphere, was perhaps Theodore, the deceased Theodore X., Negovan's adopted son, the one who had studied at the Jewelers' School in Amsterdam. Every diadem, necklace, bracelet, stud, earring—each individual piece of jewelry in his shop possessed him to the same degree as he, Theodore, was its possessor. Even more so, for Theodore was capable, in his otherwise voluntarily subordinate position, of manifesting scrupulous effort, fatherlike care, tender love, and even adoration of the particular article of adornment he owned (compare this with my attitude toward my houses), while the jewels (again akin to my houses) could only return all this devotion with an unimpassioned shine which sparkled, in all its colors, from behind the thick crystal pane of a display cabinet, with its comfortable bed of purple and dark blue satin.

Certainly those other possessors would not be capable of such things. Indeed, can I call them by that honorable name? They have become so alienated from their own possessions that, since no direct or personal link binds them, they no longer *possess* at all in the popular sense of the word, nor does the possessed have any right over them. These men no longer operate in real objects belonging to them, but in their vague, alien, shadowy affairs, such as acquisitions on

the stock market whereby industrial and agricultural products, immovable assets, land, mineral wealth, ores—in a word,
all the wealth of this planet—are transformed into paper
values, barely perceivable in concepts of rent, dividends,
shares, loan extensions, cash and terms of work, or agreed-
upon deferred payments (just as nothing at all could be
found out about my houses—about their appearance and
soul, or our mutual relations—from the concept of rent).
Inevitably, that abandoned trace of reality is finally lost by
its owner. Yet it's quite inappropriate to call them owners,
for they have acquired only echoes of those shadows—in fact,
their formless movements up and down, movements defined
by the stock exchange index, by the possessor who, specu-
lating *à la hausse,* on the rise of shares, or *à la baisse,* on
their fall, in fact possesses only disembodied differences between changeable and similarly disembodied sums, nuances
which themselves are exceptionally inconstant and changeable.

In short, between the other owners' and my own understanding of possessions there had come about—gradually, of
course—a complete difference of opinion which could, for the
sake of expressiveness, be compared with the essential difference between the theological representation of God as an
impersonal concept of omnipotence, and the real, incarnate
God which believers experience in their very soul. This op-
position had led me to suspect that all my apparent "professional friends," if by some mischance they had found themselves in my position, would have retreated before that
street of rioters, probably because everything which made it
necessary to pass through that pandemonium, through that
molten hell as over an enemy redoubt, could be postponed to
some more favorable occasion; or if it couldn't—if it really
were a question of that unique chance by which it is sometimes possible to surprise the market—they would neverthe-

less have preferred to renounce the profit involved than to risk their own life.

(My exclusive aim in pausing at this to some extent historic spot was not to reconstruct my feelings *at that time,* in the context of conditions and their meanings for me *then*— that would have been a real and useless feeling, like that which against my will had once again drawn me back to the funeral of Constantine Negovan or to the laundry room under the stone trough—but rather to subject them to a critical assessment from the considerably altered *present-day* viewpoint. To disclose the errors of my behavior which had almost brought about my demise, I had to comment on them, so as to be able to argue with those earlier feelings as if they hadn't belonged to Arsénie Negovan, but to some other person, quite indifferent to him.)

Although I wasn't stubborn in the usual sense of the word, I was embellished—if indeed it *is* an embellishment, and I believe it had to be so, Katarina's views to the contrary—I was embellished, I repeat, by that conqueror's nomad's, and traveling merchant's constancy of purpose which brought my ancestors, still bearing the Graeco-Tsintsarski name of Nago, from the backwoods of Aegean Macedonia, out of dreary anonymity, to attain first of all a separate identity, and later our enviable present-day power in society.

I would never have written all this down, of course—I was already making spontaneous use of it, living it in fact—had I not been asked to give a lecture at the Jubilee of the Circle of the Sisters of Serbia. The ladies of the organizing committee intended this to be a series of lectures about the multiple aspects of urban life under the general title "The Different Faces of Belgrade," which was to take place once a week in the large hall of the Kolarac Institute. B.P., Professor of Comparative Literature at the University of Belgrade, was enlisted to say a few words to those eminent ladies, so desirous of knowledge, about the artistic realities of the capital. (To this day I'm not clear why he thought it appropriate to deliver, in his otherwise incomparable manner, something on "The Eighteenth-Century Frenchwoman.") N.N., an experienced Treasury architect, was to summarize the architectural content of the general theme, following which the biggest names were engaged according to their own special interests. And so, as secretary of the Chamber of Commerce, I was chosen to inform my ambitious listeners about that less romantic aspect of Belgrade life, the mechanism of its economic development; in this way, apparently the part of the general title of the series promising an insight into the unknown side of the town would be fulfilled. So I had to talk about the monetary system, stock exchange speculations, exports and imports, industrial perspectives, trade and the market; about goods, clearing, rent, stocks, shares, bills of exchange, bankruptcy (both real and fictional), imposition of taxes, accumulation, profits, and wages (I remember that under wages it was suggested that in passing, *in nuce,* I should dispose of the Problem of the Workers). But all this, of course, in a way which would be both entertaining and accessible to the ladies.

I must immediately make it clear that before this offer I had never appeared at public gatherings; with the evident exception of meetings of the Chamber, auctions, and professional conferences, this particular art was for me something completely new. Without any doubt, I would have refused to take part—however flattering it was—had I not had in mind the benefit to my own business affairs which could accrue from this close and essentially intellectual contact with the wives of our most important and influential industrialists, merchants, bankers, capitalists, statesmen, and politicians. Above all, I didn't have a very able tongue, although—here I'm giving passively the opinion of others—I knew how to rise to heights of poetic inspiration whenever

I talked about my own houses or something directly related to them. On this occasion, however, there was to be nothing about houses, or at least about mine, though property ownership did come within the scope of the lecture. I was to talk about such great matters as the mechanism of economic developments which, it was naively believed, would lay the foundations for the prosperity of our flea-ridden, Levantine community. Most lamentably of all, in my statement of the essentials of the banker's profession, for example, I was expected to praise that very type of possession which is the true antithesis of real possession, and to turn real possession's living forms into a vampirelike roundabout of soulless and faceless figures on the current stock exchange index!

Arsénie Negovan could not agree to such blasphemy! I decided to make use of the occasion for myself—and, in a somewhat indirect way, for my listeners' husbands—to outline my own ideas about the subject, mainly my views about the essential difference between the erroneously favored *single-phase* ownership and the benefits of the equal, reciprocal dual-phase type. This was my own terminology to illustrate the fact that true ownership can only be one in which the subject and the object share possession mutually, in consequence of which all differences between them are erased, so that the Possessor becomes the Possessed without losing any of the traditional function of Possession, and the Possessed becomes the Possessor, without in any way losing its characteristics of the Possessed. In short, I would explain my philosophy of Possession.

Carried away by this power for enlightenment, I threw myself into the work and quickly prepared an outline of my lecture. Bearing in mind my inexperience as an orator, I thought it best to test my impact on some more experienced speaker. Not wanting to give my casual, so to speak, amateur soliloquy any prior publicity—for it was in some way to be a conversation with myself at which, quite fortuitously, the matrons of our town were to be present—I took it in type-script to Mr. Joakim Teodorović, through whom, as the initiator of the function, I normally communicated with the Circle. It would be unjust to complain that Mr. Teodorović didn't show an immediate interest in my work—perhaps "interest" is too modest a synonym for the tense expression of his face while he literally raced over the text, in which the heavy Remington letters stood out in lines like grains of wheat, like the lead beads on the wires of a child's abacus—or that he was miserly in his praise, although for my restrained taste they were a little overeffuse.

Despite this promising reception, I never appeared on the rostrum of the Kolarac Institute with my "completely original angle." To this very day I am unaware as to why this came about, and why in my place Mr. Teodorović himself gave the lecture, meekly and unintelligently retracing all those weary errors by which this vast subject is devastated. In actual fact I presume he retraced them, for it goes without saying that I didn't have the honor of being present at the lecture. But this was not important for me now, *invidia virtutis* (or as is said nowadays, *comes—invidia virtutis comes;* envy is the companion of virtue), as the Romans would have exclaimed; all this was but a pretext for me to recall something quite different. Actually, in putting together the sketch of the lecture that was not to be, I had noted down in the margin, just as they came to me, several concise definitions, paradigmatic notes which were really too exclusive to be included in the framework itself. These notes should have been read by that idiot Joakim Teodorović, for him to see what a "completely original angle" really meant, but they were indeed the barest essentials of what, in a more subtle version, I intended to elucidate for my Serbian Sisters of the Circle. As far as I remember, these notes could be reduced to a number of axioms:

1. I do not own houses, we, I and my houses, own each other mutually.
2. Other houses do not exist for me; they begin to exist for me when they become mine.
3. I take houses only when they take me; I appropriate them only when I am appropriated; I possess them only when I am possessed by them.
4. Between me and my possessions a relationship of reciprocal ownership operates; we are two sides of one being, the being of *possession*.

There were several others—probably they began to develop the above principles in individual areas of ownership—but, hesitating on the asphalt threshold of Pop-Lukina Street, looking at the pale-colored, unequally hewn-out gashes of the streets on the other side of the imaginary procession, I wasn't capable of recalling them. It was, indeed, superfluous to try. The ones I could remember were sufficient to restore my faltering conviction about the decision which I had then taken. I had to get across. Such decisiveness, whatever may be said, came straight from my possessor's heart and was therefore legitimate.

Here, of course, that ill-considered step which for many years shut me in my house cannot be hidden. Perhaps the mistake was made later. I don't deny the possibility that I even foresaw something of the sort, that I got something confused while forcing my way through the mass, or even during the subsequent incident. I can allow this—I'm only at the beginning of my reconstruction—but without any doubt, at the intersection of Zadarska and Pop-Lukina Streets I couldn't have acted in any other way than the way I did.

At that time my heart, my possessor's heart, was worrying about the house which my cousin on my father's side, Stefan Negovan, had built on Kosmajska Street, No. 41:

"Stefan's Folly" as the neighbors called the free, and certainly lighter and more intelligent, copy of Dietrich and Eizenhofer's Academy of Sciences in Vienna. Its appearance, taken from a baroque, aristocratic *hôtel particulier,* with some of the aspects and forlorn contours of a Chinese pagoda, gave the impression of a dwarf-size castle in the middle of the town, with tin, butterflylike wings as roofs from whose arch a mildewed copper dome burgeoned like a festering boil, like a breast with a circular lantern around it, with a tympanum in the middle of the façade, a blind, three-cornered Cyclop's eye from whose edge hung two pairs of (four in all) Corinthian columns like stalactite tears, with the three-sided hollow of a balcony between them and loggias to the left and right, with French windows and an ornately worked portal instead of an entrance door. Nor did the interior lag behind the façade: It was hung with expensive wall lamps, and the ceilings were of alabaster and the floors of lacquered oak, with spiral staircases and raised marble daises. Even discounting the unique furniture—in which, en route to a bearable compromise, the haphazard taste of Stefan's wife Jelena had clashed with the patriarchal heritage of her hated mother-in-law—the house recalled a padded chest where precious souvenirs were collected. And now it had come about that Stefan's Folly had cast its Cyclop's eye on me.

Not at once, of course, not the very moment it was built. When I first caught sight of it—I'd been abroad at the time it was completed—I was amazed, and that's no exaggeration; I was in fact appalled. In the humble, simple, architecturally modest surroundings of Kosmajska Street of that time—where two plots away, at No. 45, stood my Aspasia, up to then the bravest of houses, and across the way, Kleont Negovan's bungalow, the somber face of which was smooth as a serpent —in these surroundings, Stefan's palace produced a truly disturbing effect, irritatingly perverse and pretentious, like an erratum, a coarse printing error in the elegant context of the street; or, to keep closer to its essential character, like a fit of madness which had suddenly taken hold of deranged, frustrated stone and which, with hysterical joy produced its own malignant currents like cancer, its swellings, lumps, tumors, lesions, humps, ganglions, haemotomes, and all that metastasis of distorted stone forms. I could go on listing comparisons indefinitely, and still only begin to give the displeasing impression which Stefan's new house left on me at first sight.

Right from the beginning, at the moment of my first astounded repulsion, the seed of my later admiration was sown. I and Stefan's house—I'm now loath to consider it Stefan's—were like two beings at first sight divided by antipathy, but who began secretly to draw closer long before that antipathy was overcome and repudiated; moreover, quite unquestionably the initiative belonged to the house, or rather to its irresistibly extraordinary quality. I remember that, on returning to Kosančićev Venac a second time—Stefan hadn't moved in yet—I was furious. (Why that anger, when the house wasn't mine and had no reason to concern me? That a Negovan should make himself ridiculous before everyone could affect me personally only insofar as the uninformed might confuse the two of us.)

I shouted at Katarina that that irresponsible Stefan had built himself a monstrosity cheek by jowl with Aspasia—an unseemly stone aberration, *une sépulture presumptueuse des pharaons, nécropole dans la petite version primitive balkanique,* never mind what his original intentions had been; for certain, that gilded Georgian pumpkin had stuck her poisonous oar in; certainly it was far from responsible or considerate, not to mention cousinly, to contaminate the street with such a house and spoil—what am I saying, completely desolate—a whole area as if Belgrade were his patrimony, dowry, feudal domain, and not a public treasure subject to recognized laws, not to mention urban principles. "What's more," I said, "he must have greased someone's palm generously to have been allowed to indulge in such madness, with no concern at all that there are still houses being rented on Kosmajska Street. Now, of course, with Stefan's scarecrow alongside them, the question is whether they can be rented at all, never mind if there'll be any rent out of them!"

"I thought that a palace like Stefan's would raise the value of any street," said Katarina.

"And when have I cared about the money?"

She could see how angered I was by the mere suggestion that I would agree to put my pocket before my devotion to building, my only true activity, for which property ownership was simply a kind of civic alibi: that exciting and intoxicating feeling that I, with my own hands (for in the final issue, it is I who guarantee the means) take from nature as from some usurious possessor earth and ore, stone and wood, and give form to that rough clay, to that stone and wood; the feeling that with my own hands (for here too, don't I guarantee the means?) I transform them at my designers' drawing boards into magnificent visions, build them up finally into people's possessions, possessions which only by name and for a short time are mine. Seeing therefore that she had wounded me deeply, my wife conciliatingly exclaimed that it wasn't revenue she had in mind at all, nor wealth either, but standing, prestige; *la renommée bourgeoise* was what she was concerned with, in mentioning which—*la renommée bourgeoise*—she was really only repeating rather clumsily my own aired opinion that a house's standing and that of its occupants were in a reciprocal relationship, like a mirror and the face reflected in it: the inhabitants of a house heighten its reputation and the importance of its location, just as a house, by its position, its location, guarantees the importance of its tenants.

At that, I rather skillfully drew her attention to the fact

that it was indeed *my houses* which built up all those sub-
urban districts before what she understood by *address* became important, and that the opposite was not, or only very
rarely, the case. Despite the unquestionably favorable status
of those districts—and in no case would I underestimate or
deny its real effect on the continuous rise in the value of
my properties—if it hadn't been for me and entrepreneurs
like me, and our enterprise, sincerity, professional talents,
persistence, farsightedness, and even diplomatic skill (first
intelligence and then money, of course, for what can intelligence alone achieve, what good is intelligence without
means?), there wouldn't have been any addresses on the hill
at all, and certainly not those worth making any kind of fuss
about. Instead, there would have been the garrison's stables
and gun emplacements; they would still be breeding geese
on the open fields of Dedinje and Topčider; and the village
yokels would still be lightheartedly relieving themselves
against the gates of the few carelessly thrown together week-
end houses.

"That's just what I'm saying, Arsénie. If your houses built
up Dedinje, why shouldn't Stefan's help build up Kosmajska
Street."

"Because there's no need for anyone to raise Arsénie's already solid values, and certainly not that lout Stefan with his
oafish house!"

"Well, like it or not, you'll have to raise Aspasia's rent
now."

"I know. Only then I'll have to renew her façade and have
her painted, and perhaps even install central heating."

"Well, at least you don't mind spending the money."

"Of course I don't mind!"

Even without the new rental, I had intended to refurbish
Aspasia. Clearly I would have spared neither money nor effort
in putting her back into shape, but I didn't want to waste
money on making her stand out in the neighborhood. Reno-

vation was necessary for Aspasia, not for my landlord's pride, and she certainly didn't need to be surrounded by gypsy shacks.

"I don't care about money, Katarina, but I do need it for new construction."

"Always new construction," she said dispiritedly.

"Yes," I said without bitterness. "Always new construction."

There was no point in harsh words. She, poor child, just didn't understand. She couldn't understand that possession, like any other living thing—like love, for example, love or fame, power or capability, vice or virtue—must be fed, must grow, become fruitful and multiply, if it wishes to go on.

At this, I somewhat conceitedly set about explaining to her the beneficial significance of the reproductive urge for the industrial and social prosperity of the nation, referring continually to nature, and seeking out its already well-trodden paths, when suddenly she burst into tears. Seeing her distress, I abandoned my exposition. (Our personal contribution to this universal urge for reproduction was at that time, due to the ramifications of my landlord's affairs, relatively lacking, and the fate of our only son, then not yet born, would later demonstrate that it was better to put a stop to such negligence.)

"For God's sake, Arsénie, can't you forget that house just for once?"

That evening we were awake for a long time, both because of the heat, which the proximity of our overheated bodies in the marriage bed increased unbearably, and from worry.

"How can I forget it when he's ruined a whole street?"

"Sometimes I feel like setting it on fire!"

"And how do you think I feel about it?"

"It and all your own cursed houses!"

"He's loused up the whole street!"

"The whole filthy town!"

"The whole street, I tell you!"

Indeed, as regards Stefan's respect for conventions such as the unity of the object with urban space and its character, he could have put up a Chinese junk or some mammoth Polynesian idol at No. 41, had he wished to, and produced the same unseemly effect.

"What can you do now? It's there."

Perhaps I could have forced something through the Town Council. I would have received support from the property owners of Kosmajska Street: something of the sort was hinted at (with due respect for my family ties with Stefan) by Mr. Martinović, the wholesale grain merchant at the corner of Kosmaj and Topličin Venac, with whom I had the doubtful pleasure of making my first visit to the monstrosity. But the affair could never get as far as pulling it down, which would have been the only just and logical decision. God knows what kind of administrative circus we would have had to embark on—evidence and counterevidence, committees and subcommittees, complaints and petitions, applications, specialists' reports, delays and postponements—without any real administrative outcome other than to provoke a dispute with Stefan and to offer the Negovan-Turjaškis yet another chance to accuse me of the Oriental sin of disloyalty to the family.

"I'd end up being called disloyal, and envious into the bargain, but still not achieve what I wanted."

"I think I'll go to sleep now," said Katarina.

"You don't understand it at all."

"No, I don't."

"That monstrosity of Stefan's would stay where it is, but I don't say that nothing at all would be achieved. At least we could make certain that such abominations were stopped in the future, perhaps on the basis of some committee to keep watch over the town, since we still don't even have an advisory body to defend our town by law from the whims of dilettantes and the nouveaux riches. We want to build a sky-scraper—the only reinforced concrete skyscraper in Europe, and so forth—but when you get caught short in the street as I did recently, while tying yourself in knots you have to rush around to a friend's—if you're lucky enough to have one—and even then you can't rush off straight from the door. You have to kiss your hostess's hand before you can work around to your emergency. Otherwise you're left only with some statue in the park, or a telegraph post like any little dog. He has to lord it over us, doesn't he, with his Viennese secessionist horns for architectural candles. He probably thought that Kosmajska Street's deadly provincialism needed jolting, as if streets were plum trees that have to be shaken, and as if Aspasia, say, wasn't exciting enough. Some of our buildings are depressing, no question about it. But that my Aspasia with her faced stone and restrained decoration is old-fashioned, as he's been saying, and rather impoverished-look-ing, we'll have all that out in the open and soon, too. And if Stefan imagines that by building his monstrosity he's found the most effective way of reviving the street, that just shows his own obscene sense of life."

Unfortunately, that evening my reflections found no sup-port in Katarina; on other evenings she was generally less vague, more receptive. She had been asleep, I suspect, for quite some time. She was sleeping soundly as if nothing at all unpleasant had happened, and attentive as I am, I didn't have the heart to wake her and go over my decision with her. But later, whenever mention was made of Stefan's house, Katarina expressed a harsh, irrational hostility toward it for which I was never able to find a sound basis.

A day after I had ceremoniously pronounced that I was going to ignore the monstrosity, I stood before it again. Every day, Sundays and holidays excepted, according to an estab-lished schedule, I paid a visit to one of the rented houses, and on the following day I went to see Aspasia. Once en route, I was ashamedly aware of where I was really going. Stephanie of Vračar was on the list, and there was no legitimate reason for me to change the route of my inspection. And of course, when I found myself there, I couldn't, and most probably didn't want to, overcome the temptation. And so, furious at my own irresolution, I walked a few paces farther and once again found myself in front of Stefan's house.

Hardened by the first appalling impression, I was now able to look at the house in its own light, resisting the temptation to pass judgment on it because of the imagined unpleasantness it would cause Aspasia. I could cope with the unpleasantness later; for the moment, it was the house itself that troubled me. With quiet deliberation I plunged into her luxuriant forms, her butterfly-shaped roof with the upturned edges beneath which tin was curved up into the gutterings. The copper dome for some strange reason no longer reminded me of a boil but rather of a full breast straining skyward. As for that tympanum, supported on columns of Corinthian slimness, it would indeed have looked much worse if the designer had filled the simple field between the architrave and the main arch with figures of famous warriors or gods, half-gods, and quarter-gods in some farcical action such as the slaying of bulls.

Then the portal, a special feature of that deranged house which seemed to lead not into an ordinary lay dwelling but into a shrine: a shrine to Money, perhaps, and in which I failed to recognize, until I got up close to it, a wild variation of the triple-nave porch of King Milutin in the cathedral church of the Sacred Presentation of the Virgin at Hilendar. Its various divergences from the original were the obvious contribution of Madame Jelena Negovan-Georgijević to that weird house: the surround was like Hilendar, of white marble, perhaps slightly more grained, grayer, but it was outlined by the Tree of Good and Evil. The vault, also like Hilendar, was supported by three consoles; three Doric caraway trees in the form of a half-rolled leaf with protruding veins, which would suggest to the uninitiated a family crest, although no Negovan ever bore such a thing. On the plaque behind the caraways it looked as if someone in righteous anger had smashed a beer bottle against the door jamb—which, all things considered, would not have been surprising. Finally, the door itself was quite independent of its Mount Athos original: it was oak, cruciform, double-paneled, and from it, as from a gloomy face, emerged the thick yellow tongue of an engraved doorknob.

And so, when I saw her for the second time, I mollified my judgment of Stefan's house; I went on calling her a monstrosity, but there was no further mention of avoiding her at all costs, and what's more, I singled out the gutter as a successful combination of the useful and aesthetic. Leaving aside the details, the portal was the only feature which I could in no way swallow, but this apart, the house was to the highest degree an individual expression. In principle, of course, I liked such powerful and imposing houses, and in actual fact, they were the only ones I liked. Among my own houses not one could want for praise, not only for some particular feature, but for the special impression which the house made as a whole. Now, one way or another, I began to go around more often; pretexts about Aspasia were no longer necessary. With every meeting the dome, that hidden boil on her tin crown, became not a breast but a bud which oxidization had successfully changed into spring greenery; the four petrified tears which slid down the tympanum now excellently matched her troubled face (later I came to believe that they were tears of longing for me) ; while only the portal of the house stubbornly maintained its sobering role and had the effect of a single startling feature in an attractive face, a feature which, by some inverted logic, charms us more than all the other features which truly attract us.

I did not recognize my true feelings for the house, however, until the day Stefan moved into it. As I was passing along Kosmajska Street from Topličin Venac, I came upon several moving vans in front of Stefan's house. The movers were carrying in the furniture under the nervous and petulant supervision of Helena, Madame Georgijević herself. The movers were going in with the pieces of furniture and coming out empty-handed, so that they formed a kind of elliptical chain like a bicycle's, whose far end revolved around the orange, sunlike, red-lead perspective of the portico while the other end, closer to me, rubbed against the hampers of the moving vans, whose gray-green sides looked as if they'd been painted with the cadmium used for bridges. Along the diameter of that circle Mrs. Georgijević moved like some tireless pedal, scattering to left and right her hysterical and contradictory directions.

I have remembered every detail concerning what I could call a revolutionary upheaval in my relations with Stefan's house, as if my brain had been a molten copper alloy on which the mold of that moving day had stamped a lasting copper-plate impression; the cirrus clouds hung in white hempen and woolen strands against the sky, barely touched with shadows from the east; in the air was a promise of rain for whose freshness the overheated stone, asphalt, glass, and tile gasped and thirsted; and the bells of the cathedral were ringing—it was the hour for vespers, that mournful moment when color, outline, and sound merge. I stood there across the way from the newly peopled house like a snail curled up in Kleont's gate—not to be seen, recognized, or spoken to. I was struck as by a clap of thunder with epiphanic love for that building which only the day before I was calling a monstrosity, and for whose demolition I had even in a certain sense been agitating—a building which had been leading me on very effectively at each meeting, so that I now found myself in the humiliating and comical position of a cuckold who is secretly present at the wedding of his beloved to another man; or, bearing in mind that I was not conscious of my affection until the moment Stefan moved in, in the painful position of the poor fool who discovers he's in love at the moment the object of his passion is led to the altar. *Nota bene,* this comparison with all its boldness is perhaps not the happiest one, but if it doesn't lead to the conclusion that I'm mad (to marry a house is after all not such a widespread desire), it will help me even belatedly to judge the depth and strength of my feelings. For everything—that mastodon-sized entrance, like an altar in whose sacristy candles were burning; the guard of honor that the movers constituted; the mystic twilight of the street, in which I felt as if I were in the nave of a church; the insistent ritual ringing of the bells—everything made me, in the cavern of the gate, feel like a betrayed lover hiding behind a column, as in that well-known poem by Rajić, "On the Day of Her Wedding":

> *So all my finest dreams are cast asunder,*
> *Your head is covered by the marriage crown,*
> *Beside you at the altar stands another—*
> *My vibrant love for you too lowly grown!*

However, there was this difference, decisive for the future: I was Arsénie Negovan, a property owner, and not a whimpering poet; I couldn't forgive a passion, once begun, as charitably as the poet; and I was not, even then by the gate, prepared to give up so easily and promise, like Master Rajić:

> *I shall not cast my curse on him or you,*
> *Or even on bitter fate which caused our meeting;*
> *Nor can I curse myself, poor loving fool,*
> *For thus I would my own true love be cursing.*

How could I? Of course I wouldn't go around cursing anyone, there is no profit from anathema, still less from severing relations. What I was going to undertake was much closer to common than poetic sense: I'd simply try to get possession of the house.

(I must say at once that for some time I considered building elsewhere exactly the same house—without the portal, of course—but I soon gave up the idea. In the first place, however true a copy it might have been, it would still not have been *that* house, nor would it have been tolerable for me to think that I was living with a copy, no more than a lifeless imprint.)

I took my first step toward gaining possession of the house at the housewarming, when I presented Stefan with a carved ivory miniature of Michelangelo's Moses, to whose face the sculptor at my request had given, most discreetly of course, something of my features (the horns were in fact very much in accord with my position). At the same time I requested that my gift be placed at the very heart of the house: in the central, gallerylike hall, on the magnificent fireplace of light-brown Carrara marble in which half-burnt logs with skillfully installed little purple lamps behind them gave the appearance of a slowly burning fire, and on whose extensive mantelpiece, consistently faithful to her humble taste, Madame Negovan-Georgijević had set out alum-white griddles, bowls, goblets, pots, jugs, vessels, and majolica beakers, and among them, like some devilish guard, ornately dressed miniature figures which one would have thought baked of fairground marzipan rather than of Meissen porcelain. In this way I was constantly with Niké (Niké was the secret name I gave to the house as soon as we fell in love), and as it were, legitimized our adulterous relationship.

Indeed, during my ever more frequent visits to Stefan, all that happened between myself and his house can hardly be described in any other way than adultery, and since it all took place under cover of the host's innocent hospitality, adultery in the most shameful circumstances. But when did great passions worry about such small considerations? Did Abélard and Héloïse think about trifles? So for some time Niké and I illicitly, and therefore rather unhappily, carried on our affair—though I don't say that in our cautious concealment, with all its tension, there wasn't a certain conspiratorial excitement, and worthy reward in plenty in those lightninglike changes of feeling which we underwent, usually when, awaiting the arrival of Niké's master or mistress, we remained alone in one of the salons, in the hall, on the stairs, or somewhere else. Our romantic meetings in the street can also be counted here, for in the course of my business walks, which I continued according to the schedule in my saffian leather notebook, I used to pass her every day at a predetermined time. On these occasions quite brazenly, almost leaning out over her luxurious conservatories and balconies, she would give herself up to my wondering gaze, and her face, intent on keeping our sinful secret, would let slip those four clear Corinthian tears which I could only interpret as unsatisfied desire for me.

With respect to the future, however, Niké was a provocative and negligently chosen name for a house with which I dreamed of finding happiness. Viewed superficially, the name suited the house very well, for long before Katarina there had been a Niké in my life. (To tell the truth, that wasn't her real name—she was christened Gospava. I called her Niké, not at all for those reasons which led Mrs. Nego-van-Georgijević to permutate the vulgar letters of her maiden name, but because of the likeness of that powerful, ripe woman to the Paeonian Niké of Olympus, the herald and patroness of military, gymnastic, and therefore why not amorous victories—in all cases, of course, except mine.) That Niké too had been proud, vulgar, and—why should I conceal it?—ugly, yet I had had a relationship with her which no one could understand, myself included, and had embarked upon it with the greatest pleasure. So, bearing in mind the adulterous nature of our relations, I should add that the original Niké, Gospava-Niké, was unhappily married to some clerk in the Adriatic Danube Bank. So the choice of name suited Stefan's palace perfectly, except that regarding the future of our relations it was more than ominous, for it seemed to announce loud and clear the ill-fated end of my adventure.

This desire, however, which I could discern in Niké in a less and less cautious form with every meeting—a desire which by the laws of reciprocity was only strengthened by that feverish need for me to possess her—had grown so much in the meantime that it could no longer be concealed. Furthermore, its heightened suffering threatened to destroy our relationship completely, not to speak of its unfortunate effect on my work and my mental state.

So it had gone as far as it could go. I had to take action. Although I'm by no means proud of my behavior at that time, I'm setting it down here so that someone will at least know exactly what Arsénie Negovan was capable of doing, to make sure that the right house should get into the right hands—setting it down in the hope that my nobility of purpose can guarantee to these, my devious actions, at least that minimum of indulgence which history commonly affords in great abundance to other selfish human exploits. Doesn't medicine inflict pain in order to drive some dangerous illness out of us? Doesn't a mother use deception to guard her child from various temptations?

I've already said that there would have been nothing to gain from building a second Niké. To knock on Niké's door as a buyer gave no promise of success either, for Stefan was far from sated with the advantages of owning a European palace in what till recently had been a remote Turkish province; it is well known what new householders are like when they begin to be reimbursed for all the pains that building has entailed for them. Moreover, the admiration for the house which the doyen of Belgrade landlords would have shown by his offer of purchase would have gone to Stefan's head, and he might well have carried on with his building operations; instead of Niké, I might have acquired a competitor.

To keep Stefan in the dark about my intentions, I found, or rather hired, an intermediary whose special position—he was a minister without portfolio—made it natural for him to live in a magnificent house like Niké. But as I had to give serious consideration to my cousin's still unfulfilled expectations as a houseowner, I was obliged in any case to soften up the ground for the intermediary: first, by complicating Stefan's ownership of the house, and if possible even his occupation of it, by administrative subterfuges and deceptions; then, as though it were indirectly, through rumor, by hampering his enjoyment of his possessions. This latter I accomplished by undermining the self-esteem acquired by the house, and by destroying his and Jelena's conviction that they had gained some great advantage from Niké by advancing their social standing in the most spectacular way.

My preparation—"the artillery barrage preceding a frontal attack," as my brother George would have said—lasted for some time, about a year in fact, until, through the Town Hall, I had managed to obstruct the administration of his property. (In a typically Balkan manner no one could care less about the capital, and Stefan, out of spite and by means of unofficial interventions, had by now disfigured Niké with new but fortunately removable extensions.) By that time I had also managed to surround his wife with barbed insinuations, so that she completely lost her head and at last confided in me, seeking my advice as a relative and expert.

I took care to give wings to her doubts as to the taste with which the house was designed, particularly with respect to its location. It would have been well suited to Dedinje, I said, but in the middle of the commercial center, next to whole-sale dealers and department stores, it gave the impression of an artificial Siamese pavilion which, I added to heighten the effect, had been built by craftsmen from every continent and from all the differing architectural traditions. I said that the house from a utilitarian point of view was a complete fail-ure; that it was more like a riding stable with a great marble manège than the house of an industrialist. Finally, I brought her some building-industry magazines, and by showing her a number of advertised designs, pleasantly induced her to want each of them in turn instead of the house she already had; yet I took care that she didn't decide on a design to which Niké could be adapted by inexpensive modifications.

And when the former minister Mr. K.L., my secret agent, made public his offer for the house, he was not turned down. Without this mental preparation of Mrs. Negovan-Georgi-jević, he undoubtedly would have been, but after some short time taken for reflection, and thanks to my anonymous in-fluence, the formal agreement of purchase and sale was forth-coming. From then on, everything went smoothly. Even the negotiations concerning the purchase price turned out favor-ably for me. Through Mr. K.L. I kept putting the price down on various pretexts, while at the same time through other indirect accomplices—without their conscious collaboration, of course—I heightened my relations' fear that by living in such a house, a house with a bad reputation, their social standing in the town was continuously declining—declining so much, in fact, that the foolish, unsuspecting Stefan began to imagine that his work was suffering because of that house, and not because of his own ineptitude.

And then Mr. K.L.—a minister without portfolio, and a fully equipped jackass in the bargain—Mr. K.L., at the party Stefan gave to celebrate the imminent conclusion of the sale, being probably drunk, telephoned Arsénie Negovan to tell him that he had become the owner of the palace at No. 41

Kosmajska Street. Obviously, he was unaware that the time he had spent in the Ministry of Internal Affairs had been completely wasted, since Stefan was listening in on another extension.

What more can I say? I had to come into the open as the purchaser. At once, of course, all Niké's unpleasant and intolerable defects were transformed into virtues which Stefan couldn't bring himself to renounce at any price.

(At the first cabinet reshuffle Mr. K.L. took over Foreign Affairs, and as far as I could see from my superficial grasp of politics, went on to conduct national affairs with the same flippancy that he had shown in mine.)

However, I didn't give up. Under the pretext that the more prosperous people had moved out of town and into the hills, I lowered the rents of all the houses in Niké's vicinity, and reduced Aspasia's rent to suit even a pauper's pocket, thus bringing down Niké's value. While I could somehow cope with the other landlords—who, with justification, accused me of residence "dumping" and even of Bolshevism (here they made capital out of my time spent in Russia) — it was virtually impossible to convince Aspasia's inhabitants that I wasn't degrading them by this reduction of my profits, but simply giving my commercial, professional answer to the migration of riches, power, and reputation from one side of town to the other.

In desperation I had the idea of buying up other houses on Kosmajska Street, which were available above the market price, and then settling in them the dirtiest gypsy element I could find, whose proximity would have driven the Devil himself out of hell. But I gave up the notion: I couldn't subject houses to such an onslaught, not even for the love of Niké.

Finally I was so overcome by fury, never mind the cost, that I bought a plot of land adjacent to Niké. I brought in quantities of building material, as if I were going to build nothing less than a skyscraper; I set cranes and bulldozers to work, although no plans were drawn up for any building; I sent trucks up and down the street, and generally started building operations of a kind that would convince even a deaf man that the days ahead would not be easy. Then one night, thinking over the amount that my passion, my craving, was costing me, I decided that it would be better to satisfy it in a cheaper way—with patience, cunning, words—instead of throwing away the money saved up for my grandiose plans, my architect's vision of a future Belgrade. So I stopped the construction work, sold the plot of land at a profit, and once again fell into a state of depression.

The war crisis was already upon us when I decided to clear the matter up one way or another. I asked my cousin to surrender the house to me for an amount which he himself should determine. For the first time in my commercial career I compromised myself in a business transaction: I placed in his hands my admission that the object of the transaction pleased me so much that I renounced the right to help determine its price. Bearing in mind the condition, the patently unreasoning condition (for if my interest hadn't been at the very limits of good commercial practice, I would certainly not have approached him so directly, from a commercial point of view so indecently, so childishly) —bearing in mind the condition that *I had to buy the house at any price,* I said that, given my obsessive feeling toward her, I had no choice but to go to the owner with an appeal to our family ties, however much they had degenerated. He could name any figure he chose, he could himself write it on the check, here was my check book, I wouldn't even look at it, I didn't even intend to make use of that final limit on which purchases customarily depended: the hope that the sum in question would remain within the bounds of logic or of my financial possibilities. If it were nevertheless outside such possibilities or logic, even this wouldn't matter as I would sell some other houses; in any case it was Niké that at all costs I had to have.

Stefan's first reaction was one of such complete surprise that he gave no answer to my offer, but only mulishly asked what had got into me all of a sudden, after two whole seasons had passed since the house had been built, especially since it was a well-known fact that I'd never had a high opinion of it, and that at one time I had actually called the house a monstrosity, an abomination which ought to be destroyed. Given all this, he said, he decidedly couldn't grasp what I really wanted after having exhausted all those villainous, cannibalistic, and yes, even criminal means of driving him from his own house!

"Anyway, I don't know where you find the nerve to suggest something so vile, as if I didn't exist, as if I were going to sit back and watch you hurl yourself at my property. And all this because of the obsessed principles of your somnambulist taste, in a town which, I hope, despite all the houses that you already possess, isn't yet yours and never will be. I've been patient only for the sake of peace in the family. Until this meeting I kept receiving you into my house with esteem, even though I never had any particular liking for you—nor you for me, no doubt, that's something we both agree on."

He insisted on seeing in my hysterical offer some ulterior motive, perhaps a roundabout way of pulling the house down, or of rebuilding it so radically that its architect wouldn't recognize it. "What the hell was all that nonsense about the portal?" (In the heat of the discussion, I had mentioned the possibility of altering the entrance door, although I'd limited myself to that wretched piece of glass above the doorway.) "Why the devil do you have to bother with a door which *I* go in through? You don't have to go through it except as a guest. You're allowed through it as a stranger. No one makes you visit me. Never mind remodeling the doorway." And with all this in mind, his answer to my whole jeremiad was a single, simple, definite, Serbian NO.

"And as for your habit of talking about houses as if they were human beings, and usually women at that," he added with mocking concern, "with that in mind, I advise you sincerely, as a cousin, to have your head examined!"

Quite frankly, that he called me a madman didn't in the slightest affect me; Stefan was the crazy one not to see the exceptional nature of his house, and that was why he didn't deserve to possess her. What worried me more was his peasantlike stubbornness, for this excruciating conversation was repeated several times, but always with the same negative outcome. What's more, since the day of my despondent confession, his indifference toward Niké was transformed into hatred which in time would reach drastic proportions, but which already could be recognized in his coarse behavior toward her, as toward an adulteress, and a house beneath the dignity of a Negovan. To make me suffer too, he had the magnificent dome painted a bright red, so that under the sharp, stinging rays of the sun it looked as if it were bleeding. Deep under its copper skin, it was in fact dishonored. And he threatened—through mutual acquaintances, for I myself had stopped visiting him—to treat the columns with equal brutality, and, in a word, if need be, to smear the whole house with shit, to make it repellent to "that crazy Arsénie!"

However, his insolence didn't deter me. As I was about to give up all hope for Niké, I heard that Stefan, in order to cover his dealings with the German aniline dye industry, had issued a large number of bills of exchange for vast sums which were just about to expire, and that he could neither extend nor cancel, since he had already extended them several times before, and all his funds were committed to the hilt in his gangsterish plans. I knew that I had him, and that he could no longer keep me from Niké. Through Golo-

van's office I bought up his bills of exchange from all as-
signees willing to endorse them over to me. Even as he was
devising plans to have them extended further, they were
presented to him face downward so he could see both to
whom they now belonged, and the answer to his misplaced
hopes. At last Stefan surrendered, but not like a man, honestly
and openly, as fitting between relatives and businessmen.
Instead of simply selling me Niké at a moderate price, he
decided upon an auction, and to that end sent me a letter
which for its unparalleled effrontery I have kept to this day.
Above an illegible, impatient, completely flattened signa-
ture, was written:

"Your insanity has at last infected me. I've come to the conclusion, on the basis of facts which I can let you have—but
you alone, of course, as I have no wish to be shut up in an
asylum—that this house, which you call Niké, detests me. She
has tried to kill me by dropping one of her supporting lintels
on me. You have probably read about it in the newspapers."
(If this was not a shaft in my direction, then it must have
been Stefan's maniacal fancy. Niké was far too dignified to
make use of so crude a means as a blow on the head with a
blunt instrument; if it had occurred to her to commit mur-
der, she would most probably have poisoned Stefan by
emitting toxic vapor from her otherwise benign wall coat-
ings.) "Consequently, our life together has become impossible. I am therefore making arrangements for a closed
auction to be held at 7 P.M. on March 27, 1941. Although
I'm in no way obliged to you—especially since it's you who
have come between us and brought us to this—be informed
that I'll sell the house with no regard for the market price,
even if it's below the construction cost. Stefan."

Clearly, the immediate danger posed by Niké was only the
less serious half of his true reason for selling; as the owner
of Y.B.C. (Yugoslav Barv Company), he was entering into
important business agreements with I. G. Farben and was in

need of credit and liquid funds. The idea of arranging for an auction had no other aim than to inflict harm on me, for he knew that no one could match my bid for Niké.

All the same, when I received Stefan's announcement of the auction, I couldn't have cared less; now at last Niké was within my reach. All the rest—Stefan's intention of harming me with this vulgar contest, his shameless letter, his unpatriotic collaboration with the German aniline dye industry—all this had to give way before the prospect that tomorrow Niké would be mine, and I hers. So with my heart brimming over, as they say, I set off for Kosmajska Street, carrying in my saffian notebook all the house's vital statistics (her architectural *carte d'identité*), with the unchristian intention of revenging myself on Stefan for his disloyalty toward both me and Niké. Couldn't that deceitful horse trader have telephoned me and chivalrously saved Niké from the humiliation of being fingered all over by the dirty hands of the house buyers—for all the world like some African odalisque at the slave market? And couldn't he have saved me from the even worse humiliation of being present as a helpless onlooker, since, according to custom, such sales had to be preceded by an exhaustive viewing of the article put up for auction? I would revenge myself upon him, therefore, by laying bare certain features of the house of which even her original architects were unaware, and which of course wouldn't be noted on my cousin's auction inventory.

But between me and Niké, alas, stood that inopportune mob.

And what did you feel when you first saw the mob, Arsénie?

Fear.

Fear of what? Of the mob, of the masses?

Only partially. To tell the truth, it wasn't fear but rather anxiety that I might be late for the auction. I couldn't count on their waiting for me, or on Stefan's postponing the sale until my arrival!

But why then did he ask you at all? Couldn't he have sold Niké without you? If he wanted to humiliate you, wouldn't he have excluded you from the contest by selling the house to someone else?

I believe it was a question of loyalty. We didn't like but simply tolerated each other. Nor did that mutual tolerance at any specific level of danger attain a selfless clan solidarity. In exceptional instances that included even legal matters; nevertheless, there were accepted limits which only outcasts such as George's son Fedor ignored. Because of this passive loyalty, I hadn't gone all out earlier to force a decision through the Town Hall to get the house pulled down.

But putting the squeeze on bills of exchange was permissible? To drive him into a financial dead end like a dog—that you could do?

That was business. Nobody stopped him from paying them off!

So you believe, then, that you didn't hate the mob taking part in that procession?

Perhaps I did hate them, but only in the sense of their being an obstacle in my path, just as I would have been frustrated by a moat or a fortified wall. I had to be at Stefan's at a definite time!

So from the beginning it was only the will to break through the barrier which urged you on?

At first it seemed impossible to get through—those creatures were stuck together thick as dough. I reckoned that with luck and a good deal of effort—I was really in good physical condition then—I would need at least two hundred meters of street length to get across by working my way diagonally to the opposite pavement; that meant coming right up against the cordon of police who were closing off Pop-Lukina Street from the Sava side.

But wouldn't that have been the answer? The police would have let you through: you were a well-known figure, Vice-President of the Chamber of Commerce, the spokesman of our Trade Association. But most of all you were a Negovan, a name which had figured in every cabinet since Unification. They would surely have let you through and given you an armed escort.

There wasn't any time for explanations.

Is that why you tried to work your way around the procession?

Yes.

But you weren't successful?

No.

So you went back to the corner of Pop-Lukina and Zadar Streets. What next?

Next? Well, I stepped into the crowd, intending to get across the street.

Into that mob? Surrounded by frenzied people?

What is the point of these superfluous and unseemly details?

Are we carrying out an inquiry or not? Haven't we decided to discover what kept us locked up there in Kosančićev Venac for so many years with that ivy-framed window facing west? With all those binoculars which could bring the world, defined by the parapet and the oak window frame, so near to us? With Katarina and her sobriety worthy of respect? With the property owner's map—that work of St. J. Sušić from which the pinheads burgeoned like yellow pollen and sky-blue fruit, alongside the registers and leather folders with the carefully folded *cartes d'identité* of our houses? With the sided 30 x 30 photographic enlargements and several portraits in oils of the most outstanding of them? How can we find out the truth, if we conceal everything that was unpleasant or humiliating?

Perhaps after this pilgrimage you won't go back like a

disappointed fugitive to Kosančićev Venac and your im-
prisoning attic. Perhaps you will again conduct your business affairs without an intermediary. Simonida would not
be in despair at the threat of pickax and crowbar if you
hadn't retreated—deserted, so to speak. And weren't you not
an hour ago sitting by the west window holding the Mayer
to your tired eyes, dreaming of how you would extend your
ownership to the other side of the Sava—if you took a liking
to it, of course—when you had looked at it from close up?

At the very beginning, after I had cast myself into the
mob, nothing particular happened. I stood there, at the spot
where the ragged line of the asphalt joins the macadam,
while in front of me pressed the galvanized throng. I could
hear it breathing like an antediluvian monster flopping
over a marsh on its belly, across its tertiary homeland. Most
of the placards had been carried past. Now, above the
tumult, the demonstrators turned their white, ragged backs
toward me; the red banner was bleeding down there like a
wound, a purple slash on the clear stone of Brankova Street.
I still hesitated, though I knew I'd have to make up my
mind quickly. Then suddenly I was sucked into the mass.
A dozen or so demonstrators had been forced out by the
pressure of the oncoming waves, and had swirled into
Zadarska Street, like a crackling stream forced out of some
giant tube, and when this group had hurled themselves
back, they carried me along with them.

And you—did you hold back, did you resist?

Resist? Why should I have resisted? I wanted to get across.

That way?

Why not? I can't honestly say that I was altogether passive
in giving way to the pressure which was carrying me toward
the center. Somehow, I held myself up. Instinctively I must
have pushed with my back, on which I felt more weight with
each linked step. I let my legs drag along the ground like
two crooked black brakes, while my hands in their light-blue

suede gloves pushed against someone in an overcoat of rough cloth from which one epaulet had been torn, its ribbon with a brass button dangling like a piece of torn yellow skin stuck on with a yellow Band-Aid. He was not in fact a soldier; inside the ragged collar I could see the bluish-white folds of a scarf, like a bandage flecked with dark blue iodine, and a web of gray, greasy hair with a cap pulled down over it. While I was being crushed like grain by these two millstones —the invisible body from behind and that foul-smelling one in front—at that fraction of a second which divided me from the rushing torrent of the procession (with greater presence of mind, a single bold step to one side might have saved me), I felt panic swift as a shot, powerful as a heart seizure, and so unbearable in its sudden acceleration that I began to scream for help.

Doesn't it seem improbable that the imperturbable Arsénie Negovan should have given way to panic simply because he got caught up in a riot, which even so was no more unbearable than the rush hour on the Paris Métro?

In that crisis, no jovial comparisons with Paris came to mind. The thing I was absolutely certain of was that I was screaming for help as if someone were about to cut my throat. The sounds that came from my throat weren't words. Probably that's why I can't remember them. We were all behaving like wild animals.

The Honorary Vice-President of the Chamber of Commerce, a Negovan, behaving like one of a pack of wolves!

At Solovkino Station, in 1919 . . .

Unconventional behavior, to say the least.

And then my hat fell off.

How did that happen?

Those hooligans knocked it off my head. For a few seconds it bounced against my shoulders like a frightened gray bird against a wall (a rather stiff Borsalino with a curled brim, and a wide black band around its crown) —bounced like a gray bird with black feathers around its throat, then disappeared.

A hat! They're trampling you underfoot like so much dog shit, and you're carrying on about your hat!

A gray Borsalino with a stiff crown, a deep fold at its crown, an upturned brim, and a black silk band around it. Constantine gave it to me for my birthday.

Anyway, the people, caught up in a national dance, accepted you as one of them: you were striking out with your fists just as they were, and you were shouting just as they were. Deceived by your eagerness for battle, they grabbed you under the arms and took you along with the main stream?

Carried.

All right, carried—carried you off like a sack from the market, carried you off like a cripple, like a helpless paralytic.

True. At that moment I was a kind of paralytic. And not just in the physical sense. Everything had happened so quickly. It was all so incompatible with my tranquil, cork-paneled, lavender-sprinkled study where, behind the cotton curtains which tempered the harsh March daylight, I had leafed through my saffian notebook, glancing at Niké's *carte d'identité* for the last time before the auction. So incompatible with the Regency drawing room where I had said good-by to Katarina and her guests for afternoon tea. God, how sincere I had been, how approachable, even exhilarated, if such expressions weren't out of character with my normal habit: "They say it's us they're auctioning." "It's my Niké they're selling, madame, but we're up for auction too." "They say that the only thing we have is the Army." "I don't know, madame, I'm not a recruiting officer." "They say that if there's a war, we'll be in Vienna in three days." "Perhaps, madame, but with our hands tied behind our backs." "My husband says that the English will land." "Well, madame, the English are always landing somewhere." "He says that it's not a Putsch but a national revolution." "It's an officers' game, madame." "What does General Negovan say about it?" "Madame, General Negovan is a complete idiot!"

Yes, it was incompatible with that entrenched world between the fortress walls of No. 17 Kosančićev Venac, where everything from the furniture to the people, their thoughts and feelings, their actions and conversations moved, glided noiselessly, like railway cars over permanent, well-oiled rails laid down long ago.

But here in the street everything was unnatural, so that from the beginning I was unaware of what was happening to me and to my attention—if one can term "attention" that blind absorption with extraneous details of the situation: details such as my hat with the fold down the middle of its gray crown, its stiff, upturned brim, and its five centimeters of black silk band; or the semitransparent back of the placard carried in front of me, on which, since I could only read the inscription from behind, I persistently and foolishly scanned the same words: "retteB raw naht eht tcaP, retteb eht evarg naht eb a evals." My attention was disoriented, not fixed; it seized on every detail that rushed into my nightmarish field of vision, yet I could make no sober assessment of the situation. Furthermore, I had forgotten why I was there, what I was looking for, and why I was tumbling down the street like a stone.

Even so, you mustn't forget that this experience lasted only a short time.

I don't know how long it lasted.

It can't have lasted long because you yourself observed that your rank was moving in a line parallel with the left corner of Kosmajska Street.

Perhaps it was the sight of that corner which brought me to my senses. Arsénie, what are you doing, I thought, they're waiting for you at Stefan's. You're going to an auction! They're selling Niké. What's happening to you, for Christ's sake?

You'd been caught up in a howling dance, that's what. And as they carried you along arm in arm, they were chanting: "Better war than the Pact, better a grave than be a slave!" And your feet in your lacquered shoes were dangling in the air, hardly touching the ground. You were held by two fat women in suffragette's black whose biceps, wound around your arms, looked like a crab's shiny claws tearing their prey apart. The two women were breathing like two balloons overfilled with explosive gas, forcing air out of their lungs and showering you with saliva like frothy gruel.

"Better war than the Pact, better a grave than be a slave!"

I was hatless, and my light summer coat was almost torn off my back. I had to do something.

"My good ladies—"

"War grave, war grave!"

"I beg you—"

"War grave war grave!"

"I believe that all this is quite—"

Wargravewargravewargravewargrave!"

An extremely undignified situation—I would even say comical—if at the same time it hadn't all been so pitiful, if I hadn't been violently pushed, jostled, banged, scratched, pulled, tugged in that wave from whose foaming crest I was dangling like an eggshell battered against a cliff.

I think you said something else to the woman on your left?

The lady had a brigand's mustache and a voice like a stone-crusher at full blast. She wasn't a woman! She was a loading crane!

What did you say to her?

That I was sorry but we had to part now, that I was glad to have met her, and that my name was Arsénie Negovan.

I don't think she was listening.

I told her that it was our last chance to say good-by.

You said that to the one on your right.

It was no longer a woman lurching about there, but a war veteran who had pushed his hook under my elbow so skillfully that my arm felt like a telegraph pole, a pygmy-size telegraph pole along whose miniature iron crosspieces a tiny leather creature was climbing.

"What time is it?"

Yes, I actually asked him what time it was because I couldn't get my hand down to my vest. He said he didn't know, but thought Comrade N.N. would start the meeting at any moment.

Meeting! We thought with alarm of Stefan, of Niké, and the auction. And we made one more heroic effort to break out of the onrushing mass, this time without saying anything to anyone.

Meanwhile the ranks of the demonstrators had begun to shudder as if with the sharp jolt of a tender and a railway car connecting, so that my nose was brutally thrust down between someone's shoulders, while behind me some ponderous being rose up and wrapped its wet, shaggy sleeves around my head. This was the limit: to be kept forcibly in that unruly mass in the street, like a tramp, hatless, with one sleeve half torn and the buttons dangling, my nose buried in a moist, crumpled bit of cloth reeking of tobacco! The very thought of appearing at Stefan's, in front of Niké, dirty, crumpled, as if I had just crawled out of a heap of rubble —infuriated me.

Suddenly something went wrong. We had stopped on a slope, deprived of that common motion which had allowed some freedom of movement. The concentrated pressure became more unbearable, and the prospects of getting out more remote. It was as if an invisible circular press was working from the walled-in edges of the procession to compact us slowly together, so as to grind us into mincemeat, then squeeze us out into Brankova Street.

The placards had again turned their ashen, daubed faces toward me, and the blood-red banner was again toiling uphill until it stopped high above me and was spread out, its poles rattling, like the purple sky of Theophany, like an open wound in the dark, chilling air. (Made of worn crêpe de chine, it was stiff as a board buffeted by the wind.) Meanwhile the howling had diminished to a dull decrescendo in which, here and there, angry words arose rapidly and subsided into the tired strain of a rumbling chorus melody in which the themes and the instruments that bore them mingled as in some fantastic Concerto Grosso.

And then that head emerged.

Yes, perhaps ten meters from where I was standing, an egg-shaped head, fleshy and purple with cold, extricated itself from the mass. Slowly the man rose like a bather from the sea, with his arms on high, calling for silence.

"Comrades and citizens!"

He took his time to settle his thickset body firmly on the shoulders of his bearers. The war veteran whose hook was tucked under my elbow cried out, "Silence, let's hear him!" The speaker stood on high above the procession, like a statue at a religious festival, his clenched fists raised toward the sky.

"Down with the butcher Hitler!" "Down with him!" "Long live the Army!" "The Army!" The singing and responses sounded like an open-air church service with several different denominations holding forth at the same time.

"Comrades and citizens, today the peoples of Yugoslavia have washed away a shameful stain from their pure body. The overthrow of the traitorous Prince Paul and his bloodthirsty collaborators is the result of the popular struggle for peace and independence our country has been waging in recent days, days of such crucial importance for the world."

"Down with the government of traitors!"

"Down with the German hirelings!"

I pulled my watch out of my vest pocket: it was a quarter to seven. The auction had been announced for seven. I hoped that the gathering would spend at least a half hour looking over Niké's plans and financial records.

"Organized resistance began as far back as 1935 . . ."

In 1935 I bought Agatha and Christina and I was negotiating for Stephanie, but I didn't finally acquire her until 1940.

"Remember, comrades, our demonstrations for the elections of May 5, for the Civil War in Spain!"

Although my late cousin Constantine, the builder—the only person with whom I could discuss houses properly without being laughed at—was of a different opinion, I myself liked Spanish architecture, especially their plateresque. (I prefer Enrique Egas to the more famous Juan de Herrera anytime, for without that cladding which is considered artificial, these buildings would be indecently bare and ugly.)

". . . on the occasion of the Anschluss in Austria, when our sister Czechoslovakia was shamefully attacked and occupied!"

Fortunately the Germans didn't bomb Prague as they later did Warsaw—though to tell the truth, some of the most beautiful houses in the Polish capital were saved. Such preservation is crucial for a town.

"Comrades, students, and workers! At last that great day —the day we can boldly express our infinite love for our powerful brother, the great Soviet Union, invincible land of workers and peasants!"

"And soldiers!"

"And soldiers. That is why we demand a pact of mutual aid with the Soviet Union, which alone can guarantee the peace and independence of this country. And that is why we cry: Long live the Soviet Union, the bastion of peace and independence for smaller nations!"

By now the invited buyers will have assembled, probably standing around that Empire-style salon on the ground floor. Soon they will be starting off on their tour of the house. Yon (Jelena's Transylvanian variant of the name of the butler, John) will be serving drinks in conical glasses of Czech crystal, which he carries around on a gilt tray like a church collection bowl. Those fine gentlemen can choose between delicate aromatic liqueurs and harsh, fiery, warming alcohol. Before this afternoon they have seen Niké only from the outside, and each has imagined her interior in his own way. Now they will see that they have been mistaken; Niké will put their pampered imagination to shame, mysterious Niké who hasn't yet opened her doors to them or revealed her wonderful marble perspectives and her dusky outlines lit by lacquered wall lamps. *In sordine* the first cautious impressions are exchanged, concurrently misleading and covered with mimicking disguises. The guests around Stefan cordially inquire what has become of the mistress of the Negovan-Georgijević house and discover that she has asked her husband to excuse her absence. "In fact, she loves this house so much that she couldn't bear to be present at its sale." Of course the potential buyers recognize the appeal of her owner's anguish. All this is terribly complicated. Commerce is a distasteful business in which no intelligent man would involve himself if it didn't, as sociology defines it, help develop the forces of production without which mankind would perish.

Meanwhile, everyone's eyes are fixing themselves on Niké's tender innards like the moist tentacles of an octopus. Exploratory probes verify the soundness of her walls, the quality of the construction work, the individuality of the ornamentation. At the far edge of the conversation flow figures, measurements, queries, impressions, and data. Those present seem indifferent, indolent, inattentive, but in fact they are impatiently awaiting the auction, though they refrain from commenting on Stefan's delay. And so they wait with the fire of battle in their bellies, a fire that competition will ignite with every ringing stroke of the auctioneer's hammer on the improvised stand in the vestibule. The discontent at the delay keeps growing and the whole hardened gathering is transformed imperceptibly into a minefield where each careless step can lead to an explosion. In the nick of time Stefan invites them, according to custom, to follow him so he can show them the house, "which, gentlemen, I shall do without embellishment or exaggeration." No, he won't influence the buyers at the auction by a single observation—he knows he couldn't even if he wanted to: these marketeers of the capital are wolves—but he'll serve them as Cicerone, an impassive guide through his architectural kingdom which, as they probably already know, is patterned on the plans of Dietrich and Eizenhofer for the Academy of Sciences in Vienna, built in 1755.

But you can be absolutely certain that during this obvious procrastination he'll be surreptitiously glancing at the clock, that yellow sunlike face over the doorway, and listening for the ring of your arrival, at first surprised that you aren't there, later perhaps offended, and of two minds whether to abandon his personal haughtiness and telephone to find out why you haven't responded to his loyal invitation. Nevertheless, he won't reach for the phone, not because those present would suspect some kind of collusion between relatives but because, after thinking it over, he must have realized how much the absence of Arsénie Negovan was to his advantage, how well it suited his hypocritical aim of not surrendering the house to me—the customary Negovan vileness (which as usual would seem correct to everybody), entirely neglecting the fact that my desire for Niké had forced the price up to vertiginous heights. And so all of them—except me, of course—will turn to the owner and, following his advice from the hall, choose the quickest way to get around the house, while at the same time fixing as precisely as possible in their adding-machinelike heads the numbers, measurements, and impressions they note on the way. And where are *you*, just when you've been given the chance of becoming Niké's official owner (for you long ago made her your own)? Instead of cutting short that whole undignified comedy by stating an insurmountable price, you're shivering here on the cobblestones, hatless, torn, spat upon, stained with mud, trapped by fetid bodies and coarse voices of encouragement from out of whose fine net you can again distinguish the baritone of the orator:

"The deposed government was the embodiment of bloodthirsty illegality, unrestrained corruption, and willful treachery! We call upon citizens, students, peasants, and the esteemed intelligentsia to join with the workers in the struggle for the rights of the people! We call upon the army to unite with the people! We demand the abolition of concentration camps! We demand freedom of the press, a general amnesty, and a ruthless purge of the government."

Once again the chorus uttered "That's right!" Several times—a kind of liturgical "Amen, amen" in which the orator's élan was lost.

"We demand the abolition of the power of capital over human labor. We demand that factories, railways, and mines be nationalized and transferred to collective ownership!"

"And the banks—banks—the banks, too!"

The sonorous voice rang out like a shot whose crystal clarity shattered the silence. The enflamed audience was saving its breath for new acclamations.

But whose voice was that? Who appended to industry, transport, and the mines, those cancer wounds of our domestic economy, that most malignant one of all: banking?

Or has the owner of that decisive voice disowned it? For these past twenty-seven years perhaps he's been ashamed to think of it, or he's decided that the voice must have been fortuitous; an automatic reflex which burst out of the speaker's throat as an undisciplined offshoot of some inner soliloquy. Or is this the first false step that we've been looking for? Naturally the owner of that voice would gladly abandon this dangerous reconstruction and hurry on to Simonida, who anxiously awaits him.

That would be the best thing to do.

And afterward would you go back up to Kosančićev Venac, back into your ark of gopher wood, and seal it within and without, while outside those impenetrable walls of your beloved houses continue to be destroyed?

No, not for anything. That's all over and done with.

If that's really so, and I hope it is, if you really think that despite the passage of the years you can take over your own affairs again, why does it cause you such anguish to recall what made you give them up?

Because of what I shouted about the banks. Though it seemed as if it wasn't really me shouting at all.

But it was.

Unfortunately.

I hated banks, I have always hated banks and bankers. I even hated bank notes. From the bottom of my owner's heart I despised everything placed willfully between Possessed and Possessor, everything which transformed true possession into mere power over empty, hollow, emaciated figures.

So Arsénie Negovan, Vice-President of the Chamber of Commerce, sank so low as to settle accounts with the banks as part of a mob. And after he had been carried away by, let's say, excitement, and had shouted stupidly, "And the banks—banks—the banks, too!—instead of coming to his senses and beating a retreat, he went on:

"It's the fault of the Yiddisher banks!"

In such a senseless manner and quite without dignity—couldn't he see what was going on around him?—he had caused the audience to focus, as if moved by a giant hand, on him. From everywhere came resounding echoes of his ridiculous exclamation ("That's right!" "Down with the usurer banks!" "Let's hear him!"). And those nearest him —above all the bovine suffragette in black and the veteran with a hook for an arm—took hold of him and, despite his resistance, raised him high onto someone's shoulders as if into a saddle, his legs fast around someone's neck, his unsteady fingers grasping hold of someone's hair. He found himself face to face with the orator in the trench coat, who was awaiting him with encouraging approval in the shadow of the blazing sky.

As soon as I was more or less settled up there, I thought of my hat. I hoped now I'd be able to spot it. But of course it was nowhere to be seen; the rabble had demolished it.

Surely you felt an urgent need to do some explaining. Deceived by your unfortunate cry and your bedraggled appearance, they took you for one of them, a comrade as it were, and expected you to say something in the spirit of your first pronouncement. But the only thing that you should have said was that you had nothing to say to *them,* except that you disapproved of their barbarous behavior; that you wanted to be lowered to the ground; and that a path should be cleared for you to Kosmajska Street because you had more important business to attend to.

From the perspective of a promenade through more or less empty streets, dozing beneath a veil of slanting greenish light crisscrossed here and there by housewives sluggishly returning home from the market or by a civil servant hurrying to his office—from such a peaceful, leisurely perspective, that was truly all that Arsénie K. Negovan should have communicated to the people below him. But in the context of the rebellious mood of the streets, including the unpleasantness of losing my hat, the torn-off buttons, those evil placards, and especially the red banner beneath which, as under a royal canopy, the preceding orator was enthroned—not to mention my memories of Solovkino—any explanation of the kind suggested would have been devoid of reality. In that sense, my life had always differed from my work. Even if I had attempted some sort of explanation, they wouldn't have heard me. No one would have heard me. It had already gone too far.

But couldn't you have tried something else? Wasn't there something behind your acceptance of the role of street orator?

Something behind it?

Stop and think for a moment. You'd listened to the whole speech, hadn't you?

Yes. But I was looking at my watch the whole time, hoping that the crowd would disperse and let me reach Kosmajska Street. Indeed, I spent the whole time imagining the events at Niké: Stefan welcoming the buyers, serving them drinks, wondering why I'd failed to show up.

But you still listened to the speech—so carefully that even now, after many years, you can repeat it to the last detail.

Who knows if that's what was really said!

Let's suppose it was. Just as we accept without question everything else you remember. Yet at no other time had you felt called upon to intervene—even when he was talking about financial speculation. Why Arsénie? Why?

Well, there was truth in what N.N. was saying. Of course that business about our Czechoslovak brothers was all just street-corner rhetoric. But the part about our economic policy was true, primitively interpreted certainly, but the absolute truth just as I myself had preached it—and to which, incidentally, I'd dedicated my lecture to the Sisters of Serbia.

The lecture you never gave.

The lecture I never gave.

Suddenly you saw your chance, Arsénie, you still had the lecture in your head, as clearly as if it were before you in print, just as it had been before your canceled appearance at the Kolarac Institute. The audience was there in front of you, receptive and ready, like the Serbian Sisters had they been given the chance.

It was all about the collapse of the property system, the replacement of that real, human system by a new, unreal, inhuman one, the transformation of objects into symbols, things into numbers. And you abandoned caution, all civic dignity, you forgot the passage of time, the auction which would begin at any moment. You forgot your beloved Niké, you became the worst kind of paid agitator, in the middle of the street, and with no hat and a torn coat at that.

"Honored Lady President! Esteemed ladies! Gentlemen!"

Someone burst out laughing, but he was silenced by other citizens who had greater respect for the seriousness of the moment.

"I am speaking to you according to the program—"

"Long live the Communist Party program!"

"—As I said, to set out before you the economic life of Belgrade, I shall take in the economic factors of the whole country and indeed of the whole continent, tear off the mask from that incompetent and alien policy which at last, here and now, has brought us to disaster!"

"Down with the antinational government! Down with the gravediggers of Yugoslavia!"

You raise your hand to silence the audience. You need to concentrate. Interruptions disturb you.

"Esteemed ladies, gentlemen! The very last moment has arrived for us to speak without ambiguity or prevarication . . ."

"Better war than the Pact, better the grave than be a slave!"

". . . and especially the existence of the *ordre de proprié-*

taire, that toiling breed of people who, like Antaeus on his powerful shoulders, have been carrying the weight of social progress!"

"Long live the working masses!"

"And we ask ourselves what could more worthily express a nation's capacity for existence than the vitality of its ownership class, and we answer boldly at once: *rien, rien du tout, absolument rien!*"

"Louder!"

Now you must be very serious in what you remember, Arsénie; all at once the events have begun to mingle, as if emulsifying, as if they were sinking back into the anonymity of a general impression from which only your sharpest words can be distinguished. Over there to one side, no more than a few yards from you, a group of young men are laughing out loud.

Yes, those youths. Clear faces. An exceptionally favorable sign. The general mood is good, people are relaxing, and the anger is disappearing; it seems that at last, as they say, I've got them.

"What's all this about, folks?"

"Never mind, hear him out!"

"He's crazy!"

"Just you keep going, Grandpa!"

"Shut up over there—let him alone!"

"If we cast just a superficial glance at the state of our national economy, what do we see? An amazing picture of calamity: quarries shut down; speculation in timber; the synthetic cartel dictating prices to us in association with I. G. Farben; unfair increase in the cost of skilled building services; incompetent upstarts in our architectural design bureaus who are allowed to have their own way . . ."

"Enough! Enough!"

". . . the complete absence of regulatory plans and any kind of urbanist ideas. On the other hand . . ."

"Go fuck yourself!"

". . . with the helpless feelings of well-meaning owners, we see impoverished citizens unable to put roofs over the heads of their children, while the finest flats stand empty. For houses, esteemed ladies, are like human souls: if we don't inhabit them, they are lost. And most of all, ladies and gentlemen . . ."

"Shit on your gentlemen!"

". . . that the direct system of ownership is being replaced by the indirect . . ."

"Get rid of that idiot."

"This is freedom! Anyone can talk!"

"What freedom? It's a circus!"

"Listen to him!"

The crowd was exhilarated and I had to keep going at all costs. "Whereas once possession was a means of setting up a mutually corrective relationship between material and its produced forms, in the sense that work on material was carried out by the mind" (laughter), "even so it used to be balanced by the reciprocal work which material carried out on the mind" (laughter), "so that we continually had the identification of roles between mind and matter" (loud laughter). "But today the dividing lines have disappeared" (wild laughter, applause), "so that all relationship between owner and what is owned has been lost, and there are people —tycoons who call themselves owners, but don't in fact know what they own! Bremmer, Brevit, Brickhouse, British Aluminum, British Cotton, British Termo, Broom, Wade, Cable Covers, Allied Brick, Allied Insulators, Allied Textile —what can their owners know of their possessions from the interest rates and fractions which the stock exchange index shows them, or from the mathematical symbols in which the banks have drowned our assets?"

To your horror, the painted idol beneath the red sky is

leaning forward as if he wants to crawl over the heads toward you. He's shouting:

"Get rid of that madman!"

You are offended. You protest in the name of ordinary decency. You resist.

"Get rid of him—get him down!"

In such a situation the best thing is to act as if that shameless interruption in no way concerned you, to remain aloof.

"Gentlemen! If the French client could have seen with his own eyes . . ."

"Aaaahh, down with the speaker!"

". . . I repeat, if he could have seen that Louisiana on the basis of whose fatal natural riches Mr. Low from Highland Scotland" (laughter, applause, whistles) "issued his *assignats,* would any one of them have been deceived or gone bankrupt?"

"He doesn't even know how to speak Serbian!"

"Down with the imperialist agents!"

"I will pass over the unworthy invective from the gentlemen over there, and as a proof of good faith I will give as a personal example the property owner *in personam.* I don't know my Christina or Stephanie through brokers' valuations, I know them in my heart. And Niké . . ." (Indignation, acclamation, laughter, whistling.) "I withdraw, I demonstratively withdraw from the platform, I request to be put down!"

"Knock him down!"

"I've lost my Borsalino with the black ribbon—first give me back my hat!"

"Fuck your burzalino, fuck your whore of a mother, and fuck you, too!"

That is the last observation which I am reasonably certain was directed at me. Controlling myself, I ask with whom I have the honor, then everything becomes mixed up, troubled, disintegrating in a seething emulsion of colors, movement, and shouting.

"Long live the Communist Party! Down with the Bolsheviks! Slavs, unite! Moscow-Belgrade! God and Justice! Citizens! Comrades! Cattle! Long live the young King! Down with Hitler! Down with Stalin! What a crock of shit! Kill the traitors! Wretched of the world, arise! Moscow ass lickers! Get him! Police, police! Here comes the cavalry!"

Twenty-seven years later, here I am on that same corner, but not flat on the ground. I am standing, as if I had just got up, as if I had spent that unknown time—time deep as a well—in the shallow dusty gutter. I suddenly felt a jerking of my facial muscle, I was seized by *Pareze facialis dextri* (whenever I woke up that muscle began to quiver), so that at the threshold of Kosmajska Street I had to turn my back on the road and, facing the shining window of the clinic, take the muscle between the thumb and forefinger of my right hand and gently but firmly massage its pliable rubber mass until it calmed down. Only after that internal shuddering had subsided did I venture to look about.

On a dark blue plaque fixed to the lined façade of the clinic, just above eye level, there was written in large white enameled letters: MARSHAL BIRYUZOV STREET.

So they had renamed Kosmajska Street. But who was this Biryuzov? A Russian Czarist officer had once been commander in chief of the Serbian Army, but that was during the reign of Prince Milan Obrenović, and his name was Chernyaev, not Biryuzov; Mikhail Grigoryevich Chernyaev. Moreover, he hadn't been a marshal but a general, like George. I could recall only one other general. (Budyonny too, of course, came to mind, although it was inconceivable that a royal street could bear the name of that regicide.) That general who had defended Port Arthur against the Japanese—his name was Kuroglatkin—or was it Kurosatkin?

Standing underneath the plaque which shone slantwise in

the sun, I tried to think who that marshal could be. Finally I concluded that most probably he was one of those military brains whose operations George considered "infantile" maneuvers based on still more infantile premises, George being convinced that the front lines on both sides were commanded by complete idiots. There was a certain injustice in the fact that all sorts of Biryuzovs were honored in the names of the most eminent streets in the capital, whereas the man who had criticized them could only achieve a gilt inscription on a cemetery cross. And there were the most serious reasons for upbraiding the Town Council in that, on renaming the street, they hadn't consulted the citizens of the town, not to mention its home owners. On my way to Niké, I concluded that the restoration of the street's old name was one of the questions I would take up as soon as I had begun to sort out my business affairs.

As I approached No. 41, which was still hidden by the projecting fronts of the houses this side of it, my excitement grew. My reflections on Kleont and his house *avec le caractère de Cléont,* were only, of course, an excuse for keeping my thoughts away from the forthcoming meeting with Niké, a meeting which without doubt would resemble the sobering encounter of two lovers who, after years without contact, approach each other apprehensively, wondering whether their former passion—which they wish to make eternal—will have withstood the changes both have suffered. Thus I was approaching Niké with a gnawing pain inside me. It wasn't my fault I hadn't arrived at the auction, but then again it was, since I'd made that unfortunate speech.

I was so agitated that I again had to stop to calm my facial muscle, that wound-up monster beneath my right cheek whose hot and cold quiverings announced that it was again about to be seized by a convulsive spasm. When I had managed to massage it back into its den, and my lips were no longer jerking as if tied to my forehead with strings, I took the last step. I crossed over the street toward Kleont's house —to the spot where I would be able to take in Niké at a single glance.

It is impossible for me to describe at one and the same time what I saw and felt at that moment. It seemed to me that in reality I could see nothing at all, that I was inventing everything, so that I should see my Niké just as I had left her, leaning out over her conservatories and balconies, following me with her eyes filled with the violet glow of the sun. But now I couldn't see her—probably the effect of my self-inflicted punishment was still at work—for over her leveled foundations as over an abandoned grave overgrown with brambles, weeds, and briars, stretched a rectangular square with three internal walls built of stone anthills like the walls of a casemate, a square with paved paths crossing in the form of an X. Nearby were placed groups of two red and two green freshly painted benches. The houses at the rear of the square were blurred, as if, in the same band of colorless horizon, an unsteady camera had taken several pictures of buildings, one on top of the other.

Niké no longer existed. My enchanting Niké was dead, dead and buried beneath an offensively ugly stele in the shape of a public promenade. Not only she but her closest family had been brutally rooted out—probably according to some inhuman principle of coparticipation in misfortune. Everything that was there in her place seemed so unreal that, completely unhinged by this somnambulist vision, I thought— what am I saying, I hoped—that I had lost my way (this isn't Kosmajska Street, it's the street of some Biryuzov!) , and that as soon as I pulled myself together I'd find the right one, where Niké would be waiting for me. But the awareness that I was leaning on Kleont Negovan's house, and that my disappointed gaze could turn to Aspasia whenever it wanted, brought me harshly back to the fact that Niké was no more, that if I wished, I could walk around her tomb.

And you, Arsénie, you were so certain that you knew every-thing about the outside world simply because you found out about your brother's death? There are other things too which have ceased to exist in the meantime—your Niké, for ex-ample—and who knows what else. Of course, they would have stayed alive if you hadn't seen them dead.

I directed my steps toward the square as if approaching a deathbed, a deathbed without a corpse, a concrete and grassy catafalque from which the coffin had long ago been removed. Where a luxurious fireplace with Moses' hybrid face had once stood, there were now red and green benches. Dry, dusty grass grew from the vestibule; on the first step of that portal which had caused me so much irritation, there now stood a rusty hydrant; in the middle of the salon where I had imagined the gathered buyers, was a wrought-iron tube with flowers; and over it all rose the empty stories of the burning June air. Nothing was left of Niké. Not even the cadaverous breath of a cemetery. Even the most insignificant carrion leaves a skeleton behind under the sky's mantle; our own dead give off incomprehensible phosphorous signs from under the earth; ruined buildings resist destruction and with-draw deep underground, keeping their own remembrance in the scarcely discernible shape of their former foundations; shattered stars are scattering particles even now. But of Niké there was no trace—only a cross-shaped pathway stamped on the barren earth like a brand. And the picture of Niké in the Chinese embossed ivory frame on my desk.

Nothing held me here now. I walked on toward Aspasia, but with the feeling that I owed something to Niké's memory. It would have been heartless to leave without mak-ing an attempt to find out under what circumstances she had been destroyed. The most natural thing, of course, would have been to call on Kleont. But that would have required an explanation for which, at the moment of mourning, I was least of all disposed.

As I approached Aspasia I noticed a sign: a clumsily drawn shoe, and next to it white as chalk: SHOEMAKER—SOFRONIJE ŽIVIĆ—COURTYARD: TURN RIGHT. Sofronije Živić, shoemaker? No, there was no one with that name among my tenants. Nor had Golovan told me of a shoemaker in Aspasia. But it was quite clear why he had remained silent. He knew well that I didn't allow workshops in my houses, still less crude signs hung over their doorways. There could be no further doubt that my lawyer had been lying to me about many details concerning my houses. In this light, his obliging behavior became understandable and his exaggerated conscientiousness took on a different meaning. Standing beneath that chalklike shoe, I remembered another illuminating incident. I had asked that the business records be brought to me for inspection. The weather was bad, the temperature ten degrees below zero. Golovan had come personally, by car in fact, to hand over the books. Feeling guilty about disturbing him, I had asked him why in God's name he hadn't sent the books with one of his clerks. He replied that he had prepared them personally in order to provide me with supplementary information. This explanation had seemed reasonable, and it gratified me to see in it that professional pride which had disappeared from commercial affairs. But in actual fact Golovan had feared lest I question his subordinates and so find out everything he had been concealing from me. I decided that a clarification of this puzzling situation would be my first concern on returning to Kosančićev Venac.

As I feared, the shoemaker Sofronije Živić worked on his loathsome shoes in a workshop of unbaked bricks which, parasitelike, clung to Aspasia's defenseless back. A workshop resembling a disgusting tick which sucked out of the parent house's body all the strength it possessed. And of course, under such conditions Aspasia's garden was no longer a picture-book rosary but an abandoned polygon paved with bricks, halfway between a cesspool and a stockyard.

From the shoemaker, in his apron of shiny brown leather—
to whom, incidentally, my name meant nothing—I managed
to learn very little, except that he had settled there in 1950,
that he took in footwear of all European types from boots
and sandals to dress shoes and slippers, that the area had
been heavily bombed, and that before he moved here, the
ruins had been removed and the little park built in its place.

What could I do? I thanked the shoemaker and left. Only
when I had gone halfway along Carica Milica Street did I
remember that I hadn't even looked at Aspasia.

My bookkeeping had always been irreproachably accurate;
there were no inexplicable gaps or ambiguities. Subsequent
alterations, falsifications, and deletions were unthinkable
in the affairs of Arsénie Negovan. Every entry was written
down punctually and precisely in the appropriate column.
More than that, for each individual house I had kept in detail a kind of running record or diary in which, just as a
proud father notes down important dates in the margins of
the family Bible, I recorded important moments in the life of
my houses: all the stages of their development on paper and
their burgeoning growth on the building site; their short
childhood, that carefree time in which they were not in-
habited; their marriages, as I called their transitory associa-
tions with their tenants; and their temporary illnesses or
misfortunes, followed by old age and death. Even those which
for various reasons I disposed of—unwillingly, always with a
sense of shame—were still entered in that account book as
if they were mine, as if I were still caring for them, which
in fact I secretly was: I established a discreet surveillance
over them and in an indirect way I influenced their destinies,
though to all appearances they were in the hands of others.

The bookkeeping columns dedicated to Niké, however,
were half-empty. The last entries referred to Stefan's letter
(the invitation to the auction); then, under March 27, 1941,
a space had been left where I intended to note down the

price for which I bought the house. Under a later date was
the information that on the evening of the 27th, as I was
being carried back to Kosančićev Venac, the house was sold
to Mr. Jovan Martinović, a wholesale grain dealer. Beneath
Niké no line had been drawn; her account had not been
balanced.

Was it because I had been guilty of her misfortune?

Was I guilty?

Alors, suppose that I hadn't come upon the demonstrators,
or that I'd pushed my way through the mob, taken part
in the auction, and bought Niké. What difference would it
have made, during the bombing in which she was destroyed? I couldn't have protected her from the bomb: she
would have been hit anyway.

No, Arsénie, you can't give a true answer until you know
how she was hit and to what extent she was damaged. Perhaps with a certain effort and expense she could have been
put right and restored. Her plans still existed. (Even so,
would that new, resurrected Niké have been my Niké, or just
her successful imitation?) Perhaps Mr. Martinović hadn't regarded such an error as either profitable or useful. For Mr.
Martinović it had just been a heap of ruins like any other.
I had to pay a visit to Mr. Martinović. Only he could give
me the information that would establish the true measure
on my part in her downfall.

The Martinovići lived in Topličin Venac, and it wasn't
difficult to find them: my memory for houses was infallible.
There was no building which I couldn't describe in detail,
especially if it had attracted my attention because of some
unusual feature. I could hardly remember Martinović himself, but recalled his house distinctly—most probably because
of its color, since it had no other striking feature. It looked
in fact as if it had been rubbed with wet ash. And if the house
lacked character, this was entirely in keeping with the repu-

tation Martinović enjoyed as a grain dealer in the market place. Now the house was hardly upright on its foundations, it was so run-down. Its paint—still cadaverous but visible—had peeled, as if the walls had been afflicted by some skin disease. The window panes were cracked; the wood was moldering like that of old sea chests. The crooked and rusty drainpipe came down, like a tin intestine, only as far as the ground floor, and ended in a broken stump.

Although Jovan Martinović had never been a house-proud owner in the professional sense of the word—my judgment of him was for that reason more tolerant than otherwise—he was not, even so, capable of such shameful neglect. Its desolate state could only mean that he had moved on, God forbid, gone bankrupt, which would not have entirely surprised me, since against all my warnings he had foolishly involved himself in speculation on the stock exchange. Unfortunately, my worst supposition was confirmed. As soon as the door of the mezzanine floor was opened, and the warm, dark, fishy smell of the entrance hall mingled with the semi-darkness of the stairway which smelled of a cold, unwashed marble ash tray, it became quite apparent that Mr. Martinović had indeed experienced the catastrophe I had foreseen.

Anyway, in the doorway, distorted on the smoky porch, as if from the depths of a dream brought on by an upset stomach, there appeared a strange being, an undulating form swathed in a shaggy bathrobe. Controlling my uneasiness at not knowing who it was I had in front of me, I said that I should like, if possible, to speak with Mr. Jovan Martinović.

"Are you blind or something? It says there clearly: Martinović, two short rings and one long."

Indeed, on a slip of paper pinned to the doorpost it was written: two short and one long.

"Forgive me. I don't see too well."

"Go ahead, Grandpa, you don't have to explain!"

With these words, the carnival-like being moved aside and banged its fist on the board which had replaced the glass in the inside door.

"Martinović, someone to see you!"

My reception was preceded by a scurrying from the other side of the board-backed door, a hurried scraping as if furniture was being moved. As I waited, it occurred to me that I should have written or at least telephoned before barging in on them. The door at last opened and in its narrow frame appeared a dried-up woman in a dressing gown of loose violet cotton. I recognized her, I admit unashamedly, more from the location than from memory.

Of course I could see it all. I take in everything with a lightninglike glance, whose efficacy comes from communication with houses and was perfected at auctions. The room looked like a refuge in which the Martinovići, burnt-out survivors, had hidden the remains of their devastated possessions: canvas shades through which a greenish dusty light barely settled on the faded, threadbare surface of an office sofa; a table covered with a worn oilcloth; a triple Altdeutsch dresser, which creaked at every step; battered walls from which ribs of wallpaper hung down like dried tobacco leaves; and finally—there in the corner of the room, probably once the kitchen—a Moorish folding screen which in the pale glimmer from the window looked like ice overgrown with wild flowers and briars. I sensed too the bitter smell of stale medicines, musty leather, unaired eiderdowns, decaying clothes, parchmentized documents, and other petty reminders of decay: in a word, the intangible scent of misfortune. My professional experience helped me identify in it that element by which *ruin*, that final death throe of wasted riches, is distinguished from the smell of innate, inherited poverty—a smell which I had met long ago in the houses I rented out to people in the suburbs until, out of shame and loyalty to my theory of mutual possession, I sold them all without excessive loss and some even at a profit. I was at the very center of the devastation which Speculation had left behind; I was standing on the cold ashes of Possession, which had burned down in the fire of a gambler's mad rush for easy profits, made on the bitter green baize of the roulette wheel of the stock exchange, in the lackeylike service of the god Mammon. And I felt unspeakably sorry that I had come here at all.

"How could I not remember? You're Colonel Negovan!"

"You're thinking of my brother, General Negovan. I concern myself mainly with houses, my dear lady."

"Oh?" she said suspiciously. "Then you're not from the Secret Police?"

"I don't belong to any firm or company, madam. I concern myself with houses, if I may say so, in a special way, on my own account, for the love of it so to speak."

"We don't own houses any more."

"Of course, I understand. Speculation. Gambling on a rise during a fall, a fall before a rise."

At this Mrs. Martinović, with dismay out of all proportion to the sympathy I expressed, declared that she hadn't understood a thing about all those speculations; in fact she said her husband hadn't involved her in his shitty business affairs, in fact she hadn't found out about them until the trial, and she had nothing more to add to what she'd said earlier under oath.

"I told him to leave all that alone!"

"I told him that too, madam. In any case," I added cautiously, "I'm certainly far from disagreeing with you. But with your permission I'd still like to discuss this matter with your esteemed husband. If he's at home, of course."

Without turning around she pointed over her shoulder at the Moorish screen.

"Where else would he be? Of course he's at home. He's over there."

She then explained that Mr. Martinović had been ill for a long time, was in fact paralyzed and barely alive.

"But he *is* alive?"

"Barely. His whole left side is gone."

"I'm sorry to hear that. Truly sorry. With me it was my right side. Does that mean, my dear lady, that there is no way of communicating with him?"

"It depends. I'll go see."

She disappeared behind the screen; the cretonne flowers visibly darkened; I heard a scraping noise and saw a metal bedpan disappearing below the bottom edge of the partition like a tortoise beneath its white enamel shell. Then there was the creaking of the bed and mattress, and a hissing sound like escaping gas, followed at intervals by that bubbling, gurgling whistle with which sewage bursts through blocked drainpipes. Finally I could hear Mrs. Martinović:

"That Negovan is here. Do you remember him?"

I couldn't hear the sick man's answer so I thought it useful to add: "Arsénie K. Negovan from Kosančićev Venac!"

"Arsénie K. Negovan from Kosančićev Venac!" repeated the woman clearly. It was apparently difficult for the paralyzed man to give any sign of having understood. "He's here, behind the screen. He says he wants to ask you something."

When the woman reappeared from behind the screen she was holding the goosenecked bedpan in her hand.

"Try for yourself," she said sharply, "only don't move the screen. Bring your chair up. That's right. He can hear quite well, but it's difficult for him to speak. Especially when he gets excited."

Before going out she turned around and said: "He's suffered very badly."

"Mr. Martinović? Can you hear me?"

Sheltered by the Spanish wall—I knew those difficult circumstances from my own experience—the paraplegic strove
to control the contorted dam of his mouth. With my cheek
to the brown patterned cloth I could almost see the two
brittle, transparent wires of his bloodless lips twisting their
still sound ends until their painful edge dropped down the
stubbly chin, filled with a bubbling foam in which the agitated
tongue was bathed as if in pink soapy water, seeking for
words. At last I myself began to move my lips, as if only by
mutual effort would we be able to squeeze a voice from his
jaw. His voice finally broke through, greatly distorted by
the unnatural position of the facial muscles, but quite in-
telligible:

"My time's done."

I tried hard to explain to him to what an extent his recovery lay in his own hands. A man must never at any cost
resign himself to his misfortune. Medicines are mere pallia-
tives. I myself had been in his position. Even worse, in fact,
for broken bones had preceded the apoplexy, and even
contusia cerebri for which there was clinical evidence. Yet
here I am, thank God.

"You'll still feed us all, my friend," I said, having in mind
his grain-trading business. But it seemed that his contribution to our meeting would consist solely of one and the
same thought.

"They told me that my time was done."

"Of course," I said, "you'll soon be out and about again."

"What for? My time's done!"

"Well now, you just need a bit more will power."

Afraid that he might slip away from me again, I asked
him if he remembered the house that had belonged to my
cousin, Stefan Negovan, the building at No. 41 Kosmajska
Street, which we used to call a monstrosity. "**On March 27,**

1941, at 1900 hours, a private auction was arranged for Niké, at which I, unfortunately, was late in arriving. And you bought it."

There was no answer. "My dear Mr. Martinović, I most humbly beg you to give me some sign that you understand me."

"My time's done. What more do you want?"

"*Bon, excellent,* Mr. Martinović, everything will be all right, *tout va être très bien.* By the way, I suppose you didn't know that I—how shall I put it?—was linked to that house by certain intimate obligations which aren't worth speaking of here. It's all over and done with, I don't hold it against you, please believe that I completely absolve you of any impression that you acted disloyally toward me. Anyway, business is business. But while Niké—that house—never actually belonged to me, I was always sincerely interested in her development, until circumstances arose which for a long time hindered me from giving her my personal attention. And so, to make a long story short, I was left completely uninformed—about that house on Kosmajska Street, I mean. What exactly did you do with her?"

I'm ashamed to admit it, but my patience was beginning to give out. Nevertheless, I controlled myself once again and expressed my sincere sympathy for the calamity which had befallen him, to which the only answer through the screen was a dull groaning and the apathetic formula to the effect that his "time was done." Simultaneously, I was considering whether in his wife's absence I couldn't remove the screen and "encourage" the invalid just a little more, when something happened which threw me quite literally off balance.

Mrs. Martinović had stolen unnoticed behind me and now wrenched with all her strength at the rickety chair on which I was sitting, so that I suddenly found myself on the floor. Yes, collapsed on the floor, almost knocking the screen down across the invalid. While I was getting up—quite smartly, considering my years—my hostess rudely disposed of my tentative conclusion that my mishap had been an accident, for she bent over me to knock me down the moment I got up again.

"You feel sorry for us, do you? But you want more anyway. Can't get enough, you greedy monsters, can you? You'd take all we've got—money, belongings, our very souls! Well, *that* to you!" Here, believe it or not, she actually demonstrated it, *in vivo*. "There's nothing more for you to take and divide up. And you made my children emigrate, you filthy gangsters. Go steal from each other now!"

"Oh, *mon Dieu!* Pull yourself together, madam!"

"What sort of madam am I, you bastard! A madam in a calico dress, a madam who eats once in a blue moon, a madam who washes fucking old men's fucking drawers! Thieves! Pigs! Godless mobsters!"

"*Moi, je ne comprends rien, parole d'honneur. Je suis un homme de grande renommée!*"

"Pigs!"

"*Pardon, pardon! Vous avez eu la bonté de vois souvenir de moi—Arsénie K. Negovan, rentier de la rue Kosančićev Venac, numéro dix-sept!*"

Although I'm free to leave out this sordid scene *in pleno* (have I mentioned that I'm writing on the back of tax forms and rent receipts?), and although for my own posthumous memory and the Martinovići's reputation it would be well to do so, nevertheless I have included it since these events, together with other events that awaited me on my walk, were clearly and prophetically significant. And so, with a certain restraint regarding the choice of words but not the events, I'm writing down how, pursued by the lady's oaths, I cautiously beat a retreat toward the door, reflecting meantime that if there were no other way, I should have to make use of my cane. For the time being, however, the enraged woman contented herself with the coarse oaths whose sense was quite beyond my comprehension, nor was I, quite honestly, in any mood to puzzle it out.

"Why don't you leave him in peace for once, you filthy cheat? Can't you see that the man's dying? Do you want to finish him off altogether? Hasn't my husband done his time? Fifteen years he served in prison—innocent—so that those no-good bastards could get fat on our estate!"

"Madam!"

"Get out!"

"Please, I can explain—"

"Explain? What did you explain to us back in forty-four? Get out of here, and tell those who sent you that the Martino-vići have nothing more for you to confiscate. You can still get this!" She brandished her clenched fist. "Just look at him, all dressed up with a hat and a tie! Don't you think I can tell a secret policeman when I see one?"

Obviously, any explanation was useless. Also, her shouting might alarm the neighbors and involve me in a scandal. I managed to reach the stairs, but as I was going down, try-ing to maintain an appearance of businesslike haste in my withdrawal, Joška, the horse dealer's daughter, leaned over the wooden handrail and continued to hurl imprecations down at me:

"And that house that so caught your eye, you couldn't take that away, bloodsucker! The bastards knocked it down, thank God, leveled it to the ground. You could only take the stones, and take them you did, and how! You even took the rubble away from us! I hope they use them for your grave! And you can come back with the police if you want, I don't give a damn!"

I quickened my step to a pace just short of a run and didn't stop until I was in Topličin Venac. The woman's out-burst at the top of the stairs had ended in groaning, sobbing, shouting, and the devil knows what else.

My Niké, then, was hit during the Allied bombing and couldn't have been repaired at all, even if she had been in my hands. So from all the evidence, I could be considered neither guilty of, nor even an accessory to, her destruction. Unfortunately, I had to pay for the merited relief with shame at being so eager to accept it. Had I really so little feeling left for the house, that I preferred it to have been razed to the ground in order to preserve my own peace of mind?

That's right, Arsénie, that's right! If you'd really wanted to find a way around the procession, you'd have taken the streetcar and gone behind it along General Mišić Street, around Kalemegdan Park and the Zoo.

No streetcar could have got out from Kosančićev Venac onto the boulevard under those circumstances.

Or you could have telephoned to request a postponement of the auction.

Impossible! That was quite contrary to good business practice.

Why didn't you participate in the auction by phone? You had the right to nominate a representative—it could have been anyone. From Kosančićev Venac you could have raised the price until your last rival withdrew.

Yes, indeed, but I didn't think of it at the time.

Perhaps you were afraid that Niké's strength would displace all the other houses from your mind. She clearly had tendencies in that direction: she was selfish, egocentric, jealous of every thought which your affairs obliged you to devote to rival buildings.

Reflecting on all this, I have at last found enough courage to utter the word *premeditation*. It had been a hypocritical hope that Niké's destruction, over which I had certainly had no influence, would liberate me from my feeling of guilt, for the house had died even before the bombs sought her out. Niké passed away on March 27, 1941, at 1900 hours, when it became clear to everyone on Kosmajska Street that

Arsénie Negovan was not coming to the auction. And it was I who had killed Niké.

Yes, just as I was responsible for the destruction which threatened Şimonida, and for that greedy shoemaker's shop clamped to Aspasia's tender back. I had taunted George with desertion, but what had I done myself? What difference was there between my seclusion at No. 17 Kosančićev Venac and his confinement at concession No. 17 in the New Cemetery? Even the coincidence of the numbers underscored the similarity of our cowardice.

Meanwhile I had an oppressive feeling in my chest. I'd become unaccustomed to walking, even though formerly I'd been able to spend hour upon hour making the rounds of my own houses and building sites, and observing those of others, without feeling at all wearied. True, it was swelteringly hot —the warm air wrapped itself around me like a sticky band of flypaper—but more likely it was my seventy years which undermined my freshness and drove me to a bench where I could rest my legs.

That morning the park was fairly empty. Children were clambering over the jungle gym like spiders along their glistening threads, the rusty moving parts of the swings and seesaws creaked piercingly, and children's heads bobbed up and down from behind the ragged edge of the concrete sandbox like pink water lilies. (I'm ashamed to admit that I was never overfond of children. How many times had I come upon the front walls of houses defaced with their drawings just after the painters had finished their work? They all used colors in the same unexpected way, and pencils, chalk, coal, and sharp stones, too. My cousin Leonid Negovan termed these drawings "a direct expression of primitive, Altamira-like genius"—which was easy for him to say, since the houses were never his. I on the other hand—again, because the houses indeed often *were* mine—saw the drawings

as evidence of bad upbringing for which the parents ought
to be punished.)

All that equipment and ironwork for children hadn't even
been there before, but the monument to Vuk still dominated
the park. With my binoculars I made the aggressive iron
figure stand out against the green foliage.

GENERAL VUK, 1880–1916

JADAR

KONATICA

BELGRADE

VLASINA

KAJMAKČALAN

SIVA STENA

GRUNIŠTE

At that moment it seemed as if the general had rushed
out of the forest, out from behind those scattered chestnut
trees, with his chest out and one leg bent at the knee,
bandaged with a field dressing, while the other leg pushed
down at a sharp angle against the yellowed, rough-hewn
pedestal. The policeman I had glimpsed bearing down on me
before I finally lost consciousness on the cobblestones of
Pop-Lukina Street had been something like that guerrilla
general. I had been knocked down and my pince-nez smashed,
but I could still—thank God—control my movements, although I could achieve little apart from defending my face
against being trodden underfoot. Feet were trampling down
everything around me as if crushing grapes in a vat, rising
and falling with the speed and uniformity of a pneumatic
hammer, but I couldn't swear to it that I had any feeling
of pain, nor could I hear the din which had been going on
during the speech and later during the fight, while I had
still been on my feet. On the contrary, as soon as I was
knocked down everything suddenly went quiet, though it all
continued to writhe, jostle, and stagger in the artificial si-

lence, as if the tumult of a moment earlier had reached a pitch where it could no longer be heard even though still raging. Before everything went completely blank, I managed to focus my eyes, like the shaded lens of a pair of unadjusted binoculars, on a true copy of the Vuk monument: the police-man rushing at me with his truncheon swinging.

Of that rumbled period when my senses returned—the process went on for quite a while, as I regained and lost con-sciousness several times—I recall only Katarina's mistily swimming face; those jerky, ruby-red outlines which looked more like the darting tongues of a burning flame than living beings, cut certainly not like my nurses; and strangely, that green limb with the iron bandage around its joint, which, unattached to my body, plunged hissing into the furniture. My eyes finally cleared like a binocular lens at last adjusted for distance, and I managed to make out real objects from the fiery waves which, for a long while after I came to, went on flaring up from somewhere and setting fire to the corners of the room. It was our bedroom at Kosančićev Venac. Ap-parently I was being undressed, and someone was trying to pry something from my rigidly clenched fingers—something torn, hard, battered.

It was that very object, which seemed to have become part of my fist as if to give me some little comfort, that helped me back to consciousness: my lost hat, the Borsalino with the cleft crown, stiff turned-up brim, and black silk band. In a sorry state, it's true, but I recognized it. (In any case it had my name inside it.) How I had managed to find it I couldn't say, nor could the police patrol which found me, identified me, put me in a hired cab and with true deference brought me to Kosančićev Venac. The sergeant could only say with official certainty that when the red mob had been dispersed, they had pulled Mr. Negovan out of a gutter where the sewer carries the—pardon the expression—shit into Kosmajska Street. But they could not say how he had got down there among the excreta, unless he'd taken part in the riot, which, given the gentleman's reputation, they certainly couldn't believe (although one never knows). He had been in a bad, an extremely bad, way: beaten, unconscious, left for dead, and as they say, ready for the last rites; in his left hand he was gripping the aforementioned hat, from which they unsuccessfully tried to separate him while they were getting him into the cab.

The diagnosis was made by our family doctor, and confirmed by the second opinion of the surgeon George Negovan (whose professional assistance I myself would never have requested). This diagnosis, which I have kept among my papers, states: *Fractura tibiae et fibulae dextre, Fractura costarum II lat. sin. et III, IV lat. dex., Contusio cerebri et Haematoma faciae et corporis,* which confirmed that both bones of my lower leg were broken; that three ribs were cracked (the second on the left and the third and fourth on the right side of my rib cage); that I had suffered cerebral contusions (the effects of which made themselves felt in the temporary paralysis of the left side of my face); and that, finally, I was completely covered with bruises and swellings from blows received during the incident.

Afterward, when they removed my plaster and replaced it with an elastic lace-up corset such as our mothers used to wear, Katarina told me that for quite some time I had been delirious with a temperature as high as 104° F., and that in my delirium I had been taking part in an auction of Niké where I was bidding against the strangest rivals: a man called "Hook," another called "N.N.," and "Christina." I easily identified Hook as the war veteran, and N.N. as the speaker who had preceded me at the demonstration; only Christina baffled me. Then it dawned on me that this name stood for the hefty suffragette I was pressed against while we were marching toward Brankova Street.

(Christina, the sister of my architect Jacob Negovan, was

a person quite untouched by sanity; although her half-wittedness was known and accepted, it won't be out of place here for me to note the outward symptoms of her madness. She was a socialist, a left-wing one at that. Furthermore she was a jockey, a suffragette, a bicyclist, a Spanish correspondent in 1937, the first Serbian woman to fly in a balloon, a cellist, and a Trotskyite. She learned Chinese, wore demonstrative black with a red rose on the First of May, and in the fashion of Georges Sand, her spiritual grandmother, smoked with a spindle-shaped ivory cigarette holder like a Turkish pipe. Since I was of course a "reactionary," she had long ago broken off with me, and had resigned herself to awaiting the World Revolution, a revolution which never came.)

This whole experience—the lynch mob, my injuries, and the misunderstanding over Niké—wouldn't have been so important, if during my convalescence which went on for, well, almost six months, I hadn't become preoccupied with refashioning both my business and private life in some new and as yet unconsidered way. There was nothing else for it, Arsénie, you had to adapt yourself to time—I'm not saying submit to it, but come to terms with it. Avoid struggling against its headstrong changes like a mule against the driving harness. All in all, set about something fundamental, one of those lifesaving turnarounds which, according to some higher motivation, had dispersed the sons of the Moskopolje potter, Simeon Nago, to the four corners of the earth, and had subsequently kept their descendants on the sunny surface of life.

The feeling of insecurity was accentuated by the German invaders who during my recovery had stormed the redoubts of our old-fashioned life. Personally, I had nothing against the Germans: given my strained resources, the cessation of building activity came at just the right time. The Germans, it's true, requisitioned some of my houses, but they kept excellent accounts and paid adequate compensation for what

they destroyed. As far as the bombing was concerned, I as-
cribe all that to their debit, for the first raids were theirs
and the subsequent ones were provoked by their presence;
but as my lodger, Major Helgar, said: *"Das ist ein Krieg,
Herr Negovan!"* Yes, it was war, something subnatural, elemental, which opened up like a crater beneath certain of my
houses, to swallow them up and return them to the earth
whence they had come.

The Germans too brought changes whose essential nature
I strove to fathom, lying in my plaster trough which stank of
sweat-soaked, powdered chalk. I strove to fathom all these
changes, and Major Bruno Helgar, and Cousin Stefan, and
the green man with an iron hook instead of a fist; and N.N.,
the speaker who proclaimed the Revolution; and the Russian merchants in their overcoats, on their knees; the
Solovkino wire with its fivefold noose; *Fractura tibiae et
fibulae dextre;* George's unwarlike end; Fedor G. Negovan, who used to come see us lowered into our graves; the
attempt to demolish my Katarina on Lamartine Street;
Agatha's undermined health; the reason why I wasn't allowed
to give my lecture to the Sisters of Serbia; and Isidor, my
Isidor.

And a lot of other things, Isidor, when you look at them
soberly were all trifles and nonsense; but every one of those
trifles and nonsense was a fresh smear on the lens through
which I looked at my town and my fellow citizens, and sometimes even at you, my boy. Filth and dirt had piled up in
the space between us, some vile kind of filth. But you mustn't
think that my invalid reflections gave birth to my decision
immediately—I was too experienced to give way to those early
impulses. Initially they simply nourished my inclination toward the later decision of whose nature, dimension, and
scope I had no notion.

And yet, retroactively, the future decision was already in
force. My convalescence was progressing, the traces of violence

had long disappeared, and my bones had mended, so that I had to think seriously about leaving my bed. The doctors confirmed that any further confinement could lead to dire consequences for my faculty of movement; to restore flexibility to my left leg and suppleness to my body, they prescribed exercises in my room and quiet walks in the fresh air. However, by cunning excuses I postponed getting up, while in the meantime receiving regular reports about my houses from my lawyer Golovan, who had temporarily taken over my office. Thus I delayed getting up until an immediate danger of pneumonia was foreseen if I remained physically inert any longer.

Well and good: I got up and performed the prescribed exercises, but didn't go out at all—apart, of course, from going to the window, from where I had an excellent view over the delta at the mouth of the Sava, that gray, watery loop in the middle of the Pannonian plain. I supervised Golovan's activities, but the sad fact is he *did not love houses* (nor they him); he was merely the representative of my will and passion. Very soon, because of the multiplicity of my affairs, Katarina was obliged to associate herself with him, even though until that time I had always spared her my business worries.

I wouldn't be telling the whole story if I didn't report here how much I was tormented by the fear of disrupting that *personal* relationship, of transforming it into abstract, anonymous figures with which I should have contact only through accounts, receipts, and Golovan's and Katarina's reports. Would that not have been similar to banking or, God forbid, stock-exchange transactions, in which numbers —phantom symbols—took the place of houses?

In order that this should not happen, Isidor, I ordered a photographer to prepare enlarged photographs of my houses from various angles—I kept a complete file of the plans, designs, and investment proposals—and I ordered models constructed according to the very best patterns out of ebony and jacaranda. (Use was made, over Katarina's objections, of some elegant furniture which had belonged to her grandmother Turjaški.)

In this way I perpetuated the appearance of my houses at the very moment I left them. Seemingly left them, of course. In fact, from up there at Kosančićev Venac, as from an observation tower, I continued to watch over them tenderly. I also used photographs to note at quarterly intervals all the changes resulting from external action: atmospheric causes (sunshine, precipitation, frost), and movement or settling of foundations. If the climate caused deterioration, I recognized it in the cracking of the rendering like peeling skin; in the ricketlike appearance of the dried-up woodwork; in the faded pallor of the paint, which withered on the walls like the color of a person gnawed away by a malicious internal disease; in the damp streaks which lined the ceiling like a feverish brow.

At this point I can't resist the temptation—after all, I'm writing my will—to make note of my personal contribution to building experiments, a contribution which under the name of "Arsénie's glass" or "Arsénie's glass leaf" was put into general use. My experts were continually complaining that they had no reliable means of establishing whether a crack was "dead" or "live," "active" or "inactive"—an important matter, as its origin and therefore its treatment depend upon this: an "active" crack—one that's getting wider— is caused by constant activity of the ground, which has to be guarded against, whereas an "inactive" crack remains as the result of some past movement, and can simply be filled in and left. But apart from close examination, there was no practical way of determining a crack's behavior; they simply didn't know how. Of course I knew even less: I was a property owner, not a builder. But here fortune smiled upon me. *Nota bene*, something like Isaac Newton and his apple. On several occasions my property owner's map fell off the wall, for which I could blame neither its modest weight or the tape with which it was fixed. The only thing I noticed was a minute crack which ran crookedly across the paint like a fine wick. The next time, when I threw away the sticky tape and again tried to fasten the map to the wall, I realized that the crack had widened. I concluded that the plaster, paint, and my map were behaving toward the wall very much like skin over flesh, and were being affected by all the changes to which the layer beneath was subjected, just as our skin shrivels and cracks when the muscle beneath it is diseased. It became clear to me at once that quite by chance I had discovered a means of observing the behavior of a crack. The first trial experiment gave excellent results: a thin leaf of glass stuck slantwise across the crevice fell off after only the first week, showing that the crack was getting wider, was active. Despite the expense to which this discovery committed me—the wall had to be reinforced because of the unsound terrain—I was pleased: "Arsénie's glass" became part of the history of building. But I'm digressing.

I hadn't yet announced my intention of retiring, though I had hinted that I might transfer the renting and selling of houses to Golovan's agency. As I might have foreseen, Katarina was delighted at the idea of my partial retirement, for she had always been jealous of my houses. She saw in Simonida, Sophia, Aspasia, Theodora, Agatha—with the superficial, benign naiveté of an exploiter—only walled, whitewashed, and painted cages for the collection of rent. She regarded my private relationships with them as, at the very least, eccentric. Yet when we had first become acquainted she proclaimed my passion "slightly unusual, different"; I believe it was my loyalty to architecture, and my capacity for elevating commerce to the status of art, which set me apart from her other suitors.

Anyway, Katarina received the news of my retirement with

satisfaction. The poor woman even began to make plans. She said that at least in our old age—I was then fifty and she was nearly forty-five—we could live free of worries. After the war we could travel. We had traveled before the war, but never entirely for pleasure. Usually our transcontinental "wanderings"—only half transcontinental anyway, since I couldn't bring myself to cross the Curzon Line—were associated with one of my business arrangements; either I had to view some new feature of residential architecture or attend some conference on housing, or I had to conclude a contract with foreign suppliers, so that I always seemed to carry my houses along with me.

There was as yet no word of my secret intention to seclude myself until the end of the war. Somehow that came about of its own volition. I kept on postponing going out of the house until one day Katarina asked me:

"Do you ever intend to go out of the house again, Arsénie?"

"I don't know," I said. I was telling the truth: I had no idea.

"What do you mean, you don't know?"

"That's just it, Katarina, I don't."

"Get a grip on yourself, or you'll be an invalid for the rest of your life!"

"Nonsense! I feel all right. I've never felt better." That wasn't absolutely true, but I had no time for confessions. And it was better that way.

As usual, Katarina couldn't let it be: "You've been told to walk in fresh air for at least an hour every day."

"Don't you think I do?"

Indeed, I had established my regular walk inside the house. I had opened all the doors between the rooms and made myself a "track" long enough so I didn't have to turn around every minute, since a change of stride bearing weight on my damaged right leg still caused me pain.

"You call that walking in the fresh air?"

"I've opened the windows. We'll see about going out later on."

I never actually said that I wouldn't leave the house until the war was over. I wasn't in the mood, or it wasn't the right moment. Sometimes I wasn't feeling well, since the effects of my injuries were still with me. And lastly, I had at hand my most convincing reason, the only one in which there wasn't even a suspicion of pretext: I had a lot of work to do. Each day I had to read Golovan's summaries and various experts' findings, sort out the rent receipts, approve the signing or termination of leases, documents for which the powers of attorney were insufficient, bring my correspondence up to date, file papers, check the ledgers, put the card index in order, study the photographs which had been coming in for some time, and in general occupy myself with my houses even more actively than when I had had them constantly before my eyes.

Apart from all this—I note it for my own satisfaction—I now had time to complete my education in housing. I had read a great deal before, and knew more than many practicing architects and most city landlords, but it was never enough, always less than what any self-respecting property owner should know of his profession.

Here I shall take advantage of a pause in my narrative.

Article 1. Fully conscious and in possession of all my mental faculties, I hereby express my wishes concerning each section of my personal library in the field of architecture, easily recognizable since all volumes are bound in dark red calf-skin. All these books are to be excepted from the total of my immovable assets at Kosančićev Venac, which I otherwise bequeath to my lawful spouse Katarina Negovan, née Tur-jaški. The books shall be entrusted as a separate bequest to my nephew Isidor Negovan, son of Jacob Negovan, architect of Krunska Street, No. 19a.

(The list of books which makes up the legacy bequeathed to my nephew, Isidor J. Negovan, will be found with the other documents attached to my last will and testament in a white sealed envelope at the bottom of the top right-hand drawer of my desk. The key to this drawer is hanging from my belt with my other keys.)

But again, can I bid them farewell without a single good word for them? Of course I can't say that those books about architecture made me fall in love with houses. They only explained to me *why* I love them. From them I was schooled in houses' physiology, their circulatory system, their epi-dermic defensive envelope, even their stomachs, their sensi-tive stomachs, not to mention their life process. In addition to those features common to the majority of houses, I was particularly troubled by these secondary differences, I'll call them differences of class and race, which despite the same materials that created them, distinguish the Morić Khan in Sarajevo from the Carleton Hotel in Cannes; Mansart's Maison Lafitte from Eigtved's twin palaces in Copenhagen; Hood's Daily News Building in New York from Loos's House of Commerce in Vienna; Perret's building on Rue Franklin in Paris from Gaudi's Casa Mila in Barcelona; or even my Daphina, designed by J. K. Negovan, from Wright's Falling Water.

Lastly, also bound in calfskin on my shelves, were the biographies of the great master builders which I had ob-tained through the kindness of Jacob Negovan, through Mr. Kon the bookseller, or in the course of my journeys abroad. From books, then, I had come to know the mysterious pro-cess of a house's conception, initiated long before its violent birth on the building site.

So as I have said, I had more than enough work, and an abundance of pretexts: my illness, business affairs, the war, the Occupation. In the final analysis, doesn't everyone have the right to take a breather, to retire, to collect himself? When some famous person goes into a monastery, walls himself up suddenly in the stone box of a hermit's cell, we show approval, but when a businessman takes brief refuge under the roof of his own house, he comes up against strident objections. Anyway, I went on repeating, I am, my friends, in excellent shape, you can expect to see me out again very soon. Yes, yes, out and about. When? That, unfortunately, I can't say. In all probability, I'll go out when the situation clarifies itself and I manage to find out what's *really* going on outside. Incidentally, isn't everything taking its normal course? I attend to my work, my professional interest in my houses hasn't diminished. What's more, it's been strengthened through the action of an intermediary. (However much confidence I entertained toward Golovan—far better if I hadn't! —my lawyer served me almost as an adding machine, a writing implement, or a tool which, while functioning irreproachably, had to be oiled regularly, supervised, and corrected.) We entertain as before; Katarina still has her Thursday sessions—true, because of work pressures I drop in on them less often, but we listen to the radio, subscribe to newspapers. In short, contact with the outside world is maintained in all respects.

To be honest, all that about the radio and the newspapers was not exactly the truth. For some time we did indeed listen to the radio. Apart from my beloved music, especially if it could be visualized in material terms—I transposed Bach's fugues into the soaring towers of Gothic cathedrals, Mozart's concertos into transparent crystal-glass pavilions, and Schubert into family salons looking out onto a garden, but was incapable of making anything of Beethoven (I wasn't fond of Beethoven, who seemed like a storm, always in unpre-

dictable movement; I couldn't find a form for him in any
building)—apart from my beloved music we listened to the
various communiqués from the fronts until, I can't even
remember in what year, the air raids on London began. It
was not enough for those monsters to attack houses; now
they had started to demolish them as well. I responded by
refusing to listen, and then I ordered the radio taken out of
the house. As for newspapers, here I was less threatened, for
I could pick and choose what I read. They too became preoccupied with the war; when I read of how much damage
the Allied bombing had caused to Berlin apartment houses,
I gave up all my subscriptions and freed myself of the obli-
gation to suffer because of the insanity in which I had no
part.

And so it became the custom not to talk about the war,
out of respect for the owner of the house. This deterred
George from dropping in, as my brother could think of
nothing more useful than battles. Since not even politics,
the cause of this destruction, were mentioned, other family
friends stayed away who held forth on nothing else.

At first, because of their carelessness, certain events
broke through the deadening layer of cork with which I'd
lined my study at Kosančićev Venac. Thus I was made aware
of food rationing. I learned also about the curfew, though
it had little bearing on us except that Katarina had to
arrange her Thursday soirée for the early hours of the
afternoon. I knew of course that the Croats had proclaimed
some sort of independence and liquidated their Serbs, Ličani,
and Bosnian Moslems—always unreliable builders, by the
way—whose bodies, it was said, were floating down the Sava
as far as the piers of the railway bridge. I couldn't make
out a single one with my strongest binoculars, to confirm
whether such refugees' tales were exaggerated. Much was
made also of a certain Mihailović (no relation to the gentleman from the basement flat), an infantry officer of the Gen-

eral Staff, who at the head of volunteer peasants was fighting against the Communist rabble which had committed that infamous outrage against me at the junction of Kosmajska and Pop-Lukina Street. By all accounts the Russians had begun to reconquer Russia. And when, on my own misplaced initiative, I learned from Major Helgar that on January 25, 1943, they had entered Voronezh, the vision of merchants thrown on their knees in the mud—the vision which has haunted my footsteps for the last fifty years—was sufficient to confine me to my bed, from where I categorically forbade them to tell me anything more about the war.

This continued right up to the autumn of 1944—with the exception of the comforting news that the Russian onslaught on the Danube had finally been stopped, and the further news that by rapid advances through Italy and Greece the English and Americans were tightening a double pincer around the Balkans. In 1944, with the end drawing near, I couldn't hold it against Katarina when she informed me that Allied and Yugoslav troops were at the approaches to Belgrade (fortunately nothing more was said of the Bolsheviks); that, judging by the gunfire, their entry into the town could be expected any day, as I observed for myself with my binoculars trained on the street fighting down by the King Alexander Bridge.

It had been said that I had had more good fortune with the Occupation authorities and their civil representatives than other property owners due to my reputation, the name Negovan, and my maintaining relations with them only through my attorney Golovan, who (I must give him his due for *that* period) had been a forceful representative and faithful interpreter of my owner's rights. My rigorous retirement, I believe, had saved me from those unpleasantnesses to which even our nearest neighbors on Kosančićev Venac were exposed. Even so, I'm in no way ashamed to declare how elated I was to see the backs of the Germans—and the shuddering rears of their tanks like a praying mantis—crawling over the bridge to the west. My good Katarina was crying —from happiness, of course—and that was the first and last time I ever saw her cry. She was trying hard to get me away from the window, from which, quite forgetting myself, I was loudly encouraging our valiant liberators. Even more, I had completely ignored the danger to which, in the street fighting, they were quite involuntarily subjecting my houses, those same defenseless buildings for which I had so ardently prayed to God during the air raids. And so, close to the window, I wouldn't give in to Katarina, until I realized that such childish behavior didn't accord with my dignity, never mind my years, and what's more could be fatal, because the west window dominated the river, the bridge, and the Sava quays, and could be taken for a command post.

I should make it clear at once that I didn't follow my father Cyrill or my brother George in their monarchist convictions, even though, of all art forms, architecture had been the most favored by the monarchy. But that day, October 20, whose dawn on the greenish, shaken walls I greeted with all my heart, was not an ordinary one; for me it signified the explosive return to their God-given place of things violently overturned; the restoration of the lawful regime; the reestablishment of security.

With such encouraging prospects in view, I could already begin to think of going out of the house. Not at once, of course. Things had to be given time to settle down. My unhappy experience after the first war prompted me toward caution: for quite a few years after the Armistice conditions had been highly irregular. I remember the efforts I had had to make to obtain even the simplest building material, to achieve priority in litigation over building lots in the center of town, and to get bank credits. But in the Twenties I had been young and in a hurry, whereas now I had time to wait and see how the new turnabout would work. After the

Unification I hadn't possessed a single house except the two I had inherited, and they were shared with my brothers George and Emilian (his religious name); after the Liberation I had forty-nine, not counting building plots already purchased, land under option, and sites where work in various stages had been stopped to await better times. Clearly I had no cause to be rash or overbold in going out into town again.

Katarina agreed to this new postponement, although it continued to place on her shoulders the responsibility which we had originally agreed would be only temporary. But in fact, on her initiative, I now began to think of prolonging the status quo for an indefinite period, especially when she picturesquely described to me the pitiful state of the town: "*You*, Arsénie," she said, "you simply couldn't bear all those ruined buildings!" Yet eventually I would have gone into town if Katarina hadn't behaved quite as uncompromisingly as on the occasion of my first decision not to go out. She now deterred me from it with the same Turjaški stubbornness she had once used to urge me to go out, and I was thankful that she had at last understood my decision to retire. The change in Katarina's attitude was probably influenced by the unexpected visit of Dr. Simeonović, according to whom the condition of my heart had sharply deteriorated, so that any kind of movement was precluded. And so, when I asked for newspapers, I was told that the war was still going on, and when Germany capitulated, that the newspapers were still filled with war news, so that it seemed it had never ended. "You can't find a single page," said Katarina, "on which there isn't a photograph of some ruin."

Then came the crisis which I have already described: the chance discovery that my Simonida was to be torn down; doubts about Golovan, Katarina, and their professional reports; the fear that something was happening to my other houses as well.

That very morning, June 3, convinced that it was still not too late, I had impatiently waited for Katarina and Mlle. Foucault to leave.

I was actually going out!

With a feeling of relief and adventurous pride I got up from the bench and, as much as my years would allow, hurried off toward Simonida, where I hoped the professional rebirth of Arsénie Negovan, property owner, would begin.

How best to approach the house in these unusual circumstances?

It was important to re-establish our onetime personal relationship, maintained during my hermitlike seclusion by means of photographs and Golovan's suspect submissions. I cannot but admit that everything I had undertaken since going out of the house was more like the pilgrimage of a dispirited old man, searching for the past in unfamiliar places where he had erected its landmarks as memorials, than the march of the architect forging his future plans. Simonida was my last chance to end this futile wandering, to spend the rest of the day usefully for both myself and my possessions.

My pride in my house was, alas, rudely shaken when, en route, I found myself quite by chance in front of the most insignificant of them: the only house which, thanks to the builder's pigheadedness and my unforgivable negligence (I had been away on a journey) enjoyed that life in an evil way, an adequate, but truly evil way and the only one that I shall speak of without respect or love. I would very gladly leave her out, but everything that is written down here on receipts and rent accounts is nevertheless my legal testament, and in such a loan from death there is no point in lying.

This "house"—which I must summon up all my courage to call mine—did not have a name. Even her model, built as a result of Katarina's forgetfulness or carelessness of my own, was chopped up with an ax and burned the very day its illegitimate creator brought it from the office. In short, she was expelled as a monstrosity from the tribe of my houses, and the fact that she hadn't been sold was due partly to the war, partly to the fall in market prices, and partly to Golovan's negligence. Finally, to round it all off, this house was truly ugly with her blind, prisonlike walls, clumsily bared, with bilious yellow ceramic moldings on the parapets, and bands of flowery white natural cement in horizontal spurts, with windows like gun emplacements, with a gate which called to mind the sooty doors of a baker's oven. Despite this, I shall proceed with it in the following manner:

Article 2. It is my unalterable wish that my house (three stories and a high basement) at Gračanička Street, No. 18, should be given for his lifetime's enjoyment to Mr. Jovan Martinović, formerly a wholesale grain dealer of Topličin Venac, No. 11, with the proviso that after his death the house should revert to the permanent ownership of my universal heir, designated in these documents; but under no circumstances should any member of Mr. Martinović's family (most particularly his widow) have any right to the house by any word or intention of this testament.

The next building which lay in my path was the Renaissance palace belonging to the National Bank, which for numerous reasons I should have given a wide berth. Primarily because of its purpose: I had no time to idle away on structures not meant for accommodation. Nevertheless, I stopped in front of it long enough to show respect to the memory of its builder, the deceased architect Constantine Jovanović. Not at all, of course, because of this ponderous uninspired, truly masculine building, but because of our personal relations. When in 1882 the Tajsić fields had been divided up into building lots, Constantine, on the instructions of the colonial importer K.S., drew up plans for a family house at Vračar; a rare feminine house among his forceful and muscular works, which I later bought and christened Irina, having registered her on Saint Irina's Day. He also began the plans for Athenaida in Senjak, but died before he could finish her.

Since I have mentioned the first of my architects, it would clearly be unjust to remain silent about the others. I was very close to some of them: we planned and built houses which I still own today. Others designed houses which I bought and quickly resold—houses that merely passed through my hands, whose efficient fingers were ever ready to grasp anything successful, unusual, elegant, and comfortable, but let slip anything which fell below my passion for perfection. In almost every case, however, the architects' commercial interests—so incompatible with my own concerns —became a source of constant misunderstanding between us. For what builder can understand why *his* house is sold and not someone else's, or why, instead of *his* house, a competitor's is bought? Consequently, I can say that my friendship with my architects usually lasted just as long as my ownership over their respective houses. But eventually, exasperated by their hysterical irritability, I was forced to rely almost entirely on my uncle Constantine (despite his advanced years) and his son, the architectural engineer Jacob Negovan (even though Jacob's capabilities were limited) to carry out the work. This is not to say that Jacob was a nonentity, for that would be doing him an injustice, which I would like to avoid because of Isidor. But even if he had been as clever as his son, he could scarcely have kept up with all those brilliant architects whom I had had to reject because of their unsufferable temperaments. In any case I was building less by then, as most of Europe was at war; my fear for my noble houses, at the thought of what had happened to

Rotterdam and Warsaw, gradually led me to my spiritual and professional paralysis.

I can also recall those younger designers, my contemporaries. Collaboration with them was even more difficult; somehow they began to understand architecture as a free expression of their own inventiveness and not in the natural way, as the most perfect realization of the client's needs and wishes. With them (to hell with them, for all their talent!) I always risked an unpleasant surprise if I didn't define every condition by contract and supervise its implementation from the drawing-board on, watch over the papers, and check the construction on the building site; for sometimes they designed what I wanted on paper, but built what they wanted on the building lot.

Since the National Bank has induced me to mention the architects with whom I worked—to the discredit of the Negovan name—I must shed some light on the quarrel between those onetime friends and collaborators, Emilian Josimović of the Lyceum and my grandfather, Simeon Negovan, landowner. If I can't help those now dead, nothing prevents me from transferring my gratitude to those who can profit from it, and of endorsing the bill of exchange to the heirs and descendants of Isidor's generation in the following manner:

Article 3. I will that, after deduction of maintenance costs and taxes, the rent from my houses on Sveti Sava, Poincarret, and Kornelija Stanković Streets be collected in a trust fund, and at the end of each year there shall be designated by the Serbian Royal Academy of Sciences a worthy sum to reward the best work of residential achitecture within the town of Belgrade, but only that not exceeding three stories.

There is no objection in this legacy if other donors wish to associate themselves with the fund by their endowments, on the condition that the name "Arsénie Negovan Fund" be retained. As for the prizes, they may be given whatever name is deemed suitable.

We must approach the feud between Emilian Josimović and my grandfather from a somewhat earlier time.

(It's to him that I address myself, although it had never occurred to me before to write this in the form of a letter. Originally I hadn't even intended to set down these notes about my sortie into town. I sat down at my desk to write my will. I was incapable of writing it all in one go. I began to make a draft on the backs of old bills and rent receipts, with the intention of writing it out later, sealing it with wax, and stamping the initials of "A.N." with my signet ring. I shall use this pause to make a change in the legacy for the foundation of the trust fund: I think that the revenue from a single house will be adequate to show my gratitude—most probably, the house on Sveti Sava Street.)

At that time, then, the Turkish quarter still sprawled around the Kalemegdan fortress, which was bordered by the Moat stretching like a Tartar's bow from the Varoš-Kapija to the Danube. The Serbs built their homes below the Moat; the majority were houses of timber and unbaked bricks or, less often, plastered and whitewashed huts of woven branches with posts supporting roofs of straw or rushes. Then with youthful vigor they began to push their way uphill from the Sava embankment to the Terazije grazing land where, becoming arrogant, they built houses that rose up another story and were roofed with tiles, and that descended underground into largers, storerooms, and cellars: houses built in stone and walled around, and adorned with balconies and belvederes. Among them were the homes of the Negovans. These Negovans stood out, distinguished by a concept of European orderliness; they built up Gospodska and Pop-Pantina Streets (now Brankova and Marshal Biryuzov Streets), letting nothing fall from their grasp. Yet toward the mosques, fountains, bridges, and tumble-down alleyways and passages of the Turkish quarter, where the buildings of the old Austrian district lay in ruins, they displayed an Oriental impassivity. So it was hardly possible to think of an organized town—a Budapest-like way of life and means of communication—while in the upper and lower towns Asiatic chaos still reigned; each house was put up where and how the owner pleased, obstructing street vistas, cramping façades, and improving heights.

In 1864, with the financial support of Simeon Negovan, and probably at his suggestion, Emilian Josimović, a teacher at the lyceum and the high school, set about drawing up the first regulatory plan for Belgrade, which he published under the title *An Elucidation of the Proposal for the Regularization of the Area of the Town of Belgrade Situated along the Moat. With a Lithograph Plan to Scale 1/3000.* Bearing in mind the lack of technical means with which it was prepared, this work deserved respect, but found none among the population of the town or with the Administration. Josimović proposed that the abandoned Turkish Moat be filled in and the ground rearranged into esplanades and public gardens in seven crescents.

Old man Simeon, my grandfather, supported Emilian Josimović with both his reputation and his purse against the Administration, and against the landowners who feared losses in the proposed indemnification for property lying within the area encompassed by the "regularization." Of course Emilian didn't keep secret from Simeon his sketch for the reconstruction of the street network along the Moat, and certainly entrusted to his benefactor, before they were made public, all the changes which he had thought of in the composition of the town. But as early as the geodetic survey stage, Josimović took the opportunity to give a double warning of the danger of speculation in land, whose value would rise or fall for the most part in accordance with the location of the plots vis-à-vis the sketch. The government had bought up scarcely a third of the land from the Turkish expropriates, so that two-thirds were still for sale. Josimović wanted the state to take it all. In this he had Simeon's support, or so it seemed.

Nevertheless, as is often the case when commerce and science come together in a development project, interests were common but not identical. Quickly it became known that Simeon Negovan, personally or through intermediaries, had bought up the major part of the land along the projected park, exactly that area which Josimović had categorized as of prime value. Simeon had paid a hundred ducats, whereas the *valeur en recouvrement* of the land was almost a thousand, and a year later the market price rose to three thousand. Breaking off family relations and repudiating his role as godfather (to which their friendship had brought him in the meantime), the now furious architect showered my grandfather with imprecations whose bitter traces, barely hidden by the academic vocabulary, can be recognized even in the Introduction to his *An Elucidation of the Proposal for the Regularization of the Area of the Town of Belgrade Situated along the Moat*. I consider the reproaches exaggerated, since without Simeon's support Josimović's work would certainly not have existed at all. There was much lack of understanding among the townspeople, particularly the landowners, and much indifference in the Administration. Furthermore, an architect's greatest work must be exclusively in his mind and his heart: Josimović was entirely obsessed with the new Belgrade, and had no wish for anyone to make anything out of it along the way. Given all this, his complaint that he had "suffered so many unfavorable circumstances *from all sides*," which surely refers to Simeon Negovan, is in no way justified, for he didn't grasp all the favorable circumstances from which he profited, thanks indeed only to Simeon Negovan.

To somehow stop Simeon—not at all out of malice or to serve some higher principle, but to eliminate doubts about secret collusion between them, and therefore to make it impossible for Simeon to profit from this purchase of land—Josimović proposed a law to the government by which the resale of plots of land along the Moat would be forbidden, except to the State and the Municipality, and at the original sale price. To make sure that this law would destroy Simeon's speculations, Josimović also demanded that the owners of plots of land be obliged to put up buildings on them within a certain time limit, "according to the regulations affecting the place in question." He calculated that even Simeon didn't have sufficient resources to build on all the plots simultaneously. However, before it was entirely certain that this regulation would become law, Simeon had erected, practically overnight and as if by magic, a row of shacks and hovels of any material at hand. In the absence of building regulations they could indeed be considered houses, since they had a certain modest resemblance to them. Just how modest that resemblance was can be seen from a description Josimović gave after his final defeat: "The hulk of an old boat, dragged up from the Danube by mules and plastered with clay and caulked with tin plate, was set up like an unsightly pediment in the middle of a plot of land, beneath which, in my lunacy, I had imagined a French park with a patriotic monument, and an ornate pool with graceful water fountains."

And now of course, although I don't have the courage to justify my ancestor, I ask myself: if Simeon Negovan hadn't acted as he did, could Arsénie Negovan, disdaining profit, enjoy today only the beauty of what he possesses? Like it or not, in commercial affairs it often happens that you have to proceed by roundabout routes, defiles, and shortcuts, and resort to measures a more idealistic man would gladly avoid. Commerce is war: merchants must be continually at war in defense of Possession. You are attacked from ambush and you yourself attack from behind; you camouflage your own intentions and spy out those of your enemies; you sound false alarms, sign false truces, and put out false news. In such a commercial war there are no friends; everyone breaks with everyone, everyone plots against everyone, and alliances are unreliable and short-lived.

If, however, the property owner has in view the welfare of the nation and the people—even though this may not have been immediately apparent, or his act may even have seemed to harm the nation and the people—then the act can be approached with a clear conscience. Possession is not increased by profit for its own sake; it is increased in order to grow and multiply, and to live for the good of all. I know this from my own experience. Like my grandfather Simeon Negovan, I was exposed to all kinds of animosity even when my motives were the most honest.

I'll relate only one such incident. During the Great Crisis of '29 I wanted to take advantage of the ridiculously low price of building materials and also of the particularly low piecework rates. Earlier I had already bought several well-placed sites, on which I decided to build houses. But I had little ready cash available and was forced to count every penny, as they say. At that bad moment even the poorer tenants, particularly those who had no regular income or jobs, began to make excuses to avoid paying their rent, some for as long as six months. The individual sums were not large, but because of the number of delinquents, I showed a large deficit. This deficit threatened to destroy all my building plans. So I set about obtaining my rights. At first, of course, only in a gentle fashion. I paid a visit, reminded here, wrote a letter there, warned, cajoled, and where words were of no avail, began to threaten a little. In this way I finally got satisfaction from the majority. A few I had to take to court, though this was unpleasant for me and I almost became ill from the sessions. Among those evicted there happened to be an old lady living alone, a Russian woman with weak nerves, and as is invariably the case, a general's widow. It was not surprising that because of her nerves she had to try everything until at last she managed to bring it all to an end. But was I really to blame? I'm not the one who beat her husband to death in a ditch nor did I start that Revolution, to have the widow's misfortune hung around my neck in Belgrade, thousands of kilometers from her native Sevastopol! It was hardly a bed of roses for me either, and what's more, Madame General had only herself to worry about, while without exaggeration I bore on my shoulders a whole small town made up solely of my houses, and all the future buildings which I had in my head. Moreover, had I been told about her, I would have closed my eyes. But I quite honestly didn't know about the general's widow; she had just moved into No. 18 Gračanička Street. It was probably because of this woman that I hated the house so much that I pulled her flag out of the property owner's map and burned her model; the architectural reasons for that hatred must have been only secondary, although welcome in that they replaced the true ones. The widow's windows were on the first floor, but unluckily the basement was high off the ground. Her furniture was already out on the street, waiting in the van. While Golovan was trying to persuade her to leave peaceably and without scandal, she broke away from the policeman and jumped out the window. Truly, it was all very regrettable and I, inasmuch as it was in my power, amply expressed my sorrow. I paid her posthumous debts, incurred her funeral expenses, and even meant to pay damages, but didn't know to whom.

Therefore, I have the right to assert that this town was built up by people of the mettle of Arsénie, Simeon, and his other grandson, too: Constantine Negovan, whose funeral I couldn't put out of my mind that morning. For once again, as from Gračanička Street I made out the contours of Kalemegdan Park, I was assailed by memories of his cortege. I am walking slowly along an avenue glistening with rain between huge, looming graves, memorial stones, marble slabs, and granite crosses toward a grave dug in a wet ornamental grove; I am surrounded by a procession, vaulted by umbrellas like black silk flowers, like dark-membraned mushrooms, at a certain distance from the lacquered carriage from whose plate-glass body the coffin shines, a casket girt with silver in a jeweler's display cabinet; I am walking to the spot where, behind the choir of the Association of Architects, the funeral attendants were lined up in their red jackets, carrying circular wreaths of rosemary, laurel, and purple roses with gilt expressions of condolence printed on their mourning bands.

The procession's ranks have already formed, the funeral march can barely be heard above the buzz; I move off slowly, keeping myself well behind the front rows of the family in whose midst I should be. But my efforts to get away from Fedor Negovan are fruitless. Clearly, I am the Negovan he has decided to hate today. My turn at last.

" 'Make thee an ark of gopher wood; rooms shalt thou make in the ark, and shalt pitch it within and without with pitch, and, behold, I, even I, do bring a flood of water upon the earth.'—I hope you don't mind if I accompany you, Uncle?"

"Of course I mind! But under the circumstances I can do nothing to stop you."

"Quite right." He isn't grinning in his usual manner, but I'm irritatedly aware that beneath the youthful pockmarked cheeks something pleases him. "That's what I'm counting on."

He sucks air in noisily and then, barely opening his mouth, spits in front of him with a dull hiss on the spot where his next step is about to fall.

"Would it be too much to ask you not to spit while you're in my company?"

"No, but it wouldn't make any difference. I just can't seem

to stop my own body from unloading itself inside the family circle, *entouré de sa chère famille.* Just look at them, the bastards: black and gold products of Levantine and Serbian brigandry. The same black morning coats and black bowlers, the same black, egg-shaped heads on their stocky black bodies, the same thin gold wives, gold ornaments, gold teeth, gold manners, gold words, and gold reserves. The Negovans have gathered in their black and gold colors to show the world that they're still here, that they'll be here forever even though one of their number is no longer with them!"

"Do you have any special reason for making this already sad duty even more onerous?" I ask.

"Perhaps I have, Uncle," he answers calmly. We stopped for a moment. "I've decided that ordinary funerals are not good enough for a Negovan."

"What would you suggest?"

"You ought to be burned at the stake! In the main square, *urbi et orbi,* for everyone to see. In front of the Prince's statue, say. Like Sardanapalus. With your money, your wives, your servants, your horses, pictures, bonds, and your houses! With all your abilities and success."

"And coronaries," I add resignedly, "and gallstones."

"And gallstones too, of course—those most precious of stones."

I step discreetly but firmly into the front row, yet he continues brazenly: "Ashes are lasting and dry. First-class packaging. The relative is delivered after being weighed on an apothecary's scales, and packed in a transparent cellophane box with a printed obituary—in gilt lettering, of course." Taking my arm, he whispers: "Uncle, why don't you carry your dead around with you?"

Completely taken aback, I ask:

"My dead? In God's name, Fedor, what are you talking about?"

"Constantine, Uncle—Constantine Negovan. Wasn't he killed by one of your houses?"

I decided to ignore him. On no account will I pay attention to his provocation. And I'll see to it that I don't present this brat with such an opportunity again.

"You like to show your teeth, don't you, Uncle Arsénie? And not just any teeth, but your gold teeth. Even from your deathbed. Luckily, Negovans don't die, they simply replace one another, like the green baize on a roulette table. That's why you're invited to pay your last respects to the ever mourned Constantine, son of Simeon Negovan, builder, model father and son, faithful husband and brother, noble relative and friend, esteemed employer and benefactor, skillful Daedalus, architect of the city of Belgrade. Crap! It's the living Negovans you're supposed to pay your respects to!"

"What a scoundrel you are!" I say as Timon Negovan approaches me, takes me by the arm, and inquires whether I've yet found a building contractor to take over Constantine's projects. No, not yet. I'll never find anyone to measure up to Constantine. I'll have to do something soon, of course. There's no place for indecision. The building season is nearing its end, the rainy season has already started, and any further delay in construction could be disastrous.

Timon agrees and walks off. Once again Fedor is behind me:

"Is there a single person here, apart from Jacob, who has come to honor Constantine? Everyone knows that our most esteemed builder was *mad*! He built grandiose bridges across rivers to areas that had no roads—in the belief that roads would be built as soon as bridges could carry them across the rivers! He built a leaning tower fit to rival Pisa, but so crooked that it toppled over even before its completion! He would have been ruined if you hadn't restrained him through credits from Timon's bank."

Whatever Constantine built was irreproachable. However, while his bridge was truly majestic it served no useful purpose. And his tower had been undeniably crooked, and it too had no purpose. (Yes, he lacked that purposefulness which distinguishes the rest of us Negovans. In that respect, more's the pity, Fedor was right, the late Constantine had been a good but unusual builder.)

"Well, he was original," I concede grudgingly.

"He was more than just original, Uncle, he was mad, and you know it."

"Do you think I'd have worked with him if he were crazy?"

"It was precisely because he was crazy that you did! He didn't steal from you, or try to cheat you with bad construction work, or falsify accounts, or exceed time schedules. And because you were his nephew he built houses for you below cost"— (this last is a lie) —"and the houses he built were sound, strong, and solid as a rock, just like himself." (This about the quality of his work is true.)

We are approaching the mound of earth by the grave. In front of us, through the black silk forest of umbrellas, the coffin is being carried out of the hearse and placed on the bier; the mourners range themselves around it in tight rings. Yet again I try to reason with this insolent young man, having made up my mind to complain to his father George tomorrow about his abominable behavior.

"Before terminating this undignified dispute, I must point out to you that the late Constantine was my relative, friend, and business partner. In all three capacities I loved and respected him equally!"

(I had certainly respected him. It had hardly been possible to avoid an awe-filled reverence toward something that—heedless of rest, caution, and all obstacles, even of purpose—hovered round us like elemental bad weather, like a seismic catastrophe. In Uncle Constantine there was indeed something of those Biblical architects who ordered the wilderness with their bare hands, dislocated whole towns with a single magical sign, and built and destroyed palaces overnight. Even so I hadn't loved him, and if asked why, I couldn't have explained it. Perhaps my reserved nature, sensitivity, and moderation were offended by Constantine's Tartar-like behavior, the unbridled wantonness of a conqueror who lives permanently on horseback and with a flourish carries out his work from the saddle. Or perhaps in that distaste, which of course had no bearing on our working partnership, there was something of a secret hatred of scientific architects who gave birth to buildings from within themselves, whereas I, with all my money, could only be the midwife. Even though Constantine had never been to a school of architecture and knew less about architecture than I did, as a builder he was closer to that mysterious process, the *creation of a house*.)

"You may have loved him, but you certainly didn't respect him. In fact, you despised him because of his madness. And *I*, Uncle Arsénie, I loved him because of his madness. Even as a child I adored his nonsensical bridges over nowhere; his crooked, fairy-tale towers; his readiness to roll up his sleeves and mix lime just to feel the sheer joy of building something; the deep voice with which he summoned up the stone crushers; his down-to-earth Turkish oaths; but most of all, the fact that he genuinely loved those houses even though they didn't belong to him. You loved them because they were yours!"

We are gathered around the rust-colored mound dug out of the grave. Mr. Arsenijević, Vice-President of the Builders Association, is leaning over the wet lectern, preparing to make a speech. The tomb has been built in accordance with Constantine's own drawings. The rain is falling on the leaves and the dull gray marble slabs, on the umbrellas taut like drumskins, and on the tarpaulin sheet which had earlier covered the coffin. Knowing no other way of preserving the solemnity of the ceremony, I promise Fedor that after the funeral I will be available to explain everything concerning my relationship with Constantine if only he'll calm down now, if only, for God's sake, he'll keep quiet.

"And it was *your* building on which the scaffolding collapsed—should I keep quiet about that, too?"

"It collapsed on *his* building. It just happened to be a house he was building for me."

"That whore of a house killed him. He built it and it killed him. In true Negovan style, the house just shook him off once it didn't need him any more, once he got to the roof!"

At last the Vice-President of the Builders Association began his speech, like a deity whose immediate intervention renders any human continuation superfluous. If he hadn't begun, I would have hit Fedor without further hesitation— paternally, of course. I am sure that was just what he was waiting for, and that he would have returned my blow. But on all sides there were demands for silence and we were separated; I went off to take my place alongside the coffin.

The accusation that Fedor leveled at my house, and through her at me, was that I was responsible for any injury she inflicted on anyone. (The house was called Efimia, after Efimia, daughter of Lord Drama and wife of the Despot Uglješa, since her exterior was to have been a copy of the monastery of Saint George at Stari Nagoričan.) But she was mine only in the sense that she was built for me and at my expense; according to law and custom, during the building and right up to the time when she was handed over to me by the Building Works Commission, all the responsibility for her behavior rested exclusively with her builder, Constantine. This, of course, in no way diminished my regret over the accident. Constantine could have gone around to any other site that day, and climbed up on any other scaffolding;

by ill luck, any of them could have been unsoundly erected (though we mustn't ignore his Herculean weight), and under any one of them the lime pit could have been left open. Yet despite Efimia's guiltlessness, I never had the heart to move into her, and although I had intended her for Katarina and myself, I hurriedly sold her, taking care to make but little profit on the sale. As for Constantine, he didn't die immediately after his fall. He remained an invalid for some time and, strange though he was, not mad but irrational. Not in the least God-fearing or considerate of my feelings, he got his son to build him a tomb in the shape of Efimia. As a reproach to me he kept its model, just like the model of a church depicted in the donor's embrace, on his night table beside his medicine cabinet, right up until the day he died.

Here, finally, I have an opportunity to indicate how I wish to be buried, that is, if present circumstances (which bode little good) allow distinguished people to be buried at all; if I'm not buried in a ditch, like those of my class whose extermination I once witnessed; and if events generally take a turn in our favor.

Article 4. I wish to be buried according to the rites of the Serbian Orthodox Church, on the plot of land at the New Cemetery which I bought for that purpose and paid for in a proper and legitimate manner, so that no one else may have the right to be buried in that place, either by right of marriage or any other kinship.

Article 5. I wish that above my grave there be placed a stone of similar proportions to the size of the mound, and that it be constructed by taking from each of my forty-nine houses (including even the one on Gračanička Street), but in no way to the detriment of their appearance, a cornerstone, and that all be harmoniously incorporated into my gravestone so that its composite pieces freely form a pattern, and that on the mosaic thus formed be placed in Cyrillic letters the inscription THE LAST HOUSE OF ARSÉNIE NEGOVAN, PROPERTY OWNER, and beneath the name, engraved in gold, the year of my birth, 1891, and the year of my death, whenever that may be.

Article 6. I further declare that, apart from the ones enumerated above, I have no other needs in death, but desire these my wishes to be carried out just as I have stated and in no other way.

And now to describe my unannounced meeting with Simonida. Except for Niké's absence from Kosmajska Street and what was awaiting me on the other side of the river, it was the misunderstanding with Simonida that caused me the greatest distress. It was for Simonida's good that I had ignored my heart condition and concealed my going out from Katarina, exposing myself to the mortal danger of illness. In the expectation that the sight of the favorite among my houses would trouble me, I had protected myself with my pills; but it wasn't like that, far from it. When we actually met, I didn't feel even the slightest hint of the sudden and overwhelming elation of ownership anticipated. I don't say, of course, that I looked at her indifferently, as if at someone else's house, but I didn't feel her to be *my* Simonida, I simply didn't recognize her as the Simonida of my dreams and memories. A huge crane in the garden pointed to the forthcoming destruction. The house itself was not in the best possible condition: Simonida's façade was crumbling a little, flaking away; the pointing was losing its sharpness, and the rustic brickwork its healthy color of noble stone, the wreath beneath the eaves above the gate had cracked in the center, and its garland had withered and faded, as had the bouquet of stone lilies over the doorway; the iron blooms masking the cellar windows had rusted; and the plaster cast of Saint George, who on the medallion was transfixing a plaster dragon with a plaster lance, had completely lost its detailed relief and its vital strength of the Champion of the Lord.

But all my bitter sadness over Simonida's deterioration was nothing before the astonishing evidence of my eyes that, entirely without my approval, a square hole had been cut in the fence around the garden and blocked off with a three-paneled iron shutter across which, in black tarred letters and split into syllables, was written GA RA GE. Needless to say, I went over to remove that vile scrawl. Apart from my fragile gloves, I had nothing with which to erase it. Soon I began to pant so hard that I had to go back across the street to a park and find a bench on which to sit and calm myself, and then decide—while never taking my binoculars off of her—what to do for her good.

Only there on the bench, under the blue, reposing shade of the trees—positioned just as if, armed with my binoculars and curiosity beside the west window, I hadn't left my armchair, I realized that this house was no longer the house which, held in the spell of my uncertain memory and my lawyer's false photographs, I had imagined her to be. Despite the identical likeness of the exterior, she was not *my* Simonida, but another building, perhaps another Simonida, perhaps even a building which merited a completely new name. Because of my failure to recognize her, I had a premonition of futility—one that would grow from then on and become even stronger, so that these farewell lines are poisoned with foreboding—a feeling that I shall have explained fully by the end of my testament.

I must also mention that a similar feeling of powerlessness had seized me when faced with the plans of my first house. From a freehand and for my taste slovenly sketch, fingermarked and smudged with erasures, I could hardly get a conception of any house, never mind recognize the one which its overenthusiastic creator warmly commended as mine. But it was my first investment, my baptism as a builder, so I didn't utter a single one of those harsh observations which later would undermine so cunningly the inventive élan of those experts I hired subsequently. So the house was still a secret for me, carefully concealed under a veil of incomprehensible graphic figures. What she was really going to be like I found out only after her cross sections, basic plans, and frontal views, as well as her estimated costs, had been submitted for my approval, and I had put them together into a single three-dimensional view.

I judged houses as I judge a picture. I sincerely doubt that the whole turned out even as its own creator had imagined it, although on several occasions he tried to assure me that it had. In fact, he could only have surmised what the future house would be like. When the house appeared, it was nothing like the house I had visualized. It was a ponderous sculpture painted in the Greek fashion, before which I stood as before any other finished object, strictly excluded from its being, powerless to pierce the impenetrable surfaces with which it was hermetically sealed off on all sides. Only when I went into the house and wandered among perspectives permeated with the smells of paint and varnish, could I feel her inside me and see her. What I recognized from my first experience was that architecture is a *sculpture that is hollowed out,* so that man in movement can be situated in the empty space, that immediately afterward this sculpture becomes architecture by virtue of this hollowing out. This is what made of me the property owner that I am.

From then on I was remarkably mistrustful of those elegantly colored graphic representations, those unreal projections of future houses. A plan can never convey the true charm, but only hint at one of the possible realities of a building, while perspectives, despite Brunelleschi, can only

timidly indicate an intangible internal territory, but cannot
authentically reproduce it as an ordinary human step does,
or can only reproduce it wrongly. So even the best drawings
say less about a house than a web of transparent human
bones from an X-ray image say about a man. Models too express an unreal volume; they could perhaps be successful
if their dwarf-sized dimensions weren't incapable of de-
picting a building's spatial reality, which corresponds exclusively to the dimensions of a man.

Perhaps made drowsy by the sultry June air, I fell asleep
for a short while. Suddenly I was awakened by the excited
shout of a man who after a brief moment of puzzlement I
recognized as Tomaž Šomodjija, Simonida's concierge.

"In God's name, esteemed Mr. Arsen, what are you doing
here?"

If in Simonida's deterioration I hadn't detected Šomodjija's
sabotage, and if it hadn't been my intention to resume control of my affairs, I might have shown a warmer welcome (in
any case familiarity was not characteristic of my relations
with inferiors)—all the more since this Tomaž or Toma,
known as "maestro," had been one of my first *Hausmeisters*.
But all extenuating considerations had to be set aside, so
as to reassert Arsénie Negovan's authority as an employer.
So I overlooked the elation with which Maestro Toma ran up
to me, and said with some anger:

"*Voilà*, Mr. Šomodjija, as you can see, I'm sitting here
regretting that I ever entrusted one of my favorite houses
to you and allowed that shameless lawyer Golovan to supervise you. But before you hear what I think of your disloyal
actions and what I intend to do, I'm willing to hear your
explanation. If you have one, *naturellement!*"

But the former concierge (I say "former" because I had
decided that his replacement was urgent), probably faced
with the impossibility of finding excuses, leaned toward me
with both hands on his stick, completely overwhelmed

by shame, and moved from one foot to the other while anxiously striving in his meager Serbo-Hungarian vocabulary to justify for himself. He had heard, he said, from the lawyer Golovan that *méltóságos úr Arsen,* esteemed Mr. Arsen, had been taken ill from too much worry, and that he hadn't left his room at Venac since the war. But he, Tomaž, *becsulet szavamra,* honest to God, went several times to visit *méltóságos úr Arsen* to give an account of his house on Paris Street, but, *becsulet szavamra,* when he got to Venac esteemed Mrs. Katarin told him that esteemed Mr. Arsen couldn't receive him. But Tomaž, *becsulet szavamra,* was sorry, but understood and went back to Paris Street. Two months later he again went to Venac, but esteemed Mrs. Katarin again told him that it was strictly forbidden that *méltóságos úr Arsen* see Tomaž and worry. Then later lawyer Golovan, at night in October, told him: "Maestro Tomaž, we're very sorry but you can't take care of esteemed Mr. Arsen's house any more, though you can still live upstairs, *padláson,* in attic."

I was on the point of asking him if he meant to complain of the manner in which the lawyer had given him notice. But I realized that, in the heat of my desire to renew my professional authority, I would have acknowledged that he had worked here for years without my approval and knowledge. So instead I confirmed that certain instructions of that nature had indeed been given, but that they seemed to have been taken too literally.

"That's right, esteemed Mr. Arsen, that's what Tomaž thought. Tomaž knows what goes on, like in October when Bela Kun and the mob came, shouting no more masters, no more *méltóságos úr Arsen,* now all are equal, all brothers! But Tomaž knew that would be catastrophe. And Tomaž thought that maybe *méltóságos úr Arsen* would come back one day, so from his own good heart he painted windows, brought new tiles, and swept every day. Then a man from the Magistrate came and said the house would be pulled down, so Tomaž should repair nothing more. Then Tomaž went for the last time to see Mr. Arsen, but esteemed Mrs. Katarin came outside the house and said, *becsulet szavamra,* let them pull it down, let them pull all down! So tell me the truth, esteemed Mr. Arsen, what more could I do?"

What more, indeed? Although he hadn't yet reached Martinović's distracted state, his thoughts often wandered, and he mixed up people, events, and years. Thus his dismissal had become entangled with Bela Kun's violence, and he spoke unhappily of Simonida, as if for some time she hadn't belonged to me at all. But at the same time it was certain that my suspicions had done him a painful injustice, and I was left with only one means to redress it: Tomaž Šomodjija would be the first person honored with the announcement of the "return of Arsénie Negovan," and the first one invited to share in it.

"Does that mean that esteemed Mr. Arsen has come back?" His body straightened up, his every word was accompanied by a hearty bang on the bench with his ironclad stick. "Esteemed mister is again taking work in his own hands?"

"*Bien sûr!* That's why I came."

"And Maestro Tomaž will again be in the service of *méltóságos úr Arsen,* caring for the house on Paris Street?"

"Of course."

"*Becsulet szavamra?*"

"*Becsulet szavamra,* Maestro Tomaž. From this very moment on!"

Even now I feel a tingling of pride when I recall with what pleasure, eagerness, and hope we took pencils and notebooks from our coats—he the battered account book which I had given to him with Simonida's keys, and I the saffian leather notebook which I had always taken with me on inspections. In the latter, under March 1941, I had written the date of Niké's auction—my last *pro memoria*. As for Šomodjija's account book—all my superintendents had similar ones—he jotted down in it all the important events in Simonida's life, and whatever was needed for her care. I used to read it on the spot, crossing out the unnecessary requests but transferring the appropriate ones to my saffian notebook, so that I could verify their implementation.

Before crossing over to Simonida, I opened the notebook and immediately below the note about Niké (as if the narrow white space beneath didn't signify an absence of twenty-seven years), I wrote clearly: June 3, 1968, *Simonida.*

"That's it," I said. "Now we can get down to work."

To get to the house, we had to go around the crane, which had dug itself in like a wooden catapult in the middle of Simonida's weed-infested garden. It was rusted, broken in pieces, and full of dust, but from its greedy, protruding iron head hung a hook with a weight. The iron ball hung there peaceably, as if gathering strength to launch itself upon my last-born's tender walls. I went up to the machine and noticed with pleasure that it was itself quite damaged by the blows it had inflicted on houses. Still, the foul and ugly machine was awaiting its moment, not knowing that it would never come. For I had already thought of a plan by which Simonida could defend herself from demolition.

"Maestro Toma, that garage must be removed and the barrier fence restored as soon as possible."

"Remove garage," said the concierge as he wrote. "Restore barrier fence."

"Fill in the façade, wash it, and spray it with paint."

"Wash, fill, and spray façade."

"I'll decide on the color later, but I think it's going to be pearl."

"And what about the pointing, esteemed Mr. Arsen?"

"Scrape out the pointing neatly, scrape the grills on the

cellar windows, the courtyard wall, and the balcony with a wire brush. Coat with red lead and paint in black."

While I fingered the oak front door, tapping like a doctor on the peeling outer layer of its surfaces, I heard Maestro Toma explaining my presence to the neighbors.

"That *méltóságos úr Arsen*, he will not allow his house to be pulled down."

"Maestro Toma, note down: restain the front door and varnish it. What state are the other doors in?"

But we were already inside Simonida. From the athletic hallway one might think that the bulk of the house lies to the left. But no, there she quickly ends in a side wall; only on the right can one move forward into attractive perspectives. If you open one of those doors, you find yourself in a totally unexpected gallery lined with elegant carved woodwork reminiscent of the icons of a Mount Athos altar screen. Where you think you'll find a palatial room, you'll encounter a warm, dark chamber. Your view will break out into open space just where you expected a wall. The walls are not subordinated to any known geometrical system; the ceilings change heights with disturbing agility. For this unusual house there are no valid laws, no rules. At first you feel deceived, humiliated, perhaps angry. Then, just as you're on the verge of losing patience, you realize that you cannot rest without penetrating her secret, and so you go around her again, taking the same route. But now the rooms are entirely different. You know no more of her than before, but whatever the rent, you accept her. That was what my Simonida was like: unexpected, mysterious, inconstant, magical—a conjuror's box whose gifts never end.

"The key is her unexpectedness," I said, "but that key is lost."

"Pair of new keys," wrote the concierge.

"Do you know why?"

"*Nem tudom*, esteemed Mr. Arsen."

"Because right up to the quattrocento, architects thought themselves masters of their buildings. And owners of houses, too, of course. And why, Mr. Tomaž, why did they believe that?"

"*Nem tudom*, esteemed Mr. Arsen."

"Because for centuries—ever since the dolmens and menhirs—it was thought that buildings were ordinary manufactured articles, inheriting the inanimate nature of their materials. It was thought that a stone in a wall was as dead as a stone in a field, that a beam differed from its oak ancestor only in the form it was shaped by the carpenter. What a mistake, what an unforgivable error!"

The time had come for me to leave Simonida. Although there was no threat that my sortie would be discovered—Katarina had not planned to return from town until the afternoon—it was essential for me to rest and gather my strength for the delicate conversation which I intended to have with her. Before going, I wanted to draw Šomodjija's attention to several additional repairs. In that connection, I experienced so pleasant a surprise that here I must break off my confession for a moment.

Article 7. As a special legacy, to Mr. Tomaž Šomodjija, the caretaker of my house on Paris Street, I leave for his lasting ownership the basement of my three-story house on Rigas de Feras (No. 24), and a cash sum totaling the twenty-three years of caretaker's wages of which, through no fault of mine, he was deprived.

Before I had made a single one of my additional observations, Maestro Tomaž said:

"If the esteemed Mr. Arsen will allow, I will show him a list of repairs."

From his account book he took out a long list which he began to read from; it left out neither the replacement of the broken guttering and the worn stair treads (seven in number) nor anything else. In view of all that, how could I have not written in a legacy for him?

After I had promised to return the next day, I gave Maestro Toma one last instruction of which I wish to leave no record. I'll only say that it concerned the crane in Simonida's garden.

"*Becsulet szavamra?*" I asked.

"*Becsulet szavamra!*" promised Simonida's caretaker.

As I walked away to the streetcar stop, I heard Maestro Toma's excited voice behind me: "That *méltóságos úr Arsen*, he will not let his house be pulled down!"

I got on a Number Two, certain that when I returned the next day, the crane wouldn't be lying in wait for me in Simonida's courtyard.

I got on the streetcar—which I calculated would carry me as far as the underpass named after the Blessed Late King Alexander. There, I would be but a few steps from home. I never dreamed that this restful ride wouldn't bring my outing to an end, and that in its unplanned but voluntary prolongation the most unusual events still awaited me. Compared with these events, everything that had taken place that morning was only a gradual introduction, a restrained prelude before the furious scherzo that was to threaten both me and my houses. But everything in its turn.

And so the Number Two moved off along Paris Street and came out on the bend jutting out toward the delta, from where the view was so familiar that I could count the buildings from memory and describe in detail every human trace within the wide sweep of my binoculars.

As a result, suddenly I felt at home again, as if I'd returned from some foreign city. This nostalgic feeling of the returned wanderer would doubtless only have increased with the approach to Kosančićev Venac, had not the New Township made its appearance out of the sunlit haze in the west. Of course it was as familiar to me as all the rest, but for the first time my view of it was linked to the possibility, if I was so disposed, of actually going around it, touching it, smelling it, of understanding it from a spiritual angle. And so, while the streetcar accelerated downhill along Karageorge Street toward the King Alexander Bridge, it was clear to me that my pilgrimage hadn't yet come to an end, that I would rapidly find myself en route to the New Township, and that nothing I could do now would stop it. For my motivation was no longer fear of growing old, which I could overcome by gathering my strength, but fear of spiritual death, of becoming outmoded, of succumbing to what in architecture is known as *obsolescence.*

I got off the streetcar, and, breathing rapidly, walked over the bridge. This was most unusual, for I had never held any esteem for the Township, and certainly no liking. It could more truthfully be said that from the very moment when the foundations had been laid, I had been in dispute with the invisible designers of those termitelike buildings. Now I was hurrying to meet them, paying scarcely any attention to the white carcasses of reinforced concrete which, like some dissected giant caterpillar, were scattered along the main road; or to the auto repair shops behind their wire fences; or to the abandoned building sites with heaps of ballast, pebbles, and sand; or to the billboards, traffic, passersby. Having relinquished my neutral position at the window, I had shaken off old prejudices and was approaching the new constructions like a modern and fully operative property owner.

Five hundred apartments, I thought, covering a site of 25,600 meters, with four sides 160 meters in length as against 500 family houses with foundations and Lilliputian gardens, which as a result of the insatiable horizontal spread would take up dead ground of 202,500 precious square meters, with four frontages of 450 meters each. In the former case the electrical conduits and the water and gas mains would come to barely five kilometers; in the second, to at least fifty-six. The apartments would need four structural units: a floor and three walls; each family house would require six, and those six the most complex ones. The floor and walls had to be built into expensive foundations and cellars, while the roof structures would be more expensive still. Five hundred roofs! Five hundred foundations! But the apartments had common foundations and a common roof. What a financial saving!

Finally I would have to think most seriously—and without old-fashioned prejudices—about those hanging façades. And about prefabricated ceilings, too. Expensive, unreliable, time-consuming tradesmen's crafts would undoubtedly be replaced by industrial work in the factories. For cost and speed of erection, there could be no competition for that kind of construction. But would those factory-built houses devalue the space they dominated, depersonalize it, take away its soul? No, because my houses wouldn't look like upturned car bodies or armored tanks. Though machine-made, their faces would still be varied, personal, unexpected. And the benefits of garden cities would be preserved: every apartment would have its hanging garden, its compact flower plot à la Semiramis. But of course no one would be able to peer into it; my buildings would defend their tenants' privacy. And the insulation would be such that they wouldn't be subjected to noise of others. Free of soot, smoke, and dust, the air which my tenants breathed would not originate in other people's lungs; the view they rented could not be stolen from them; and even the sun would be brought nearer to them, and while it warmed them it would belong to them alone. With the keys of their home, my tenants would also receive the keys to their own lives, which they had almost forgotten about—keys whose duplicates would belong only to me.

Such gigantic dwellings, particularly if concentrated in the Arsénie Negovan Housing Development, would be placed under complete owner control. Arsénieville would be safe, stable, unchanging, and when in time the buildings were combined into a single mass, into a symmetrical Chauvin-Mazet-like block, they would be as eternal as the tombs of the Pharaohs! Such constructions would no longer have to adapt to anything; everything would have to adapt to them. Hermetically sealed, impenetrable, indestructible, they would thwart forever all hysterical attempts to reconstruct our cities or our lives. There would be no place for subversive dreams of dynamic cities, behind which lurk Bolshevik yearnings for a change of regime.

I was just concluding my revolutionary concept when on all sides I noticed an unusual excited movement. I would have noticed it earlier had I not been so preoccupied with my calculations. The people were all hurrying toward the railroad embankment. And the roadway was jammed full of red fire engines and military trucks with rubberized green canvas tops. I had no particular urge to join that animated movement, and certainly not to let it carry me along as a current carries a splinter of wood. I stopped an agitated passer-by who seemed, despite the camera slung around his neck, a reasonable-looking man, and asked him: "Excuse me, sir, can you tell me what's happening on the other side of the embankment?"

The man looked at me pleasantly, but without understanding. "*Je m'excuse. Je regrette bien. Je ne parle pas serbe.*"

"*Oh, excusez-moi, je voulais seulement demander ce qui se passe la-bàs derrière la digue.*"

"*Une révolte, monsieur,*" the man said enthusiastically. "*Une révolte!*"

"*Quelle révolte?*"

"Une révolte magnifique!"

Was it really happening again? At first I couldn't believe it. Being a foreigner, the man could easily have misinterpreted the disturbance. It must be a huge fire menacing the town, and now the soldiers and firemen were on their way to control it.

But I too was hurrying toward the embankment. Fortunately, none of my houses lay on the Zemun side. Since I wasn't personally threatened by the fire, and furthermore was incapable of looking on helplessly while houses were being destroyed, I would have returned home if I hadn't known how unpredictable the whims of fire are. I considered it opportune—and all the more so since I was once again committed to my business affairs—to take a closer look, and to undertake my own defensive measures should the blaze be spreading toward my houses.

"Is the fire a big one, young man?"

"What fire? It's a riot, old man, a riot!"

I was astounded. "Are you saying things are out of hand down there?"

"What's the matter with you? They're marching on Belgrade!"

Still hoping to clear up the misunderstanding, I addressed another onlooker who was limping toward the embankment.

"In heaven's name, sir, somebody just told me that a mob is trying to force its way into town. Is it true?"

"It's true," he said without stopping. "But they won't make it, the bastards!"

I fell in beside him. "No one could be happier than I about that. But how do you know they won't?"

"I used to be in the army."

"My late brother was in the army, too. Perhaps you've heard of him? General George Negovan? I'm Arsénie K. Negovan and my business is houses."

"I was a colonel. I was in command of a battery."

I knew nothing about military units, but despite his unduly direct speech and behavior, which I put down to barrack-room upbringing, the colonel inspired me with confidence. I kept as close to him as I could, all the more so since he shared my disgust at what was happening on the Zemun side of the embankment.

The citizens from behind were pushing me toward the underpass, on whose arch was written: BOAC LINKS ALMOST ALL THE COUNTRIES OF THE WORLD. As I began to be drawn up the slope, I made up my mind to see with my own eyes what heights of incompetence the royal government had attained in their defense of owners' interests—an incompetence which I had described in my talk about banks and bankocracy. For a property owner on the threshold of a large-scale building operation such as I had conceived during the journey to the New Township, it was of the greatest importance not to have to worry about the future of financial investments.

Even so, it's difficult to believe that this was the real reason for my ill-considered approach. The direction I took must have been influenced by a secret hope that there along the railway embankment I would obtain satisfaction for the mob's malicious attack on me on March 27, 1941, that here at last I would be revenged.

The railroad tracks crossed a sandy stretch and descended toward a dusty field covered with thistles, on which lay rolls of rusty metal fencing, concrete pipes, torn sacks of cement, and broken bricks, as if on some abandoned building site. Along the tracks and in the curve of the underpass the army, in steel helmets and standing three deep, had formed a cordon to block off the approach to the town.

"That's not the way to do it," said the colonel. "They ought to block the road with trucks, set up road blocks."

I took my binoculars out of their canvas case and trained them on Zemun. At first I could see nothing. Adjusted to a different range, the lens was blurred and opaque. As I turned the regulating knob, from out of the thick winter fog in front of me *they* swam into view; at their head was a standard-bearer waving a red flag, and it seemed as if I was drawing them toward me, luring them forward out of that fog, and not at all as if they were moving forward of their own murderous volition, gathering speed from way back in '41 when they came down Pop-Lukina Street. With a sharp twist of the knob, I sent them hurrying back into anonymity. The strength of my index finger and thumb, between which I held the tiny wheel that adjusted the lens, was for an instant greater than all the soldiers waiting there beneath the embankment.

Nothing was moving out there where I'd seen them a little earlier. Then they reappeared with the flag-bearer at their head, swarming forward of their own accord, although I was careful not to move the knob of the binoculars again. Clearly I hadn't removed them far enough—only a few steps back into the fog, out of which they now surged toward me again. I spun the wheel sharply: they disappeared. But this time a shorter period elapsed before, unaided by me, the red flag appeared out of the fog into which I had banished it. I knew that the intervals would get shorter and shorter, that my binoculars wouldn't halt them, so I stopped adjusting them. I stood on the embankment as if in a theater gallery, and waited.

Soon they appeared. They dispersed the powerless mist of the lens and came on. There were more and more of them. It was as if the diseased, cataractlike fog from which they kept soundlessly appearing would never stop producing them. They were carrying their red flags, of course, and Yugoslav flags, but with the Jewish-Bolshevik red star, as if they had already seized power and were giving it a visible symbol. They were also carrying some sort of pictures, and placards which I couldn't make out because they were too far away. And I had no need to, for I knew in advance what was written on them. *They* always demanded the same thing. *They* wanted my houses. *They* had wanted them in March 1941 and *They* wanted them now in June of 1968!

"I can't see what's written on their placards," I said.

The colonel handed me a pair of bulky binoculars with a black metal casing. "Here, use mine."

"They look powerful."

"Artillery binoculars. None stronger."

"Thank you. But then they'll be too close."

The colonel looked at me askance. "They will be, very soon."

The man behind me, against whom I was pressed, spat noisily. I could feel his breath on my neck.

The colonel was right. Soon, even my binoculars couldn't keep them back. Now the pictures that they were carrying on poles could be seen with the naked eye. One was Lenin. I didn't recognize the others, but they surely belonged to the same coterie. Scrawled across one of the placards in red was: FREEDOM, TRUTH, JUSTICE! DOWN WITH CORRUPTION! (I had no quarrel with that, though I would have added, "and banking.") NO MORE UNEMPLOYMENT. I HAVE BEEN BEATEN UP. (I was, too, I thought, looking at the young man with the bandaged head who was carrying the placard.) THE REVOLUTION IS NOT YET FINISHED! (It needs to start first, you son of a bitch. But it looks as if it has started already.) DOWN WITH THE RED BOURGEOISIE!

Yes, take good note of that, Isidor: *down with the red bourgeoisie!* They probably meant *bloody,* but they said *red.* For them the bourgeoisie was bloody. For them Arsénie Negovan was bloody! Arsénie, whose forebears had built this ungrateful town with their sweat and skill. Arsénie, who let people off from their rent, and whose building workers were the best paid in the country—that same Arsénie was bloody, and ought to be dragged out of his house and clubbed to death in a ditch like a dog!

All at once I was conscious of something which in my excitement I hadn't noticed: I was standing on a wooden tie between two rails just as I had at Solovkino, where beneath me the track had lain glistening in the rain. There had been firing in the town from all directions, but I can't remember whether the Reds were entering and the Whites fleeing, or the Whites entering and the Reds fleeing. I only remember a small shunting engine that rumbled slowly toward me, on whose engineer's platform was fixed a pole where five men were hanging from a single wire noose. Because of the unbalanced load, the engine was tilting to one side, and it rocked like a boat sliding down the ways to the water. It clattered on past me so quickly that I had no time to read the sign hanging around the necks of the dead men. It went on around the gentle bend behind the railway station and, picking up speed, disappeared into the gray steppes of the Ukraine.

The rioters stood opposite the cordon of soldiers, singing. I'm not sure that I can remember the words exactly, but they went something like this:

> *Awake the East and the West,*
> *Awake the North and the South,*
> *Steps thunder into the onslaught,*
> *Forward, comrades, shoulder to shoulder!"*

But still they hadn't attacked; the lines simply rippled as if the force of the rear ranks, who could see nothing, carried forward into those in front with a violence that didn't abate despite the sharp warnings from the soldiers.

"I wouldn't even talk to them," said the colonel, taking the binoculars from his eyes. "If they'd let me, I'd teach them a lesson!"

The man behind me spat again. "What would you do then?" he asked.

"I'd go straight at them—what else? Attack both sides. I'd surround the column and smash them before they knew what was happening!"

"It's easy to attack," said the man behind us. "Why not meet their demands?"

I had to intervene. "In heaven's name, sir, *de quoi parlez-vous?* Can't you see what they're demanding? They want our property!"

"Only property unjustly accumulated," said the man dryly.

"The only property unjustly accumulated is what belongs to the banks!" This was my own ground, on which I acknowledged no superior. "I've always maintained that those damned Yiddisher banks would be the end of us! On no account should they be allowed to make a middleman's profit. Yes, by the law of the land, those industrious people who've been bearing the whole weight of social progress for centuries . . ."

"I wouldn't even talk to them!" repeated the colonel. "They've been given freedom, and now all kinds of scum are wandering about the country!"

". . . before the most illustrious gathering of the C.S.S., but to be honest with you, they didn't listen to me then, nor do these people now."

"Hirelings, that's what they are," said the colonel bitterly.

"Of Moscow," I added.

"Not just of Moscow. All sorts."

The man behind us spat again.

"Why are you spitting all the time?" asked the colonel. "Are you on their side?"

"I'm not on anyone's side. If all were well they wouldn't be worked up, that's what I'm saying. I spat because I feel like spitting."

"Well next time you feel like spitting, just read that." The colonel pointed his finger at the placard: DOWN WITH THE RED BOURGEOISIE. "Who's the 'red bourgeoisie?' Me, do you think, because I own a house?"

"You own a house?" I was sincerely pleased.

"Over there, to the left," he said. "That yellow two-storied house. A beautiful house, don't you think?"

I took the binoculars and directed them toward the house he indicated. The building was revolting from every point of view—squat, with harsh colors that reminded one of an Oriental eunuch. But it was *his,* and judging by the pride with which he spoke, very close to his heart. It was a primitive stage of the feeling of ownership.

"A fine house, colonel," I said, putting the binoculars down. I felt almost ill just looking at it. *"C'est une vraie perle!"*

"Those hooligans have almost destroyed it! Smashed the windows with rocks—not a single one left! They opened the hydrants and turned them on the police! And after that you expect us to talk to them? If it was up to me, I'd get rid of them all."

"That's a political error," said the man behind us.

"It's an urbanist error, gentlemen!" I shouted. *"C'est une faute urbanistique!* The workers' suburbs have been located in an encircling belt which grips the commercial heart of the city like a vise. This has concentrated the proletariat in breeding grounds of revolt and destruction. Why, gentlemen, didn't they place those people in closed-off Soleri cones?"

"What's all that crap about?" said the colonel.

"I'm speaking of Paolo Soleri, who designed a town like a beehive, or rather a conical anthill with internal passageways. All its exits can be easily controlled, and production carried on without any fear of revolutionary ideas or attitudes. In a word, a real town for workers. *Si l'on avait appliqué les plans de Solerie, cela ne nous serait pas arrivé, je vous le garantis, messieurs!"*

Suddenly the crowd below the embankment became agitated and began to sing:

> *Arise, you prisoners of starvation,*
> *Arise you wretched of the earth.*

It was my last chance to leave. I had to think quietly. Although I knew what conclusions I would reach, I had no idea that afterward it would induce me to write my will, and to make the decision that I'm now carrying out. One thing, however, was beyond all doubt: Arsénie Negovan's city of thirty thousand inhabitants would not be built, nor would any of his houses ever again feel the hand of a true property owner.

The man behind joined in the chorus:

> *'Tis the final conflict, let each stand in his place,*
> *The Internationale shall be the human race.*

"What in God's name are you singing about?" Despite the cramped space on the tracks, the colonel managed to turn around; from the side, his profile stood out like a worn ancient coin. "Well?"

"Why shouldn't I sing the *Internationale?* I'm a Communist."

"I'm a Communist, too, but I'm not singing—not with that rabble. I fought for this country, comrade!"

"I fought too, comrade!"

"For what?"

"That's just what I'm asking myself!"

I couldn't understand a word of it. They sounded as if they'd taken leave of their senses.

"Gentlemen, get a hold of yourselves!"

But they'd already come to blows. They were grappling with each other as violently as the cramped space allowed, and in doing so pushed me right up to the edge of the embankment, above the sandy field where at that very moment the military cordon was under growing pressure from the frenzied mob.

I cried out once again: *"Mais s'il vous plaît, messieurs!"*

(Whenever I was excited or in a difficult situation, I always resorted to French, probably because I went to school in Grenoble and first began to think maturely in that language.)

But already I was falling off the embankment. I have no proof that the two of them intentionally pushed me (although

I wouldn't vouch for the man sympathetic to the rioters), but they didn't hold me back either. And so, still clutching my stick and my binocular case, I rolled down toward the ditch, and surely couldn't have stopped myself at the foot of the embankment had I not been taken back into the terrible past and imagined that I was falling from the mob's shoulders in Pop-Lukina Street after my talk about banks and bankers. As it was, I understood that if I didn't manage to stop myself I'd once again be trampled underfoot, and this time—considering my advanced years and health—without any hope of recovery. And so, thanks to my earlier experience, I arrested my fall without great bodily harm; my stick and binocular case were still firmly in my grip, nor were my pince-nez broken. But my hat was no longer there: it had fallen off and rolled right down into that rioting mob. Having a wide, stiff Boer brim, it rolled easily. I followed it with my eyes for some time, for it was black as pitch and its width made it clearly visible. And its quality, of course. Miraculously, no one had yet trampled it: the rioters' heels just pushed it away, and like some lame black bird it continued to bounce elastically over the sand.

I was proud of it.

I followed it until at last it stopped under an enormous heel, crushed. Bitterly I raised my eyes: it was the red standard-bearer. He still held the red flag aloft, even though he was being beaten. The soldiers had formed a circle around him and were hitting him with their batons, but the great ox wouldn't let go of the flag. He was brandishing it like a club and fending off the soldiers. All around, as George would have said, they were fighting "hand to hand." I couldn't discern any enthusiasm among the soldiers. They were shouting "Charge!" and "Kill!" but they weren't shooting or using their bayonets.

Crouching there in the ditch, it seemed to me that this wouldn't stop the mob. I'm not disputing that the soldiers were hitting them in the back, grinding their boots into their stomachs, trampling them down unmercifully. I couldn't see everything that was going on in the field because bodies continually blocked my view, and anyway I had no stomach for violence. The standard-bearer hadn't fallen yet. He was bloodied but still on his feet, waving his flag like a battle-ax. Hammering at him from close quarters, the soldiers were trying to force him into the ditch, where the cramped space wouldn't allow him to defend himself. They were pushing him toward me and hitting him all over his body, which jerked convulsively but wouldn't give in.

"*A la tête, frappez-le sur la tête!* Hit him on the head!"

Let me elaborate the reasons for my unseemly involvement *dans une bagarre*. Though the riot was of direct concern to me, since on its outcome depended the safety of my possessions and my personal status, it was unlike me to become involved. Without question, angered by the soldiers' incapacity to deal with the hooligan carrying the red flag—and all the more, since it was he who had trampled my hat—I shouted loudly: "On the head! Hit him on the head!" Of course they didn't hear me over the screams and cries of battle. But I have no reason to hide it: I urged our soldiers on. But my encouragement was devoid of passion: a business commitment, so to speak, rather than participation from sheer enjoyment. I did not throw rocks. The soldiers and rioters were throwing rocks at one another—I actually saw that. Completely forgetting myself, I had recourse to what were in fact only ordinary pebbles, no bigger than a child's fist. Anyone who has ever been on this embankment knows that there are no large rocks there, only a few round pebbles. And I threw them only at the man who was holding the red flag.

It seemed, however, that new and more decisive orders had been given, or that the soldiers roused themselves of their own accord, for they charged into the mob with savage and heroic force that would have pleased even my brother George.

The attackers wavered, yielded ground, and then, pursued by the soldiers, took to panic-stricken flight across the field, where only the injured and unconscious remained and among them my trampled hat.

With a certain effort I got up off the ground and went to pick it up. Perhaps I should have gotten away from there as quickly as possible, instead of wandering around after this very ordinary hat. But it was a question of principle: That hat was *mine;* it belonged to me by inalienable right of ownership. One might say that all revolutions began with hats, with the destruction of the outward signs of dignity.

I had to get it back and put it where it belonged.

"Well, pop, do you want a bash over the head, too?" The soldier blocking my path was pressing a blood-soaked handkerchief to his cheek. "Is that what you're looking for?"

"The man whom you intend to strike," I said with dignity, "—only *intend,* since whether you'll do it or not remains to be seen—has reached the age of seventy-seven. Sir, with due deference to your situation, I inform you with pride that I am Arsénie K. Negovan, property owner of Kosančićev Venac, *Who is only looking for his hat.* There it is! Over there! Here are my papers. *Voilà.*"

Unfortunately, I didn't have time to show them. The mob was swarming back again, pushing the soldiers against the embankment. I found myself at the very center of the fray. But I didn't care: in such circumstances the best thing to do is not to submit to events but be oneself. So I continued to search for my hat, which unfortunately lay once again under the mass of infuriated feet. At that wretched and brutal moment it was the sole guaranty of Arsénie Negovan's dignity.

A young man was lying crumpled on a torn sack of cement. Judging by his appearance, he was seriously injured, but since his eyes were open I assumed he was still conscious. I went up to him and asked if by chance he had seen a rather large hat, *un chapeau de Boers?*

He didn't answer, as if he hadn't heard me. Indeed, there was so much noise that any normal conversation was impossible. I described the hat with my hands.

"Black—large—a Boer hat?"

I don't know how long I wandered about. Probably I went around and around the same spot repeatedly. I did receive a number of blows. At one moment I stumbled and was pushed. What then followed was as incoherent and absurd as a nightmare. Did I really kill that Bolshevik flag-bearer, beat him to death with my stick with the silver greyhound's head on the handle? Judging by the strip of red cloth that afterward I found in my hand—it's right here on my desk in front of me—I would say that I certainly came in contact with him. But that still doesn't mean that I attacked him because he refused to help me find my hat. When I asked him about my hat, did he provoke me by his foolish flag-waving while there on his knees (for he'd already been brought to his knees)? Did he so frighten and confuse me that I raised my stick in self-defense and felled him with a blow to the back of the head? Did all that happen near the underpass or was it much, much earlier—way back in 1919 when that man, or at least a man very much like him, seized the merchant Mr. K. S. Pamyatin by the hair and dragged him out of his house, where I'd been hiding during the worst of the pogrom? Did it happen when he herded us all—me and Mr. K. S. Pamyatin and his friends in fur coats, cloaks, and capes—into the ditch in front of the house, and raised his club to strike me, but I wrenched the club away from him, knocked him down in the mire, and kept hitting him and hitting him and hitting him?

Whatever actually happened, I must be prepared for all eventualities, and so:

Article 8. As an exceptional legacy, with no possibility of modification, I determine that, should an untidily dressed, dark-haired, thickset man with a reddish birthmark on his left cheek make application to the executors of my will, and show undeniable proof that on June 3, 1968, around noon or shortly after, he was at the underpass of the Zemun embankment with a red flag, then to that man, if he be so injured as to be unfit for work, financial compensation shall be paid, the sum of which is to be decided by my lawyer Mr. Golovan and my nephew, the engineer-architect Isidor J. Negovan. If by chance the said person is no longer living, but all the above conditions can be satisfied, then the compensation shall be transferred to his heirs in direct line of succession.

I was sitting on the seven steps which led down to the quayside, sitting on my handkerchief which I had spread out on the third step down, and resting my feet on the fifth; but I couldn't have said how I had got there. That wasn't important; though after all that had happened, many things were no longer important. Even the steps weren't as I had imagined: seen through binoculars from Kosančićev Venac, they had glistened out of the clump of graying ivylike shiny purple sealing wax; but only now could I touch their rough gray crust. It was somewhat blurred before my eyes. Everything around me, particularly things near to me, were somehow vague and blurred, because my pince-nez had been lost. My stick was there, however, resting between my legs, and the binoculars were in my pocket.

I couldn't yet feel the effects of my participation in the incident at the underpass; I certainly had bruises on my body, but they weren't giving me as much pain as now. All I really felt was fatigue, as if I'd had a heart attack. Indeed, I had been fortunate, for the circumstances of my tour might well have provoked such an attack.

But what had really happened?

I fumbled in my pocket for my handkerchief, to wipe away the sweat on my forehead. It was hot and I had lost my hat.

I missed it very much. I felt for my handkerchief and at the very instant I found it, I asked myself what I was sitting on. With an effort I raised myself slightly and pulled from under me the piece of cloth which was spread out neatly on the step. It had been torn from a larger piece, bright red. Bright red and very cheap, judging by the quality. It belonged to *their* flag, the flag which *he* had been carrying.

That could only mean that I had come into direct contact with him. Most likely he had rushed me and I had to defend myself by hitting him with my stick. He had fallen in the sand without letting go of the flag. He had tried to get up, turning toward me while still on his knees. Two thin streams of blood were running down his left cheek, forming between them the swollen dark little island of the birthmark. And I had struck him again with my stick, this time not from behind on the back of the head, but in the face and on the crown of his head.

I kept on hitting and hitting and hitting.

When was that? How many years had passed since then?

On the hatstand in the hallway, amid the other sticks, is the one with the dog's muzzle for a handle. I put it there when I returned from my walk, and I haven't had it in my hands since. Probably I should interrupt my work, pick it up, and examine it—I would know what to look for. I haven't been able to do it. Perhaps later. Yes, I shall certainly do it later. When I get to the end of my will, and there's nothing left to do but pile the furniture against the door and wait.

From a distance, my window shone in the dark rear of the house, like a tiny sun in a universe of stone. Its light dimmed and brightened, as if summoning me back to the protection it had offered for so many years. I brought it so close with my binoculars that it seemed as if I could touch the gleaming glass. When I put the binoculars down, the illusion disappeared. That was how it had always been with those useless instruments. They had pretended to help me but in fact had just deceived me. They had cunningly convinced me that I knew and understood the objects which they had brought near to me, whereas in fact those objects had remained just as distant as before. Perhaps even more so.

There on the steps, I knew what I had to do. First of all, I had to pull myself together, tidy myself up. Then I would go home and get to work. Katarina wouldn't have returned yet. She had gone off with Mlle. Foucault to buy a ticket for her trip to the spa the next morning, and to take care of other matters connected with her journey. Mlle. Foucault was to look after me during her absence. On any other occasion such an arrangement would have infuriated me, but now, as a result of this wretched affair at the underpass, it admirably suited my intentions. Katarina would leave without any idea of what was going on. Even if, as was probable, she eventually found out about the disturbances, she would be too far away to grasp their seriousness. And they wouldn't spread as rapidly as that. They would meet resistance, delaying things at least long enough for Kosančićev Venac to hold out for several days.

I looked at my watch (now, too, I'm checking the time left me to finish what I'm writing) and verified that I should start for home if I didn't want Katarina to learn of my absence. Before putting the watch back in my pocket, I listened to the beating of its heart; surrounded by rubies in its gold casing, it looked like a tiny model of the planetary system. The mechanism still worked perfectly, although it had belonged to my father. Inside its cover was an engraved dedication: *To Canon Cyrill S. Negovan, Chaplain of the 1st Infantry Regiment, Drina Division, for the faith and fear of God which he instilled in us, and his exceptional skill as a marksman. Colonel Živojin T. Maksimović.*

The heart of that watch was beating surely and regularly, but my own was suddenly beginning to hesitate and flutter. For the second time that same day it let me down. The discomfort beneath my rib cage advanced rapidly with antlike steps into my hands, which were shaking treacherously as, blinking to disperse the mist from my eyes and gasping for breath, I tore the cellophane wrapping from the pills. I swallowed them hurriedly, though in fact I hadn't a single valid reason for doing so.

I must admit that this afternoon, the third since the events that have so dominated my confession, I'm in a particularly happy frame of mind. Until recently I was disturbed, troubled by anxiety, even dismayed, but today I'm composed. No, I'm by no means calm—I'm not completely prepared for what's coming—but I'm composed, and its clear to me what I have to do. With regard to the fate which awaits me and my houses, there can be little ambiguity. It's like a big business deal. As long as the affair he's involved in swings back and forth, like a pendulum between victory and defeat, the businessman's heart spans the amplitude of uncertainty. But as soon as the affair is decided one way or the other, and turns out a success or a failure, the businessman relaxes: nervousness gives place to the calm reckoning up of accounts, the calculation of profit or loss, and preparations for some new project to recuperate the loss or multiply the gain. But if, as in my case, the commitment has already taken the irreversible route toward catastrophe, and the pendulum of fate has adopted its final position, then nothing remains but to plan how to submit to it in the easiest possible way.

Only the presence of Mlle. Foucault still bothered me. I have mentioned that on that first day Katarina had packed her things to go to the spa; now I must add that on the following day she left without having found out anything about the time I had spent out of the house. I have the impression she was surprised at the tenderness with which I said good-by. It was not our custom to show openly any of the devotion we had for each other, but I considered that the unusual circumstances allowed me, even required me, to make an exception, for I hadn't the slightest doubt that Katarina's kiss, which I tenderly returned, marked the end of our fifty years of happy marriage, and in a modest way, of course, our golden wedding anniversary.

Before leaving, Katarina gave Mlle. Foucault the instructions necessary to satisfy the demands of my way of life, having no idea that in the meantime it had changed radically, that it had evolved new demands which no one could satisfy for me. Indeed, it would be unjust if I failed to acknowledge the diligence and loyalty, however superfluous now, with which Mlle. Foucault carried out her duties, particularly if one bears in mind the intolerance which had always colored our relationship. Naturally she had to treat me for the bruises I had received. In a moment of inspiration I explained them away as the result of falling on the parquet floor, whereupon she upbraided my "childish lack of caution," *mon imprudence,* and as she swathed my aching welts with raw meat, muttered:

"I do not understand, Monsieur Negovan, I really do not understand how a grown man could fall down just like that! *Je ne comprends pas cela—un homme de votre agilité!*"

"You don't understand anything," I answered in exasperation. *"Précisément rien!* Absolutely nothing!"

"On the contrary, you are the one who understands nothing!" The malice with which she made this pronouncement I attributed to the inventiveness with which she kept up the subterfuge that was meant to preserve my mental security. "Absolutely nothing. *Précisément rien!*"

"Tell me, Mademoiselle Foucault," I asked, imitating the guttural pronunciation of her *r*'s, "the French marshal, his Excellency Franchet d'Esperey, didn't he ever fall down?"

"Monsieur Negovan," she said authoritatively, like a teacher of military history at St. Cyr, "marshals, and especially French ones, fall down only when hit by a bullet!" And with that she withdrew, exclaiming, "*Quelle insolence! Quelle insolence!*"

Making use of one of the few pieces of military data at my disposal, I shouted after her: "And what about Pétain? What shall we do about Pétain? *Et que ferons-nous de Pétain, du Maréchal Pétain?*"

This dispute—my personal war of independence—was repeated every time the compresses were changed. Nevertheless, the raw meat was doing its job: I felt stronger hour by hour, especially in my arms, which were of importance to me, not just for the writing of my will—that was in fact almost finished—but in order to move the furniture, without which my plan couldn't be brought to its conclusion.

Mlle. Foucault came in early each morning when I was already writing, but fortunately she fussed around in the kitchen without showing any interest in my work. Only in the afternoons did she take her knitting and sit down in the armchair opposite my desk as if she were the mistress of the house. She reassumed this touchingly familiar position after my evening meal, which by habit I took in the study, until nine o'clock, when she gave three yawns—always three but brief, one right after the other—and said: "*Enfin*, I think it's time for bed." She then rolled her knitting into a neat ball, pushed it into her nurse's bag, took away my writing implements in the middle of a sentence, and despite all my protests led me off to the bedroom. For obvious reasons I undressed even though I'd get up again as soon as she had left. Meanwhile on the one-legged table in the study, she prepared the bottle with my drops and pills, which I would use if I became ill in her absence. Then with irritating zeal she would tuck me in on all sides, put out the light, and having wished me good night in French (always in French), she would leave. The last thing I heard before I got up and resumed my work was the sharp rattle of the key in the lock.

Today for the first time I dared to pull my pyjamas over

my shirt and underclothes so that, in my struggle for time, I could reduce its waste to an absolute minimum; I could hear her clattering her heels and the bottles, but she still didn't come into the bedroom. I was really getting angry: she exasperated me with her attention and at the same time spied on me; because of her, I hadn't managed to take a look at the newspaper which I had bought on the way home and was keeping hidden under the carpet. If she saw me reading it, I would have to offer some awkward explanation. But I intended to glance through it rapidly, as soon as I finished my will.

This last I have to finish in the course of the night; by tomorrow morning everything must be ready and sealed. Sealed with sealing wax, stuffed inside a white envelope, and placed in the bottom of the top right-hand drawer of my desk, whose key will be hanging with the other keys at my belt.

At last Mlle. Foucault came in. "Perhaps you would like me to sleep here, Monsieur Negovan?"

"Thank you, no."

"*Vous me paraissez éreinté, un peu pâle, n'est-ce pas?* You're not feeling ill?"

She felt for my hand to take my pulse, but alas, under the blanket she touched my shirt cuffs, confirmed her suspicions, and snapped:

"*Grand Dieu*, Monsieur Negovan! What do these childish tricks mean? Sleeping in your underclothes, I wouldn't have expected that from a man your age! Such vulgar behavior—honestly! *Une telle conduite ne s'est même pas passée dans les tranchées de Salonique!*"

"To hell with your Salonika!"

"If you please, get undressed at once. *Vite! Vite!* And don't think I won't come back to make sure!"

While she waited in the study, I got undressed. Quite

honestly, I hadn't been so furious for years. I must ask, therefore, that my rather violent vocabulary not be misconstrued.

"Such a thing," I shouted, "Marshal Franchet d'Esperey would obviously never have done! He wouldn't have been brave enough! Isn't that right, Mademoiselle Foucault? Nor would my blessedly departed brother, *monsieur le général,* have ever so degraded himself, *n'est-ce pas,* Mademoiselle Foucault? But there was no mob of louts with clubs waiting at the gates of their houses! No, Mademoiselle Foucault! But Arsénie Negovan refuses to die in a nightgown simply because—without any permission from me—you take it into your head to play governess! I categorically refuse to die in my pyjamas! I won't die like those Russian merchants who hardly had time to throw fur coats over their nightshirts! Some didn't even have time for that, they were beaten to death in their nightshirts! Can you hear me, Mademoiselle Foucault? *Est-ce que vous m'avez entendu?*"

I don't know if she heard me or not; if she had, it would have had no effect at all on her behavior. She came in with a firm, masculine step, tucked in the edges of the blankets, put out the light, and said arrogantly:

"I'm going now. We'll keep all this from Madame Katarina, of course. *Bonne nuit, monsieur.*"

"Go away, mademoiselle!"

Stretched out in the warm, slack darkness, I listened to the sound of Mélanie's heels fading away. Suddenly I was back in the children's room of our house on Gospodska Street. George was squirming about in the next bed (Marko, the future Emilian, was already away at the seminary), and those steps dying away like the ticking of a clock were my mother's. My mother had been there just a moment before; the sweet smell of lilies still hung in the air. Together we had said an Our Father and a Hail Mary, then she had covered us up, and kissed us on the forehead. Lying there, I listened as her steps receded, ready to jump out of bed and set off with my brother on pirate adventures over the vast and mysterious continent of our darkened room.

Then I got up, and, while dressing myself even more meticulously than usual, I thought about Mlle. Foucault. I in no way approved of Katarina's fondness for this naturalized Serb, even though her social origins were beyond reproach, and her services to Serbia had been rewarded with military decorations. Nor was I moved by Katarina's story about how during the Occupation Mlle. Foucault had sold her own possessions but preserved the general's, in order to support him—most probably because I despised his games with tin soldiers from the bottom of my heart. In all fairness, though, I'll add that the dominant trait of her personality was loyalty, the loyalty of a domestic animal, which after George's death she had transferred to Katarina and in part to me. If that devotion hadn't been combined with such an authoritarian will, arrogance, and insistence, I swear I'd have written of Mlle. Foucault in a far more kindly manner. And so, still retaining my hateful memory of her, but in the knowledge that Katarina will be pleased:

Article 9. To Mlle. Mélanie Foucault, retired army nurse, along with the apartment on Lamartine Street I leave, for her enjoyment during her lifetime, the basement house in Tadeusz Koszczuski Street, so that she may receive the rent until her death. Afterward the house is to revert to my universal heir as designated by this will.

Now that's done. Katarina will see that, despite my stern demeanor, property owner's affairs have not alienated me from those everyday sentiments which she herself has cultivated. The legacies to Mlle. Foucault, Mr. Martinović, and the caretaker Maestro Šomodjija—not to mention those to Katarina, Isidor, and Emilian—give proof of my finer feelings, which have been disputed all my life. And since I've firmly resolved to leave nothing to that double-dealing lawyer Golovan (apart from the sad duty of certifying this will as cosignatory), and since I have no reason to leave anything to my country, which tomorrow will take everything it can lay its hands on anyway—*voilà!*

It is precisely *that* possibility which has worried me whenever I turn from my reminiscences to my will. All the time I've felt a certain resistance whose origin I haven't been able to grasp. I attributed it to my hesitation as to what to leave and to whom, when I passed from my memoirs to my will, and to the sparseness of my own story, when I returned from my will to my life. But my anxiety was a natural consequence of my action; it resided in the irreconcilable contradictions between the *order* which I prescribed in this document—order which calls for legality, continuity, and justice—and the *disorder* which brings with it revolution: disorder which, constituting the life of the lower strata, calls for force, discontinuity, and illegality. Therefore one of the two, my memoir or my will, must be in vain. These incidental jottings of my memoir surely can't be futile; they didn't have to be and don't need to be acted upon. But my will must be, if it is to be a will at last, if it is to be upheld as a document which determines the future of my property.

And when did a revolution ever have consideration for property?

When did it ever recognize the right of inheritance?

When did it ever respect any rights of ownership at all?

Perhaps this revolution will do all that.

Perhaps it will show some concern for that man who was carrying the red flag—the one who ruined my hat—if he's still alive, of course.

Will it or any of its Aramaic brethren perhaps see to it that Mlle. Foucault gets what she has justly merited, or the humble caretaker Šomodjija? And that my houses are distributed as I have determined in this document?

What is it all for? Why am I writing a will?

To abandon it now, half finished—wouldn't that be an act of surrender to the mob, quite incompatible with the dignity of a Negovan, and even more dangerous than the loss of my Boer hat?

No, not for anything could Arsénie allow his bookkeeping, of which this will is the crowning glory, to be left unbalanced. That would be beneath his professional honor.

And then, well, even the Revolution would have to give way to some kind of order and proclaim laws to be observed, among which those concerned with personal property and personal relations would occupy an honored place—even if the sense of possession was to all appearances abolished. And tomorrow, when Arsénie Negovan will be no more, people will accumulate personal property, and having done so will want to leave it to their children. And their children will want to go on accumulating and add what they accumulate to that already accumulated, and leave it to their children—and so on for ever and ever. The sense of possession is ineradicable; it will go on for as long as man exists, and heart and mind and character, and virtues and vices, and memories and goods and houses, and all this is only one huge estate under mortgage to death which during our lifetime we can augment or disperse.

Because of this, I won't lay down my pen until I have concluded my testament, after which come what may!

Not counting Emilian, whom I don't consider an heir, I still have two legacies to make, two further paragraphs in which I will leave my library to my nephew Isidor (insofar as it's concerned with building), and an appendix to the one in which, along with all my movable assets, I will leave No. 17 Kosaničićev Venac to Katarina. In these additional paragraphs I must take care of the most delicate part of my last wishes: my efforts on behalf of my beloved houses.

By good fortune at least the most eminent of these buildings—by virtue of their incomparable beauty and because, by a coincidence in which their owner (I swear) played no part, they have served as setting for some of the most important if shameful events of our national history (I will mention only the officer's plot against King Alexander Obrenović, which was hatched in Eudoxia before she belonged to me) — the most eminent of these buildings, I say, must come under the protection of the State. *Nota bene,* just before the war I presented a memorandum to this end to the appropriate ministries; but with a revolt beneath my windows, it would be unreasonable to hope that the State will take a sincere interest in houses, except to confiscate and destroy them. Originally I had planned, as is our custom, to leave my houses to Katarina. But as I've already pointed out, she has no affection for them; though as my heir she is in everything else a trustworthy person, she offered no guarantee of treating them well. And when I so recently discovered that she had conspired—it's true, from the noblest of motives—with my lawyer Golovan in his miserable negligence, my desire to observe convention (which would surely have cost the life of my beloved possessions) lapsed entirely.

Therefore I have decided to leave my fortune to my nephew, Isidor Negovan, since in my opinion he is the only one of my blood relations who understands my houses, both as an architect and as a person, and who in the status of owner, may perfect that healthy relationship and at the same time—why not?—make it identical with my own.

Isidor J. Negovan is my nephew in the second branch and the fifth degree.

It is not the custom for a testator to justify his decisions, except of course if they go against the natural order of succession or deny someone their so-called rightful share. I nevertheless feel the need, for my own satisfaction, once again to go over the reasons which led to my choice.

First, Isidor loved and understood houses. More than that, Isidor was a builder, one of the most skilled in the business, and therefore the kind of person who, next to their owners, was closest to houses. Isidor was the only person with whom I could talk freely and openly about them. Isidor showed respect for my way of life, visited me regularly, and supplied me with books and especially information of vital importance for my work. Finally, he was alone: his father had left the country in 1944, driven out by the accusation of having built a building—a House of German Culture, or something —which was considered an act of national treachery; recently his sister had also left; and his mother was in an asylum with little hope of recovery. During the last few months Isidor had fallen into deep creative apathy, from which he would be roused only by busying himself with real buildings, instead of using his God-given talents on cemeteries, euphemistically called memorial architecture. Involvement in the possession of real, living houses could well encourage him to build them himself, and in this way he would gradually come back to his earlier grandiose plan to design the *perfect city*.

It was beyond all doubt that he was undergoing a crisis. It was a crisis that had come over him soon after he had accepted the government commission to build a monument on Banjica to perpetuate the National Triumph. At first he was full of enthusiasm, carried away by the same passion which defines my own relationship with my houses. But even then there was something unhealthy in his interpretation of the projected task. The sketches he brought to show me grew progressively more emaciated, and each time more mutually contradictory, so that the purpose of the building had been changed. Meanwhile Isidor became more and more depressed and ill-tempered. I interpreted his despair as the result of his exhausting struggle with a material which remained unresponsive. How wrong I was! I should have known that for a passionate enthusiast of his temperament, such resistance could only serve as stimulation, and that in his best works —I've seen them only in photographs—Isidor succeeded in breaking down the material's resistance, and in forcing on it a form which at first seemed impossible. In short, I should have known that he was in the middle of something far deeper and more serious—that it involved a much greater alienation from his own art, or perhaps the greatest alienation of all: from life.

Our last conversation took place in my study last October. He had come to show me photographs of his monument before the official opening. Though I haven't seen him since, several days after that I received a letter from him, apparently written right after our meeting:

Dear Uncle Arsénie,

I don't think you'll be surprised at my departure. Our last conversation at Kosančićev Venac will explain my action. Don't take it badly that I didn't come see you before leaving. I felt that we said good-by during our talk. Please pay my respects to Aunt Katarina. Very affectionately,

Isidor

Isidor had sat in the chair in which I am now writing this will. I was in my Chippendale armchair, at my lookout post by the half-open window. I felt cold even though Katarina had put a blanket around my knees. It was drizzling, and the rain and dampness covered the double glass wall through which, with the help of my binoculars, I was watching an empty building site in the New Township.

Isidor had spread the photographs of his monument across his brief case and was looking at them closely. From there, in the gray, cold, watery light, the pictures looked like celluloid X-ray plates, dark patches crisscrossed with a network of transparent canals. He had already shown me the first twelve. There were eight more.

I must say at once that the monument was truly magnificent. But—and I hope Isidor will forgive my honesty—there was scarcely anything human about it. Nor again was there anything divine. It was quite beyond my understanding—magnificent and incomprehensible. Possibly he was expressing some ancient forms.

I asked Isidor if he had had any news of his father recently.

"None."

"And your mother, how is she?"

"The same as ever."

"Not getting any better?"

"No."

"What do the doctors say?"

"Keep waiting."

"Is there any hope?"

"A little."

"Do you visit her?"

"Every day."

"Does she recognize you?"

"Sometimes she seems to, but often she doesn't. I also get the impression that she thinks it would harm me if she did."

"Does she speak at all?"

"A few words."

"What do you do with her?"

"I sit and wait for her to say something."

He gathered the photographs together again and laid them out on the table as if dealing a game of patience, a game he was never going to finish. "I sit and wait for her to speak. And when at last she says something, I don't understand her."

"What does she say?"

"Hours pass and then she says, 'table,' 'glass,' 'letter,' 'tree.' As if she came from another world and is trying to learn our language."

"Angelina used to be a great lady, Isidor."

He stared at the photographs as if unable to recognize them. Again he gathered them together in a pile and laid them out in a new pattern.

"When did you say the opening is?"

"October twenty-sixth."

"I'm sure there'll be a lot of people. Katarina says they're going to hold a military parade, and afterward fireworks and a national celebration. I'd like to be there, but I can't stand crowds. Will His Majesty be coming?"

"Probably."

"You've become famous, Isidor. I want you to know how happy that makes me, and how proud I am of you. The Negovans are a mighty breed, eh?"

"Indeed they are." Then he asked, "Do you remember that Le Corbusier church, Uncle?"

"Which one? The one in Brittany?"

"Yes, the one in Brittany."

How could I not remember it? It wasn't distinguished by excessive piety. It looked like a home for the mentally ill.

"Why is it," he asked, "that his church looks completely different from each side? Other buildings have different aspects, but their façades proceed one from another; when we look at them from one point, we can easily predict what they'll look like from another. Why is it that when you stand in front of the north face of the Le Corbusier church, you can't describe the south side, or any side?"

"I told you the building is deranged. It's like someone mentally ill whose actions you can't foresee."

"Her four faces represent four different artistic entities, don't they? Each façade is planometric in nature, and not a part of the structure."

"That church does not *exist*."

"The church exists, but the *building* doesn't. Only its appearance exists. You can go inside a hollow beech tree, but you don't call it a building. Something unreal can't produce something real. Those walls don't exist as architectural elements, and no linking of them can give form to that internal space with which we identify architecture."

"So?"

"Because that space isn't there—in the architectural sense, of course, since in reality it does exist—there is no architecture either."

"In the case of that church?"

"In all cases. *Architecture does not exist.*"

"*Merde!* That means my houses aren't there either?"

"That's right."

"But they *do* exist! I love them! And I've always considered my houses first-class architectural works."

"You are wrong. We are both wrong. Everything on the basis of which we call architecture *artistic* belongs to other more authentic arts."

"All right, in the final analysis it doesn't matter to me whether or not my houses are artistic works. They're buildings. And what buildings! Architectural pearls!"

"But Uncle, *buildings aren't architecture.* If what can be seen is art, then it isn't architecture. And if what can't be seen —emptiness, a system of hollow spaces and nothing more—if that again isn't architecture, then architecture doesn't exist, at least it doesn't exist *yet!*"

Suddenly I was struck—horrified—by the thought that Isidor was passionately asserting that his work has been for nothing, or at best a mere illusion. I asked him frankly what he thought his work to date had encompassed. He answered dryly:

"Myself."

"Yourself?"

"Yes, myself. I agreed to work on the monuments in the hope that I'd achieve *true* architecture. It was an experiment in the direction of art. But at the building site I at last grasped why I hadn't succeeded yet and never would: I'd been working on myself! I hadn't been looking for architecture, but for myself. I hadn't built anything, I'd demolished myself. Here, look!"

He moved his armchair closer to mine and placed a photograph of his monument in such a position that the window softly and slantingly illuminated its surface; then he presented proofs taken from his own work to justify his shatteringly disappointing revelation. I have neither the strength nor the will power to repeat them here, all the more so since his "proofs" only in a roundabout way correspond with my recollections. As the photographs of the monument silently succeeded one another on the carpet, Isidor's argument followed them right up to sunset, interrupted only twice: by Katarina's return, and by the coffee she brought us.

After he had exhausted them all, he began to gather up the pictures from the desk and the floor. I asked him to leave copies for me, and he said that he would; they were of no further interest to him.

"Well, time to go."

"What are you going to do?"

He stood in the doorway, his shoulder against the jamb, tall and dark like an elegant tree which had been uprooted. He smiled.

"The same as my father! I'm going away."

And he left. In front of me are the photographs of the monument, alongside the enlargements of my houses. I can sense a certain kinship between them, but I don't know yet where it lurks. I hadn't thought of it earlier, but now I'll take some account of it. I must do my very best for my houses and also take care of Isidor, in the reasoned hope that both will profit: the houses will acquire a most reliable defender, while Isidor will find in them his life's *causa finalis*. With this in mind:

Article 10. I incontestably determine that after my death Mr. Isidor J. Negovan, an architectural engineer of Krunska Street, shall be given the lasting ownership of all houses belonging to me except for those disposed of in individual legacies, and except for the house in Kosančićev Venac, which I bequeath to my wife as set forth later. In addition to my library the bequest includes everything in any way associated with the houses: records, photographs, dossiers, account books, correspondence, and models.

Article 11. The testator of course hopes that what now seems certain to him will not come to pass, and that no hindrance will impede this testament, or any conditions attached to it. But *in causa,* if in fact this testament cannot be carried out in any way, then I ask Mr. Isidor Negovan to use all the means in his power to keep in his possession the photographs, models, and documents of my houses, and if he be allowed the opportunity, to care for those houses as if they were his own kin. And further, if things do in fact turn out badly, I leave to him the charge of remembering in his blackest hour that once before, under the name of Nago, the Negovans lost all their possessions and were scattered to the four corners of the earth; that they started once again from nothing and by their stubbornness and ability again attained the uppermost heights of commercial, social, and political life; that although more than two hundred years have elapsed from that first downward plunge of our breed, and although it has twice more to date been repeated, we are now once again in a position from which many people have tried to dislodge us.

After all this, and despite the fatherly sentiments that I feel toward my nephew, I cannot shake off the conviction that this last instruction would have much greater sense if

I could leave it to the conscience of my own son. But I don't have a son. I did once, but that will be the only episode of this story which, long buried, I will not disturb.

And so, instead of speaking of my son, I shall offer my adopted son the last explanation I owe him, concerning Fedor's insinuations that I was the cause of his uncle Constantine's accident. But first I shall relate the spectacle which Constantine's funeral degenerated into.

Coming to the end of his oration, the Vice-President of the Builders Association, Mr. Arsenijević, gave up his place on the rostrum as planned. The very fact that Constantine's family had no objections to me, the employer of the deceased, showing my respect for him, is evidence enough of the groundlessness of Fedor's incriminations. But more of this later.

I don't believe that Mr. Arsenijević provoked the mis-understanding on purpose; probably he was carried away by his subject. Even so, in conjunction with Fedor's incessant mutterings and interruptions, Arsenijević's lapse initiated the scandalous scene beside the open grave. Enumerating Constantine's virtues as a builder, Arsenijević, himself a builder, ventured to say that the artistic abilities of the greatly mourned deceased would have attained still greater expression, had he not been frustrated and fettered by the miserly small-mindedness of the property owner for whom he had built his houses.

Such an injustice I could not overlook. It was well known that during the two building seasons prior to his death, Constantine had worked almost exclusively for me. Proceeding in my turn to the rostrum, I declared first that I couldn't compete with the esteemed previous speaker in honoring the deceased, since my posthumous respect as his business partner was of a different, less conventional nature. That respect, I said, by force of unpleasant circumstances for which I was not in the least responsible, had to be supplemented by an explanation which, superficially, was perhaps not very flattering to the deceased, but which was nonetheless necessary to preserve his illustrious memory. That explanation, I said, must refer to another vocation without which the builder's reputation could not have been merited: the vocation of property owner. For if this vocation is unworthy—and a moment earlier I had heard something to this effect—how could the vocation of builder be worthy, a vocation that only serves it and is subordinate to it? To defend the vocation of property owner was in effect to defend the building trade, and therefore our own dear deceased and departed, from accusations that they served usury, cupidity, and the selfish interests of an antisocial coterie.

Complete silence reigned over the mound; only the raindrops sprinkled like glass on the silk bellies of the umbrellas. Looking back, I recognize in it the silence of amazement, but at the time I took it for attention to my words, which gave me still greater encouragement.

"Ladies and gentlemen, is there a single person among you who thinks that I've built my houses haphazardly, or that in doing so I've frustrated and fettered the builder's capabilities? Always I've known what and for whom I was building! I carried out complete scientific surveys, took every factor into consideration: the future tenants, the dimensions of the human living space, the parameters of heating, the effect of color . . . !"

Probably it was Fedor who shouted out: "Who are we mourning here—Arsénie or Constantine?" But I didn't let myself be interrupted.

"And I had to calculate all those factors myself, gentlemen. Who could I have learned from? Could I have copied the Turkish Beys' houses, or the three-room Serbian ones? Only in 1892 did we bring in piped water, and electricity barely a year later! And our streets were first macadamized only in 1886!"

Someone from behind tugged sharply at my sleeve. The umbrella, which up to then had been held over my head, was removed abruptly, so that rain began to soak my hat. But my allotted time wasn't up yet, so I proceeded to sum up what I had to say about the late Constantine.

"When family homes in Paris, Vienna, and Budapest were adorned with gold, silver, silk, brocade, and elegant wood, what was there in our backward country? Here, we property owners were obliged to create everything! Property owners, ladies and gentlemen, among whom the late Constantine occupied a preeminent—"

"—role of victim of your greed!" cried Fedor Negovan, at which point events began to get out of hand.

"What does that mean?" I shouted.

"It means that I've got something to say about it, too!" And the impudent scoundrel shouldered me away from the rostrum.

"I demand that the order of this ceremony be adhered to!"

"And *I* demand," yelled Fedor at the rostrum, "that this man here"—he pointed at me—"tell us if it's true that at the time of the accident Constantine Negovan was ill! And if it's true that he visited the site where Constantine was building a house for him, and was dissatisfied with the progress of the work. And if it's true that—"

"Gentlemen! Ushers!" I shouted, as I and others tried to get the troublemaker away from the rostrum.

"Is it true, I ask this man, that he went straight from the site to Constantine's house and accused him of negligence, so that a violent quarrel broke out and Constantine, pressured by him, rushed off in a high fever to the building site and passed out on the scaffolding!"

I cried out that this was calumny, that the accident occurred because the scaffolding hadn't been erected according to regulations. But Fedor, now struggling with the gravediggers, went on asserting that Constantine had passed out because of anxiety due to my malicious attack on him. In the general pushing and jostling, one of us stumbled and jarred the coffin from its low bier. As it slithered down the mound with a rumble, its lid fell off—why it wasn't nailed down was never established—and Constantine's swollen body sprang out of its violet satin-padded resting place like a jack-in-the-box, covered to the waist in its shroud. It was as if, by stretching out his black-gloved fist, he wanted one last time to touch the earth with which he had worked so long, before being committed to it forever.

And now for the explanation due Isidor. It was true that, indignant at the chaotic state of Efimia's building site, I went to see Constantine, and that I upbraided him and a quarrel broke out. But it's a base lie that Constantine was seriously ill. He was in bed, perhaps with a temperature, but it was only an attack of the flu. Certainly he seemed basically healthy to me, enough at least to visit the site nearby. "Somehow I haven't felt my best," he said, and I asked him, "Shall I get someone else?" "No," he said, "I'll soon be better." I answered caustically, "I can't wait till you get better— I haven't the time or the money!" Had I realized how ill he was, of course I would have been more considerate, though I do think I would still have taken him to task. I would have rebuked a dying man, had the fate of my houses depended on him! And then the scaffolding—why hide it?—was in perfect order. According to the commission's findings, all its bolts were in place, all its points were solid. Yes, the scaffolding was in perfect order.

Constantine is dead. My son also: perhaps because what I wanted wasn't a son but an heir. Ownership is maintained by inheritance. If you have no future you can have no past either. Katarina wanted a child—how she wanted one!—but I myself, because of my obligations toward my houses, could think only of an heir. Haven't I said that I won't write about that?

And is there any purpose in writing at all, any sense in speaking out? Do words have any purpose if nothing more can be done for my houses? Quite recently—for how long I can't say, but that *recently* is measured in hours—an unusual dejection has come over me, an indifference, an apathy. Ostensibly, as a businessman with a sense of reality, I evolved it from the conviction of an inevitable upheaval; but it could be that my mental paralysis has no connection with that at all, but originated of its own accord on the backs of the accounts and receipts, among the words concerned with my past. In ignorance of its causes, there can be no treatment. At first I suspected that my discontent—for that is what it is —had arisen from the fact that my assets couldn't bear serious comparisons with the magnificent palaces, mansions, and castles that I had seen in my travels through Europe. But I was consoled by the fact that size, or rather volume, was never a crucial factor in building; some miniature Chinese pagodas are more beautiful than ill-proportioned emperors' palaces. As everybody knows, a dwarf has all the attributes of a normal full-grown man. As for a soul, all my houses possessed a soul; on this count my mind is at rest.

But did *I* have a soul?

Without the slightest equivocation I can declare that I loved my houses more faithfully than any houseowner; that my devotion didn't lapse even when they brought me no revenue; that I didn't have an official relationship with my possessions, but a spiritual one of the purest kind; and that I sacrificed for them all that time which others would have squandered on social life and for their own enjoyment. And what was that if not a soul—a soul in action?

No, the sources of my discontent have to be sought elsewhere. They are certainly to be found here somewhere, perhaps close by me; I can feel them like an elusive word on the tip of the tongue.

It has long been dark; bent over my manuscript, I can see a pitch-black, empty sky in which the transparent reflections of the street lamps shine, and maybe even those of fires. Perhaps Belgrade is already alight. Now the fires are burning only in the suburbs, but at dawn they'll reach the roofs of Senjak, Topčidersko Brdo, and finally our Kosančićev Venac. I have no idea what time it is. My watch has stopped. It no longer seems important to know the time. Nothing seems important anymore.

Morning must be a long way off. I don't feel cold yet. When I start feeling cold I'll know it's getting light. From down below on the river comes the wail of a steamer's siren. Probably they're bringing in reinforcements from the provincial garrisons: the Bolsheviks have barricaded the roads, so troops are being transported by water. But what sort of troops are they? Probably peasant riffraff, ready and willing turncoats! It was wrong to allow the workers' suburbs to encircle the city; our cities are made for civil war and for massacres: the business center with its shops and offices, then a defensive ring of urban residents, and then the workers' districts. The latter are encircled in turn by upper-class villas, beyond which lurk the peasants. Everyone lives behind everyone else in concentric rings: rows of the rich alternate with rows of paupers as far as the eye can see. So is it really surprising that instead of houses they put up barricades? Who knows if they've already occupied the radio station?

The printing presses may be in their hands already; they'll be issuing proclamations by tomorrow. And then the creaking of wheels in the distance, and the locomotive, that moving scaffold of the steppe snaking back and forth with its dead load, and its bell on the top of a squat pole, ringing, ringing.

But nothing can be heard from the street; probably my

hearing isn't good enough, or the fighting is still some way off. But if they're fighting around the barracks at Topčider, my Sophia is there; they must be encrusting her with bullets. That doesn't matter, I can claim damages. If only they don't set her on fire. If they're up there on the hill, they'll never reach Kosančićev Venac by dawn. Kosančićev Venac has no strategic significance. They'll take it when the expropriation starts, when they come to drag us from our beds and batter us to death in the ditches. It's a good thing Katarina's not here. They wouldn't touch her, but she'd be humiliated, and she'd have to watch; and if she tried to defend me, she'd suffer my fate, too. Poor Katarina, your life with me can't have been easy. I don't know of a single woman for whom things worked out well with the Negovans. It's been especially hard for you since I retired, when you had to take on my business affairs and work with the houses you hated. And before that, when we lost our son, little Isidor.

I've pulled down the blinds. I won't raise them again. I've no reason to look out the window. From now on my attention must be directed toward the door. Toward the door and this will. I have only Emilian's legacy to make. I have no idea what to leave him. What can you leave to someone who will share your fate? Things are very black for the clergy, particularly high church dignitaries. And for possessors. And for army officers. If George were alive, they would certainly have killed him, but he died in good time. And if he *were* alive, he would have stayed at home up there on Lamartine Street. Mlle. Foucault would have gone on knitting in the armchair, while *son bien aimé et courageux général* pored intently over the map of Belgrade, spread out on the dining table and held down at all four corners with coffee cups and little plates with biscuits on them—there might even have been some cognac in one of those cups. With the help of little poles, he would have moved government forces with irreproachable tactics, and finally won a textbook victory over the rebels at the very moment when, smashing down the double-paneled doors, they'd break into his staff headquarters. Lead soldiers and officers, little flags made of prewar toilet paper, clockwork tanks, cardboard fortifications, storm troops of tinfoil— models, nothing but models! Mlle. Foucault was only a model too. And for George I, his own brother, was a comical, old-fashioned, worn-out model which (together with my houses) could be ignored in his exemplary military operations. Houses could be razed to the ground and we could be taken as hostages, or we could be dragooned into digging trenches if we were unfortunate enough to be his compatriots. For George, I was a model made of expendable material which he threw into the wastepaper basket once its uselessness annoyed him. Or was it the other way around? *I* had consigned *him* to the wastepaper basket. Who can tell after all these years?

I remember when he came to talk about the house on Lamartine Street. *Mon général* was in the full dress uniform of a brigadier general, with a yellow sash across his chest. In 1943—in a cab, it's true—but in 1943! It would have been better if he'd worn his decorations at the right time—he died at the front door of the house in Lamartine Street, in slippers and a dressing gown with hussar's tassels that Mlle. Foucault had plaited for him from curtain fringes. Poor George, he'd always insisted on preserving his martial appearance, and since it wasn't given to him to immortalize himself by operations that might have borne his name—the Negovan bridge-head or George's flank attack—he was forced to pay attention to the personal impression he created. I'm not suggesting he was incompetent—all those mighty military schools in France couldn't have given poor results. All I'm saying is that George had no luck. In 1914 he was the first Serbian soldier to be captured by the Austrians. And when the Germans attacked in 1941, George was again taken prisoner—this time, the third Serb captured. So much expense and effort, simply to slip from first to third place!

We had inherited the house on Lamartine Street from our father; the whole house was in fact bequeathed to George, but for half of it I had exchanged a much more valuable property. After his return from captivity, however, George announced that he wouldn't share the expenses of her up-keep. So I offered to buy my brother's share from him, with the proviso that his tenancy would be rent-free for life. To my dismay, George declared that an officer of his rank couldn't be a tenant. I pointed out that *volens-nolens* he already was, since he used that half of the house which belonged to me. He retorted angrily that only on condition that he pay no rent would he cede me his half of the house in exchange for—as he put it—that piece of wasteland at Mačva. I once again became angry: I could be accused of many defects, but never of money-grubbing! Most of all, I said, I would no longer tolerate his brazen refusal to take care of the house.

"We'll go to court, if need be!"

"You can forget about that *tout de suite!*" The sash across his chest shone out in the half-dark room. "I'm standing in your line of fire, Arsénie!" (He was fond of juicy barrack-room expressions.) "And I warn you that I won't spend a penny on the house, especially in the middle of a war!"

"But she has to live, even in wartime!"

"You've no room in your head for anything but houses!"

"They deserve more consideration than some people!"

"Don't you realize they can all suddenly go up in smoke? They and all the rest of us!"

"*Tu es fou?* Don't you dare say such a thing!"

"Brother mine, not a single one will be left standing when the real war starts! We'll destroy everything with barrages or air raids! Everything! Bridges, factories, railways, towns. Everything will be blown sky high!"

"You're a madman!"

"This house will be destroyed, too! Into dust and ashes. All your goddamn houses!"

If Katarina hadn't intervened, I'd have assaulted him.

He was at the front door when I ran to the head of the stairs and shouted down that he was just a harmless lunatic—a lead soldier!

"*Tu es un soldat de plomb! De plomb*—that's what you are!"

After that, he never entered my house again, nor did I ever again visit that half of the house in Lamartine Street which belonged to me. The very idea—my houses destroyed! My Sophia, Eugénie, Christina, Emilia, Katarina, Natalia, all razed to the ground; my Barbara, Anastasia, Juliana, Angelina demolished; my Theodora and my Simonida reduced to rubble. Really, the very idea!

From where I'm writing, each of them comes within my range of vision: in the glass case to the left of the property owner's map—on the right is the bureau with their files—are kept their faithful models. Perfect facsimiles to scales from 1:50 to 1:100, made with different model techniques and materials. Simonida, for example, is made entirely of ivory, whereas Theodora is sculptured from Rumanian amber which imitates her warm greenish-yellow color and noble bearing. It doesn't follow, however, that all the models are expensive copies. Emilia, for example, is molded out of plaster with fine glass shells in the window openings, whereas Christina is built of blond maple with cork floors. For the larger flat surfaces of Juliana, teak is used; and for the pilasters and ornamentation in general, because it's so easily worked, mahogany. Juliana's windows are of celluloid. Tiny sheets of celluloid cover Katarina's windows also, but her walls are made of ash, and the impression of her woodwork is conjured up by light-brown oak.

I feel some discomfort in my rib cage, something like a

slight muscular spasm. Probably I've been sitting in the same position for too long and the edge of the desk has been pressing against my chest. If it doesn't stop soon, I'll have to take my pills. They must be on the shelf, Mlle. Foucault set them out before she left. Really I ought to take them at once, but those drugs make me sleepy, and I don't dare sleep. It's stuffy in here. I was wrong to shut the blinds before morning. Perhaps it's already light. Perhaps I was wrong. What was it that Isidor said? He'd been concerned only with himself, not with architecture. But my concern hadn't been with myself. I've dedicated myself to my houses. To my beautiful But where are they   Where are those houses   *Tout cela est un mod*

--ᴇᴛ Postcriptum ᴊᴇᴏ--

As editor of the manuscript of the late Arsénie K. Negovan and also as the self-appointed chronicler of the Negovan-Turjaški clan, I, Borislav V. Pekić, would like to explain how the manuscript came into my possession.

On June 7 of last year I was summoned to Kosančićev Venac at approximately eight o'clock in the morning. There I found my cousin Katarina Negovan-Turjaški with Mlle. Foucault and Mr. Martinović, their tenant from the basement flat. Katarina informed me of her husband's death. She had been out of town until that morning. Worried by the student demonstrations, she had hurried home from the spa.

But it wasn't Katarina who discovered Arsénie; it was Mlle. Foucault. She had arrived at Kosančićev Venac at six o'clock in the morning, her usual hour. As a rule Arsénie was up by that time, and Mlle. Foucault instantly suspected something was wrong when she didn't hear noises from his study. She called him but got no answer. The study was locked from the inside. She aroused Mr. Martinović, who broke down the door. Arsénie was on the floor dead. The manuscript was on his desk. Glancing through it, Katarina discovered the legacy to Isidor. I had been Isidor's closest friend, so she asked to see me. She gave me the manuscript to decipher and use as I saw fit.

My request to see the dead man was granted. I went into the study: a roll-top bureau containing a card index, an oak table, and a huge armchair were piled by the door. Arsénie had improvised a barricade, as if to defend himself against something. The shades were down. The desk lamp was still lit. Arsénie was lying in the middle of the room, his head on the carpet, one arm stretched out toward the window, the other squeezed under his body. Judging by the position of the corpse, the heart seizure had come just as the old man had gone to open the window. He was wearing an austere black suit and light summer shoes over black cotton socks. A semiprecious stone gleamed in his tiepin. In his pocket we found his watch, which wasn't working, and a Mauser automatic. I don't think the automatic was working either, but I can't be sure.

The manuscript was made up of two separate sections, the private notes written on one set of account forms, and the will on another, although Arsénie was not always consistent. Toward the end his generally legible and decorative handwriting had become somewhat untidy, his thoughts rambling.

From a purely legal aspect, the will was valid. However, except in the case of Katarina, its provisions couldn't be carried out. All Arsénie's houses had long ago been expropriated, and the more dilapidated ones pulled down. But even if that hadn't been the case, and if by some chance the Revolution hadn't come about, Arsénie's will could still not have been followed as he had conceived it. At the time the will was written, Arsénie's universal heir had already been dead for six months (Isidor committed suicide on October 20, 1967). The only other provision that could possibly be carried out concerned Arsénie's gravestone, and that only partially. As stated earlier, some of his houses had been demolished, making it impossible to obtain a cornerstone from each. I can't guarantee anything, but I still hope that, as the voluntary heir to Isidor's obligations, I shall be able to fulfill at least this one wish of Arsénie's—as soon, of course, as my financial situation improves.